The Punishment
of Sherlock Holmes

Selected Sherlockian puns

Collected and Edited by

Bob Burr and Philip K. Jones

Paperback ISBN 978-1780920443
ePub ISBN 978-1780920450
PDF ISBN 978-1780920467

Published in the UK by MX Publishing
335 Princess Park Manor, Royal Drive,
London, N11 3GX
www.mxpublishing.com

Cover design by www.staunch.com

Introduction

This collection of puns was amassed through several accidents. The senior member of this partnership in perfidy (Bob Burr, "The Rascally Lascar") has been collecting, publishing and perpetrating puns for many years, often in Sherlockian periodicals such as Plugs & Dottles and Wheelwrightings. A few years ago, this predilection for punditry bubbled over and caused him to start posting puns before the very respectable Sherlockian discussion group, The Hounds of the Internet. In the fullness of time, this venerable punster was asked to cease and desist, the normal reaction of any respectable literary discussion list. When he continued in his madness, he was asked, politely, to take his mental affliction elsewhere, ANY elsewhere.

The junior editor (Philip K. Jones, "An Ill-dressed Vagabond") contrived to continue posting bootleg puns, supplied by his venerable Fagin, until asked to cease as well, by the long-suffering listmeister of the Hounds. The problem was that this infected soul, was no longer able to function in a semi-rational manner without a regular "fix" to slake his horrible addiction. He had even arrived, in his madness, at the point of actually producing his own puns, the final, fatal stage of this progressive degeneration.

Indeed, the poor man was also involved in cataloging Sherlockian pastiches, parodies and related fiction. In his madness, he insisted that the narrative format of these puns should actually be classified as pasticherie and was busily engaged in listing every last one of these hideous travesties in a database. Both editors obtained some temporary relief by participating in a new, Sherlockian forum, The Shamlockians, which allowed free rein to their warped imaginations and actually accepted their efforts as fit subjects for discussion. This relief was, however, short lived and the progression of their addiction has now forced them to share their madness with others through the medium of the printed word.

So, here it is! A collection of the worst PUNishment available to Sherlockians, a monster agglomeration of puns involving The Master, The Good Doctor and other Canonical characters. These are not amusement for the lighthearted. They are mainline, perverted, Sherlockian scholarship, truly twisted views of the Master and the Holy Canon. They are meant to disgust true Sherlockian scholars, not to inform or to uplift, but rather to appall and to astound.

We warn you! Prepare to be offended! We strive to be equal opportunity offense producers and to offend **Everyone**! If we haven't offended you, it is not from a lack of effort, we merely have not yet got around to your particular hang ups. Our scriveners are working feverishly on new and more offensive materials, as we aim to offend everyone who can read. Wait your turn. Take a number. But, if you are really in a hurry, drop us a note through the Publishers and monitor your favorite Sherlockian list while you wait for our writers' genius to ferment all over your suggested sensitive subjects.

Items included in this collection are all Sherlockian narratives; that is to say that they detail some events involving Canonical characters. One liners are not included. Each and every one of these is supposed to be a tale describing events, not a comment or an observation. In light of this requirement, each follows a standard pattern. It has a title, a narrative portion, an author's line and one or more publication lines. Finally, the SHPUN number is given. This identifies the item uniquely in the database of Sherlockian pastiches, parodies and related fiction. The value of this identifier becomes apparent as the number of puns on file grows. Each pun is associated with a SHPUN# and one of its punch lines in the database and can be retrieved by either. With more than 300 such items on file, confusion involving similar items is certainly possible. This is especially true about the items in the final section (THE STONES, et al…).

To:

The late "Sage of Santa Fe," John Bennett Shaw, a punster in his own right as well as the numerous other pun addicts of the Sherlockian world.

Acknowledgements

Listed, more or less, in the order their work is included:

Robert Brodie
Chuck Neblock
John C. Sherwood
Donald A. Redmond
Richard Milne
Jack Kavanagh
John Ruyle
Melanie Hughes
Ann Margaret Lewis
David R. McCallister
G. Earle Hamerstrand
Carolyn Low
Rev. Dr. Benton Wood
David J. Milner
Karen Murdock (May Blunder)
Howard Einbinder
Frank Darlington
Dr. James Taggart
Suellen Kirkwood
Marla Elmore
Howard E. Burr

Dave Galerstein
Frank Darlington
Rosemary Michaud
Lee Shackleford
David Galerstein
Sandy Kozinn (Esmeralda)
Brad Keefauver
Gary List
William Ballew
Art Moger
Gordon R. Speck
Tom Simpson
Newton Williams
Edward B. Bagley
Don Dillistone
Marion Parker
W. W. Higgens
Dr. Neil Taylor
Bret D. Wortman
Peter Blau

Contents

BIBLICAL

As many serious literary efforts begin, we too, resort to the Bible for inspiration. Sherlockian scholars (and Sherlockian hacks, as well) are unable to avoid drawing inspiration from this most seminal of Literary Sources. Unfortunately, as is the way with punsters, Literary Sources quickly are made mock of and I'm sure the inspirations to be found in our Biblical puns will offend at least a few of the truly devout. Be consoled that we shall move on to other sources of inspiration with equally offensive zeal.

The Case Of The Devious Painters [SHPUN068]

Sherlock Holmes had been bent over his deal-topped chemical table for almost an hour as he analyzed some samples of paint supplied to him earlier in the day by the rector of the church of Saint Monica. Finally, with an expression of satisfaction, he extinguished the Bunsen and remarked:

"Well, Watson, it's as the rector and I expected."

"How's that, Holmes?"

"Simply this, my good fellow. The rector recently hired two gentlemen to paint the new addition to the church, and to realize a larger profit the two scoundrels diluted the paint with solvent to make it go further. My tests this afternoon prove it beyond a doubt."

"Very dishonest, Holmes," I remarked. "And what is to be done now?"

"I shall contact the two knaves and admonish them accordingly."

"And what will you say?"

"I think, Watson, that 'Repaint and thin no more' would be most appropriate."

This was written by "The Rascally Lascar."
This was first published in Plugs & Dottles, Issue #88, January, 1986.
It was later published on the Hounds of the Internet List on January 30th, 2005.

John 8:7 [SHPUN291]

Professor Moriarty, that evil genius, had succeeded in producing a clone of himself. The clone, who was even viler than his original, proceeded to murder a young woman whose body was eventually found in the nets of a fishing trawler. The enraged crew brought the case to Sherlock Holmes.

"Find the murderer, Mr. Holmes," their Captain exclaimed, "then turn him over to us. We'll tie an anchor round his neck and pitch him into the Thames."

"And which of your crew will feel qualified to do so" asked Holmes.

"Qualified? What do you mean?" queried the Captain.

"Well," replied Homes, "I was simply recalling to mind the old Biblical injunction: 'Let him who has never seined cast the first clone'."

This was written by Robert Brodie and Dave Galerstein.
It was first published in Plugs & Dottles, Issue #160, January, 1992.

Matthew 22:14 [SHPUN292]

In December of '86, my wife having left to visit an ailing friend, I returned briefly to the old lodgings in Baker Street I had so long shared with Sherlock Holmes. A chill wind howled through the deserted streets and Winter rain beat a heavy tattoo on the window pane as Holmes and I sat before a cheery fire reading the morning papers. Languor slowly crept over me, and I was on the verge of nodding off when an article suddenly caught my eye.

"I say, Holmes," I remarked. "have you seen the announcement of the January footrace in honour of the Queen's Jubilee? Surely the heavy clothing they will be compelled to wear in this frightful weather will chafe, and there will be constant danger of hypothermia".

"I shouldn't worry." replied Holmes. "As you well know, though many are galled few are frozen."

This was written by Chuck Neblock.
It was first published in Plugs & Dottles, Issue #161, February, 1992.

Row, Row, Row Your Boat [SHPUN014]

Some years after the events of SIGN, Holmes & Watson once again found themselves upon the waters of the historic Thames, this time in pursuit of Manicotti of the cleft palate and his abysmal mistress.

Having secured a small dory, the two headed swiftly down stream, Watson furiously at work with the oars, and Holmes loudly shouting directions. As they neared the Deptford Reach, Holmes spied a half submerged network of steel rods, part of the device which had recently been used to capture the Thames Monster but which had not yet been removed. Watson, so engrossed in his rowing, failed to hear Holmes's frantic warning. With a sickening crunch, their boat smashed into the structure and was literally skewered by one of the steel rods.

"No cause to fret, Watson, Manicotti can't get far," said Holmes. But let this be a lesson to you -- such is found in that old biblical adage. I believe you'll find it in Galatians."

"And what might that be?" questioned Watson, in a tone bordering on rage.

"My good man ... as Ye row so shall Ye seep."

This was written by "The Rascally Lascar."
This was first published in Plugs & Dottles, Issue #061, October, 1983.
It was later published on the Hounds of the Internet List on December 16th, 2004.

Critic's Choice [SHPUN111]

Holmes and Watson were whiling away a late winter Saturday afternoon at Baker Street. Both were reading the various newspapers that Holmes perused on a daily basis.

"Holmes," said Watson with a hint of exasperation in his voice, "I simply cannot tolerate some of these drama critics. Especially this Christopher Koonan of *The Evening Standard*."

"What has you so upset, Watson? The poor man is just trying to make a living," the great detective replied.

"All the same, Holmes, it's simply wrong to write that the amateur cast of the Camford Little Theatre's production of 'A Shamrock Grows in Belfast' is 'far superior in all ways' to the professional actors and actresses of the original London production."

"Well, Watson, I guess one might say he stoned the first cast."

This was written by "The Rascally Lascar."
It was first published on the Hounds of the Internet List on February 22nd, 2005.

He that Is without Sin... [SHPUN277]

'Twas a beautiful evening in late September. Holmes and Watson were leisurely strolling along the Strand, having just taken in the first theatrical performance of the season at the Lyceum Theatre.

"Well, Holmes, what did you think of the play?" queried Watson. "I myself thought that the actors were extremely amateurish. When not forgetting their lines, they more annoyingly read them without injecting a trace of emotion. Very poor – the whole bunch of them! Don't you agree?"

"To be perfectly frank, Watson, I would rather not comment," was Holmes's terse reply.

"But why not, my good man? Surely you have an opinion."

"Elementary, Watson. I simply don't want to be the one to stone the first cast."

This was written by "The Rascally Lascar."
It was first published in Plugs & Dottles, Issue #132, September, 1989.

Canonical Bits

Sherlockians have a Bible of their own, referred to as The Canon; those 60 tales of Sherlock Holmes published by Watson's literary agent, Doctor Sir Arthur Conan Doyle. Sherlockians naturally tend toward puns that fit into it. Although the titles of these tales are the preferred target, quotations or images from the Canonical tales are also acceptable for paranomasical efforts. Some, of course, require a fair knowledge of the Canon as well as a tad of imagination. Others may well seem to be blunt instruments used to bludgeon the reader into submission.

Mycroft's Lodgings [SHPUN306]

After meeting Sherlock's elder brother, Mycroft, during the Melas affair, I became aware of the depth of the relationship between the brothers. However, it took many years for me to gain even small pieces of information about Mycroft's personal life. Of course, he was unsociable by the standards of the times, with no membership in gentlemen's gambling clubs and no participation in the social world except for attendance at official functions.

The Diogenes Club provided him with the standard gentleman's amenities of a place to dine and to entertain, all be it sparingly, the social contacts required by his position. The nature of that position was never, ever specified, but it became increasingly apparent that his contacts were with the highest levels of government and, indeed, numbered members of the Royal Family, including Her Majesty. Aside from these social contacts, only a few friends seemed to be included in his circle, with Sherlock as his most intimate friend as well as his sole surviving relative.

His history in government was strangely cloudy, with very little information ever given about his earlier assignments. At one time, I heard, he had served abroad in a diplomatic capacity after the American Civil War. There had also been some mention of a position in the Exchequer on loan to the Scottish government. Sherlock once claimed that Mycroft "audited the books of a government department" but that was merely a short explanation for a complex position that really defied description. Of course, at another time, Sherlock said that Mycroft "...occasionally is the British Government..." but that was another approximation. His position was ubiquitous and all pervasive, but he once explained to me that he carefully avoided ever attempting to set policy, merely preferring to advise policy makers.

There seemed never to be any details of any personal life to be found. The single indication of any human contact that I ever encountered in Mycroft's life was a painting hung in his rooms. It depicted a striking young lady in an outmoded ball gown surrounded by gentlemen in unfamiliar grey uniforms trimmed in gold. The group were gathered in a paneled room, with a large fireplace, many books and a number of leather covered chairs and divans scattered about. A Negro attendant was passing out a tray of drinks and the lady was laughing impishly. It was apparent that she was the social center of the room, surrounded by a court of handsome attendants.

I once asked Mycroft what was the subject of the painting and he replied that it was titled "Scarlett in a Study."

This was written by "an Ill-dressed Vagabond."
It was first published on the Shamlockians' List on November 17th, 2006.

A Bardic Source For The Hound [SHPUN171]

A recent perusal of an esoteric exegesis of the plays of the Bard, including notes on variant versions of all the works printed before 1700, brought to my attention a singular and illuminating bit of fugitive text that is not to be found in he Globe edition with which most of us are familiar. Credit for this discovery goes to a signore Ben Trovato.

In an early version of *The Tragedy of Othello*, Desdemona, while being courted by Othello, receives an unsigned letter in the form of a half sheet of foolscap paper folded into four. Across its middle a single sentence had been formed by the expedient of pasting printed words upon it. It ran: "As you value your life or your reason, keep away from the Moor."

This was written by Frank Darlington.
It was first published in Plugs & Dottles, Issue #176, May, 1993.
It was later published on the Shamlockians' List on April 22nd , 2005.

The Incident of the Digital Diversion [SHPUN050]

Dr. Watson opened the door to 221b to discover Holmes sitting in his usual armchair, one of his shoes and socks on the floor, playing with his toes.

"This little piggy went to market, this little piggy stayed home..." Holmes was reciting as he looked up to see his friend in the doorway. "Ah, Watson! Welcome back!"

Watson closed the door in a state of wonderment.

"Whatever are you doing, Holmes?" he asked.

"Watson," said Holmes as he donned his sock and shoe. "You have just missed my most recent client, a young woman who had a babe in arms. The case itself was a trifle. But, as
she played with the infant, I realized that all my life I have been incorrect in one of my axiomatic statements."

"Really?" said Watson. "And what did you learn?"

"I learned, Watson," said Holmes, "that the foot is a game!"

This was written by John C. Sherwood from a suggestion by Mike Royko.
It was first published on the Hounds of the Internet List on January 18th, 2005.

Knowledge of Athletics—Nil [SHPUN018]

It was in the fall of '88 when the noted polo coach, Roder H. Blaggard, consulted Holmes on a rather serious matter. It seems someone had stolen all of the team's mallets. Blaggard, in a state of excitement, launched into a description of the circumstances, using much of the game's vernacular as he did so. Holmes, being uninformed concerning such non-crime matters as sports (especially polo), was quite baffled by what was to him an almost foreign tongue. When the subject of the polo mallets came up, the great detective made a comment as to the unusual length of their handles —

"It's a wonder the players don't trip on them as they run about the field," Holmes remarked casually, causing Blaggard's mouth to drop open in absolute astonishment.

Blaggard was just about to ask Holmes what the devil he was talking about, when Watson leaned over and whispered in his ear:

"He doesn't know whether the game is afoot or on horseback."

This was written by "The Rascally Lascar."
This was first published in Plugs & Dottles, Issue #67, April, 1984.
It was later published on the Hounds of the Internet List on December 20th, 2004.

Skullduggery [SHPUN305]

Long after the conclusion of the Baskerville case, Sherlock Holmes continued his association with Dr. Mortimer, from whom he greatly increased his knowledge of skull formations. In one instance in particular, Holmes's ability to identify the origins of a mysterious skull was the clue which set the authorities on the trail of the murderer. The case began when a dockworker at Gravesend discovered what appeared to be a human skeleton concealed deep in the cargo hold of a Mexican freighter.

"This is no ordinary skull, Watson," said my friend as he began his examination. "It is quite unique. As you observe, there are many characteristics of the native tribes of Mexico. I should place this specimen as a member of those people indigenous to the Yucatan Peninsula. And yet there is also a suggestion of the Eskimo here. No more than ten percent Eskimo, I should judge, and probably less."

"Holmes!" I cried, "Does this mean -- ?"

"Yes, Watson. It is a seven percent Aleutian of Cancun!"

This was written by the Rosemary Michaud.
It was first published in Plugs & Dottles, #224, May, 1997.

The Curious Incident at Loo Fan Chew's [SHPUN266]

As readers of my little tales have undoubtedly noticed, the eating habits of my friend Sherlock Holmes were both sporadic and, at times, peculiar. Just how peculiar I was not to know until one particularly cool evening in July. Mrs. Hudson was out of town for the week, and Holmes and I were left to our own devices as to where to take our meals. On the night in question we had reached a quandary as to where to dine.

"Simpson's," I suggested.

"No, not Simpson's," Holmes retorted. "His wife is nice enough, but he always tries to get you drunk."

"The Diogenes club?" I tried again.

Holmes shook his head. "I have serious doubts about a place where the members are forbidden to speak to one another and tongue is constantly turning up on the menu."

"The Copper Beeches Inn?"

"Last time I was there I found a hair in my soup, and a long chestnut-coloured one at that!"

"At least it was not so bad as when we ate at Victor Hatherly's new plathe – thumb food, heh?"

Holmes shook his head in utter dejection. After a moment, however, a spark lit in his eye and he slapped the arm of his chair with a laugh.

"Loo Fan Chew's, that's the ticket!" he exclaimed.

"Who?"

"No, Loo. An Oriental culinary creator … a veritable vizier of veal and vegetable; he's always inventing the newest dishes for his customers. You shall have a unique dining experience tonight, my friend."

And so, we were off to Loo Fan Chew's. Holmes proved to be right. A more unique dining experience I doubted I would ever find. Two items in the beverage section appealed to me in particular. One was a mixture of nectarine and lime juices that Loo called a "Nime." It was served chilled and was said to be very low in calories. To my dismay, however, the waiter's coat sleeve, a long loose affair, was hanging in the glass as he carried my drink to the table. So as not to embarrass the waiter, I pretended to change my mind, and ordered the second beverage that had appealed to me. It consisted of an egg and milk mixture that was served in a very small cup fashioned out of an American ten-cent piece and fitted with an exceedingly tight cap to maintain the freshness of its contents. With great difficulty I removed the cap and sipped the odd drink, only to find that it was made from powdered egg and powdered milk.

"Holmes!" I exclaimed in disgust.

"Is there something you'd like to call to my attention, Watson?" my friend asked. "The injurious incident of the tog in the diet nime, perhaps?"

"The tog did nothing in the diet nime," I replied. "I refer to the spurious instance of the nog in the tight dime. That is the injurious incident!"

With that we left Loo Fan Chew's establishment, went to Simpson's and proceeded to drink ourselves pence less.

This was written by "Anonymous."
It was first published in Plugs & Dottles, Issue #071, August, 1984.

No Way to Curry Favor [SHPUN304]

There were frayed nerves indeed at Baker Street when Dr. Watson began experiencing strange, periodic episodes of sleepwalking. Every Sunday night for a month, he arose from his bed, shambled to Sherlock's bedroom, and stood there – sound asleep – hurling vicious insults at the friend he so revered in his waking hours.

When the next Sunday came, Holmes was determined that the

midnight harangues should come to an end. He persuaded Watson to go on a long walk in the evening, and, after a light supper at Simpson's, the two returned home to bed. Sure enough, Watson did not sleepwalk that night! Next morning, Holmes explained his reasoning to his grateful friend.

"Mrs. Hudson had got into the habit of serving us curried mutton for supper every Sunday night," said he. "It was this spicy dish which so upset your nervous system that it caused both your somnambulism and your uncharacteristic impudence."

"Splendid, Holmes!" cried Watson. "I shall write up this case so that it may take its place among the catalog of your successes."

"Indeed? What shall you call it?"

"That should be obvious, Holmes: 'The curry-ous Impudence of the Doc in the Nighttime'!"

This was written by the Rosemary Michaud.
It was first published in Plugs & Dottles, #223, April, 1997.

Holmes the Cubs Fan [SHPUN302]

"Ah, Watson!" exclaimed Sherlock Holmes, tossing aside the newly arrived telegram with a flourish. "There is good news from America! Wilson Hargreave wires that the Cubs will start their Spring Training in a few weeks, and that there are no labour disputes to delay the start of the season this year."

I looked up in considerable surprise at this statement. "Why, Holmes, I had no idea you were such a sports fan."

"Indeed," he replied with a smile. "I am lost without my baseball."

This was written by the Rosemary Michaud.

It was first published in Plugs & Dottles, #211, April, 1996.

Make Mine with Everything [SHPUN300]

"But why hot dogs, Watson?" asked Sherlock Holmes, as I unpacked my luggage. I had recently returned from a holiday in New York City, and the contents of my bag had attracted his ever-active attention.

"Surely you have heard of Nathan's Famous Hot Dogs," I replied. "It seemed a pity not to sample them while I was in New York. But I confess I cannot tell how you knew it."

"The train of reasoning is very simple," said Holmes with a mischievous twinkle. "It belongs to the same class of deduction which tells me that you made a romantic conquest at the same time. No, my dear fellow, don't trouble yourself to deny it! Observe the many stains of ketchup(sic), mustard, and relish upon the lapels of your jacket. Knowing you as I do, surely it is not too great a stretch of the imagination to say that you can now boast of an experience of women extending over three condiments and many Nathan's!"

This was written by the Rosemary Michaud.
It was first published in Plugs & Dottles, #205, October, 1995.

Stick out Your Tongue and Say 'Ah' [SHPUN284]

In a slightly modified version of SIGN (Sherlockian shorthand for *The Sign of Four*) we find Holmes and Watson discussing various aspects of the case following its dénouement.

"I say, Holmes," remarked Watson, "it is quite evident that Jonathan Small was a man driven mad with an idea of vengeance, but however did you ascertain that he was seriously ill in a physical sense?"

"That should be elementary to a man with your medical training," replied Holmes. "I simply looked at his Tonga."

This was written by Donald A. Redmond.
It was first published in Plugs & Dottles, Issue #150, March, 1991.

A Change in Habiliments [SHPUN264]

When not involved in his renowned criminological pursuits, my friend Sherlock Holmes was a man of varied tastes and activities. So it was that in October of '83, I was totally unsurprised to find that he had purchased a set of headgear usually worn by the men who shovel coal into the mighty engines that power the Queen's steamships. We spoke little of the matter, and two days later he appeared carrying a cloak made entirely of asbestos cloth under one arm. Sensing a pattern emerging, I then asked him what the cloak was for.

"For walking amidst flame," he succinctly replied.

As the days passed and no criminal activity came to his interest, Holmes grew more and more fond of his new headpiece and cloak, even to the point of wearing them around his sitting room in place of his smoking jacket. Eventually a case did come, yet Holmes insisted upon wearing his beloved outfit, even to investigate the crime, a murder in Fleet Street. The newspapers there went wild with the story of Holmes's new garb, and before long everyone in London knew of the distinctive apparel.

So it is that even today, hardly a likeness of Sherlock Holmes ever appears without his dear stoker cap and in-furnace cape.

This was written by "Anonymous."
It was first published in Plugs & Dottles, Issue #069, June, 1984.

What Really Killed the King [SHPUN149]

"Holmes, are you telling me that you foresaw the death of this Elvis, the rock and roll singer?"

"I can tell you nothing but the truth, Watson. I did, in fact, have every reason to believe that this self-styled 'king' was quickly approaching his demise because of his poor dietary habits."

"Ah, you mean his helpless addiction to saturated fats and cholesterol?"

"Precisely, old fellow. I merely noted the depth to which the Presley had sunk into the butter."

This was written by Lee Shackleford.
It was first published in Plugs & Dottles, Issue #198, March, 1995.
It was later published on the Shamlockians' List on April 3rd, 2005.

The Adventure of the Prodigal Niece [SHPUN251]

"I am a bit puzzled," said Holmes as he faced the rather fierce looking baronet Sir Jasper Fairfax who had arrived to consult him just after breakfast, "as to how I can help you, Sir Jasper."

"Well sir," said Sir Jasper, "I was given your name by a gentleman at Scotland Yard because they explained they could not help me either."

"I see," said Holmes. I could tell he was not entirely pleased by being sent a Scotland Yard castoff.

"The fact is I have, or should I say had, a younger brother named John. He was two years younger than myself but something of a scapegrace. Twenty five years ago having been sent down from Oxford, John was given a sum of money by my late father Sir Roger, to depart to the colonies and never darken our door again, as it were."

"I see, pray continue," said Holmes still a little nettled.

"We never heard from him from that day until very recently when we had a very attractive young lady turn up on her doorstep with the name of Sybil Fairfax. This young ... er ... lady claimed to be John's daughter and, although she claims to be independently wealthy courtesy of my late brother and has a considerable amount of knowledge of our family, I have my doubts. She has quite plainly set her cap at my eldest boy and I think she is nothing more than a colonial adventuress come to cause trouble. I want you to investigate her past and spare no expense in exposing her – I'll even throw a shilling or two myself."

"Most generous. Well, I shall send Watson down to your estate."

"What?" spluttered the Baronet. "Not yourself.?"

"No, I fear not Sir Jasper," said Holmes, "I am tied up with the Admiralty Rope affair. Watson will be an able substitute - as I have said on at least one occasion the Fairfax is Watson's department."

This was written by Richard Milne.
This has not been published before.

Poor Lestrade! [SHPUN011]

And then there was the time when a bunch of hooligans kept stealing Inspector Lestrade's trousers from the clothesline when his wife hung them out to dry after washing. The mighty Baker Street Sleuth finally brought the miscreants to justice, and when Watson wrote up the case he titled it:--

"The Adventure of the Copper's Breeches"

This was written by "The Rascally Lascar".
It was first published in Plugs & Dottles, Issue #58, July, 1983.
It was later published on the Hounds of the Internet List on December 12th, 2004.

Silver Blaze II [SHPUN020]

Following the original case in which this equine figured so prominently, he was again the victim of villainy. It seems a mischievous little girl named Kristi Rodine, actually Lord Backwater's niece, fed the noble steed two pints of castor oil, the results of which need not be detailed here.

The horse's owner, Colonel Ross, once again called upon Sherlock Holmes to ferret out the culprit, which he readily did. When Watson published the case, he titled it "The Adventure of the Empty Horse."

This was written by "The Rascally Lascar".
It was first published in Plugs & Dottles, Issue #208, January, 1996.
It was later published on the Hounds of the Internet List on December 22nd, 2004.

Too Good To Refuse [SHPUN078]

Following a delicious supper of kippered enchiladas one early February evening, Watson began reminiscing about the many famous cases his fidus Achates had handled but which the good doctor had never published.

"Tell me, Holmes," he queried, "just why was it you decided to take on that case for the Grice Patersons?"

"Elementary, my good fellow, they made me an Uffa I couldn't refuse."

This was written by "The Rascally Lascar" from a suggestion by David Galerstein.
It was first published in Plugs & Dottles, Issue #094, July, 1986.
It was later published on the Hounds of the Internet List on February 5th, 2005.

Chomp & Barf [SHPUN221]

"Ha, Watson, you're finally back. You've been gone for over two hours. Your patient must have posed some problems."

"A very strange and difficult case, Holmes. It involves a sixteen-year-old girl who has a gluttonous appetite for food, but soon after consuming same retires to the WC, where she induces emesis by sticking her finger down her throat."

"In addition to concern for their daughter's condition, her parents are desperately trying to keep others from knowing about it."

"Alas, a true scandal in bulimia, my good fellow. Not so?"

With apologies to John Ruyle author of "A Scandal in Bulimia" [1986]
This was written by "The Rascally Lascar".
It was first published on the Shamlockians' List on February 10th, 2006.

The Case of the Spattered Chapeaux [SHPUN180]

Mrs. Abercrombie wrung her hands as she took Sherlock Holmes into her millinery shop to show him the damage that had been done to her new spring line of hats.

"It's the second time in a month that vandals have been here," she wailed. "I'm at my wit's end! Do you see? Twelve brand new hats, all spattered with blood."

Holmes examined the shop doors and windows, and finally held up his pocket lens to one of the hats. "There is no sign of forced entry," said he at last. "and these are not blood stains."

"Then what are they?"

"I noticed that the shop directly above yours sells sweets and nuts. The red stains upon the hats are nothing more than the food coloring used to stain pistachio nuts from their natural color to the more appealing red to which we have become accustomed."

"A few repairs to the vats and drain pipes upstairs will prevent any further seepage of dye into your shop."

"Bless you, Mr. Holmes, you've solved it! Do you think Dr. Watson will write up this mystery as another 'Study in Scarlet' or 'Second Stain'?"

"No, no, my dear lady. Surely, this case will be called 'The Adventure of the Red-Hatted Leak'."

This was written by Rosemary Michaud.
It was first published in Plugs & Dottles, Issue #228, September 1997.
It was later published on the Shamlockians' List on May 5th, 2005.

Watson Cops a Plea [SHPUN211]

It was not one of Dr. Watson's better days. He had purchased a bicycle with the idea of getting some useful exercise while making the rounds of his medical practice more quickly than on foot. Alas, after one late night house call, he had fortified himself for the trip home with one too many pulls from his hip flask, and as a result he and his bicycle collided with a hansom cab. And now, his bicycle in ruins and his arm in a sling, the good doctor found himself brought up before the Magistrate, charged with PWI (Peddling While Intoxicated).

"Dr. Watson," said the official of the law, "this is a very serious charge. The punishment is a gaol sentence of thirty days. However, as I see that you have been injured in the accident, I will give you the option to pay the court thirty guineas in lieu of your sentence, if you so prefer. Which shall it be?"

"Your worship," replied Watson, "I would definitely prefer not to become the cyclist in solitary, and therefore, I elect to pay the fine of the sore."

This was written by Rosemary Michaud.
It was first published in PLUGS & DOTTLES, Issue #225, June 1997.
It was also published on the Shamlockians' List on September 9th, 2005.

<u>A Pilfering in New Orleans</u> [SHPUN182]

It was, without doubt, one of the most bizarre cases Holmes had ever tackled. And to make it doubly difficult, he was required to solve the matter from a distance. Through the medium of cabled messages from London to New Orleans, he helped Police Captain Pierre Beauregard recover a musical instrument that had been purloined after it had been in use by one of the members of the brass band playing for a funeral cortege as it made it's way to the graveyard.

When Holmes gives his permission, I shall make known the details of this strange affair. In the meantime, I have kept my notes filed under the rubric:

"The Adventure of the Burial Cornet."

This was written by Frank Darlington.
It was first published in Plugs & Dottles, Issue #236, May 1998.
It was later published on the Shamlockians' List on May 16th, 2005.

An Archeological Find [SHPUN183]

When Holmes and Watson were involved in "The Addleton Tragedy", they were presented with "the singular contents of the ancient British barrow." After clearing up the mystery to the satisfaction of the authorities and explaining all to the innocent victims, there remained the matter of the barrow contents to be explained.

"Holmes, I just don't understand the significance of this find."

"I think it is clear enough, Doctor. This is a community burial site for a Neolithic matriarchy."

"Why do you say that, Holmes? I see skeletons, each with a marker or identifying grave item of some sort, but no clear indication of the type of society involved."

"Watson, you look but you do not see. Note that the larger skeletons, clearly the males, each have a wooden item buried with them, usually a spear or a digging stick. The very small ones, the children, were buried with organic matter, probably baskets or clothing items. Finally, the medium sized remains, most likely the women, are buried with fertility statues of chert and even of obsidian. Some even have what seem to be carved portraits of the decedent."

"Well, yes, that describes the dig pretty well, but how do you infer that this society was a matriarchy, Holmes?"

"It couldn't be clearer, Watson! The ma's are in stone!"

This was written by "An Ill-dressed Vagabond."
It was first published on the Shamlockians' List on May 19th, 2005.
It was later published in The Gaslight Gazette, V11, Issue #12, December, 2005.
It was also published in The Pleasant Places of Florida Communication # 258, V12., Issue #01, January-February, 2006.

A Message From The Great Beyond [SHPUN113]

Two Sherlockians, Bob and Christopher, often philosophized as to whether their wonderful hobby of Sherlockiana existed in heaven. They both agreed that the first to die and enter the Pearly Gates would attempt to contact the other still on earth and inform him of the existence or not of a heavenly Holmes cult.

Bob was the first to go. A few months later, while watching a Jeremy Brett rerun on TV, Christopher suddenly heard an ethereal voice:--

"Christopher ... Christopher ... can you hear me? This is your old friend Bob."

"Yes, Bob, I can hear you," answered Christopher. "Please tell me -- IS there Sherlockiana in heaven?"

"Christopher," replied Bob, "I have both good news and bad news for you. The good news is that there IS Sherlockiana in heaven. All the great Sherlockians are here -- Smith, Starrett, Burr, Baring-Gould, even Conan Doyle. We meet every month and have the greatest of times!"

"Wonderful!" cried Christopher, "but what is the bad news?"

"The bad news," came the solemn reply, "is that you are scheduled to give a paper here in two weeks on 'The Speckled

Band'."

This was written by "The Rascally Lascar" from a Suggestion by David Galerstein.
It was first published in Plugs & Dottles, Issue #120, September, 1988.

Fishing for Trouble [SHPUN272]

It was in the Summer of '85 that Holmes and I travelled to Bakershore Lake in the West of England for a few days of relaxation and fishing.

"I think we should fish for crappies*, Watson," Holmes said as we approached the shore.

"But, Holmes," I protested, "Bakershore Lake is noted as a haven for some of the largest bass in the world. Why not fish for bass?"

"You've not heard the full story of the Bakershore bass, have you Watson? Fish for them if you like, but I shan't be responsible for the consequences."

Holmes's manner provoked me to do just what he advised against, and in no time I had hooked a beautiful six-pound bass. I placed it in my creel and was about to re-bait my hook, when a soggy projectile struck my leg with sufficient force to knock me off my feet. "What on Earth was that?" I cried.

"A day-old hot-cross bun,**" said Holmes. "The local bakery dumps their unsold baked goods into the lake. A shocking practice, especially since the bass have learned to fling the hot-cross buns with their tails when provoked. When you just caught one of their kinsman you earned their water-soaked vengeance."

"You should have warned me, Holmes. I'm going to have a

nasty bruise where that thing hit me."

"Don't worry about it, my friend. The locals are so accustomed to the fish that they have developed a gelatin that, when placed on the bruise overnight, heals all by morning. We can procure some at the Inn."

"Well, let's go then," I grumbled. "I shall certainly be happy to see the last of this place."

"Yes, Watson" Holmes mused. "But, somehow I feel that our names will someday be associated with a bass-al wrath-bun and a night-gel bruise."

* We were NOT aware that the 'crappie' was indigenous to the British Isles. – Ed.
** Definitely a Watsonism, since it's Summer and hot-cross buns are only made during Lent. – Ed.

This was created by a prominent Morton, Illinois Sherlockian who shall be otherwise anonymous.
It was first published in Plugs & Dottles, Issue #115, April, 1988.

The Sumatran Horror [SHPUN258]

"And now, Watson," Holmes said quietly, "the source of those large, malodorous chips so prized by the native pygmies, as well as the probable fate of Bishop Henesley, young Gerard Gill and Lady Ruth Eringray."

Holmes pushed aside the vegetation with a sweep of his arm and a wide-eyed look of amused astonishment. The look upon my own face had to have been less amused and more wide-eyed and astonished, if not totally aghast.

Within the small clearing, a beast in the form of a rat, yet larger than an elephant, sat upon its hind legs. Instantly, I realized that those large teeth in the creature's awesome mouth could very well have been responsible for the demise of our missing three. Without any need for Holmes's usual explanation, I recognized the source of the organic chunks, which made up the pygmy temple: giant rat droppings! But one thing baffled my stunned brain. Who was the tanned old man who was commanding the monster to sit up, as if it were a Scottish terrier?

"Dr. Oeht, I presume?" Sherlock Holmes said casually, as if our lives were not in direst peril.

"Howdy." The peculiar doctor waved to us and returned to leading the awful rodent through a series of tricks. Finally, he ordered the huge creature to lie down and wait, then turned to face us once more.

"You must be here 'bout them killin's," Dr. Oeht said in a friendly fashion. "I 'spected somebody'd turn up sooner or later. Me and Hugh been awaitin'."

"Hugh?"

Dr. Oeht nodded toward the monstrous rat as he picked up a large clay jug and took it to where the creature laid its huge head.

"Hugh's medicine," he told us, holding up the jug. "Poor fella's been a mite constipated of late, and I hate to disappoint the little folk. Hugh's sort of like a god to them, y' know? And they seem to take whatever gifts from god they can get."

"We've seen their temple," Holmes replied. "But as to the murders, we …"

"Now don't go blamin' Hugh here!" Dr. Oeht exclaimed violently. "Hugh didn't have nothin' to do with killin' the bishop or that boy! I know!"

"But what of the missing Lady Ruth Eringray?" Holmes asked.

The deeply tanned doctor turned as white as his skin allowed.

"The truth, doctor," Holmes demanded with subtle firmness.

"Well ... I, uh, Hugh ..." squirming under Holmes's steel gaze, Dr. Oeht was unable to form coherent sentences. Gathering himself, he took the jug and poured its contents into the monster's fearful mouth.

"When Hugh gets rid of whatever's blockin'him up ... that is, if those pygmies don't grab it, well .." Dr. Oeht struggled to get his thought out.

"To quote you, Mr. Holmes," the doctor finally said, "once Hugh has eliminated the impassible, whatever remains, however imp-robbable, must be thet Ruth!"

This was written by Brad Keefauver.
It was first published in Plugs & Dottles, Issue #051, December, 1982.

A New Look at an Old Maxim [SHPUN303]

In the Summer of 1896, Holmes and I found ourselves in Aldershot, investigating the case of an entire company of soldiers who had gone missing from their barracks. The Great Detective traced the men to the remote farm of one Bob Miller. The farmer could scarcely have made much of a living, as all the farm buildings were in a state of almost total ruin.

As Holmes and I approached, the only sign of life was a fierce bull, which stood blocking our path. The huge beast showed no inclination to move, and our investigation seemed to have reached an impasse. Holmes, however, whipped off his Inverness cape,

32

and with a flourish of a matador, maneuvered the animal into a nearby paddock, where we locked him safely out of our way.

Then it was the work of but a moment to find the hapless soldiers, who had somehow gotten themselves trapped in the rubble of what had once been Bob Miller's barn. As their comrades from Aldershot freed the men, I asked Holmes how he knew that we would find the soldiers in the barn.

"It is an old maxim of mine," said he, "that once you have eliminated the impasse-bull, then whatever remains, however in Bob's rubble, must be the troops."

This was written by the Rosemary Michaud.
It was first published in Plugs & Dottles, #219, December, 1996.

Gilbert and Sullivan

The music and charm of Gilbert and Sullivan's operettas share the Gaslight era with Holmes and Watson. Although never mentioned in the Canon, it is sure that the partnerships were acquainted, one with the other.

Der Französische Glöckner [SHPUN296]

'Twas in the Winter of 1885 that the famous British comic opera team of Gilbert and Sullivan decided to do a musical version of Victor Hugo's classic *Notre Dame de Paris* (The Hunchback of Notre Dame). Unable to come up with one themselves, the two collaborators offered a prize of £100 to the person who could provide the best title for their upcoming musical.

Dr. Watson, in need of extra cash as usual, was churning over in his mind one evening a myriad of possible titles when he suddenly exclaimed: "I've got it, Holmes, I've got it – the perfect title for the new Gilbert and Sullivan play. How about 'Ringing in the Seine'?"

This was written by "The Rascally Lascar."
It was first published in Plugs & Dottles, #172, January, 1993.

The Adventure of the Malevolent Orchestra Leader [SHPUN252]

"Well Sir Arthur," observed Holmes, "I wondered when you would consult with me. The loss of one orchestra conductor may be a misfortune, the death of two is clearly a disaster, three looks like something from the Ring saga ."

"Indeed," said Sir Arthur Sullivan. "As you would be aware as a relief from having to write music for another one of Gilbert's infernal magic lozenge plots, I undertook to chair a committee to select a suitable conductor for a newly created London Symphony Orchestra. Four candidates applied for the post -- Alphonse Des

Habille a Frenchman, Luigi Savaratolli, late of La Scala, Hermann Eisenbahn from Bayreuth, and a Joseph Green who claimed he was the English Guiseppi Verdi."

"Is he?" I asked.

"In name only," said Sir Arthur. "Each candidate had to conduct a passage of music and it was decided that the length of applause by the audience would determine whom the successful conductor would be. After all four had performed we would visit each gentleman and inform them of the result after the concert was concluded. The Englishman was to go last and I must say the first three lead magnificently and the difference in applause length was only a matter of seconds with the Frenchman a narrow winner. Mr. Green, who went last, was appalling, he could not lead or keep time and was in fact inebriated. If Gilbert had been present he would have said the man could not have conducted an omnibus. The applause was a few slow handclaps so he was obviously eliminated. Just as he finished, a freak thunderstorm struck the Albert Hall. To our horror the dressing rooms were hit by lightning and all the candidates except Joseph Green were electrocuted. Only Joseph Green was alive and it would appear we will have to employ him, by default, as there is little time to find a replacement."

"No, you won't" said Holmes. "You must find some one else."

"But why Holmes?" I asked.

"Because Joseph Green is *obviously* a bad conductor."

This was written by Richard Milne.
This has not been published before.

<u>With Apologies To Gilbert & Sullivan</u> [SHPUN181]

"Holmes, did you read in the paper that Penn's Bakery in the

Strand, which is run by the two maiden aunts of owner Josiah Penn, has been closed by the authorities because of an infestation of rodents?"

"No, my good fellow, I haven't."

"Seems like the pesky creatures have overrun the bakery and have been nibbling on the tarts, pastries, and what have you."

"Ha, Watson, brings to mind a work by the team of Gilbert and Sullivan."

"How's that, might I ask?"

"Elementary, old chum—'The Pie Rats of Penn's Aunts'."

This was written by Melanie Hughes
It was first published in Plugs & Dottles, Issue #226, July 1997.
It was later published on the Shamlockians' List on May 6th, 2005.

Spying in the Bristol Channel [SHPUN231]

During the Great War, Holmes was employed by the Government in a number of instances. I only learned of some of these services long afterward. One fall day, after I had moved to the South Downs to share Holmes' retirement, his housekeeper served us a succulent Mulberry Pie. Holmes began eating and then began to laugh. Naturally, I asked the reason.

"The pie reminded me of a strange case I handled during the War," he said. "It was in the late Fall and Winter of 1914 and we were beginning to lose merchant shipping to German raiders, both small surface ships and submarines. The losses were not frequent, but they were persistent and always seemed to be ships with particularly needed cargoes. Most of the losses occurred in the Irish Sea and the approaches to the Bristol Channel, so I was asked to look into the matter."

"After a careful check of shipping records and Port logs, it became apparent that most of the valuable ships that had been lost were, indeed, headed into Bristol. Further, they had notified the Harbour Master at Bristol of their expected arrival by radio and had asked that an escort be sent to meet them at an appropriate time and location. In almost every case, the ships had been attacked and sunk only hours before their escort was scheduled to arrive. Naturally, my thoughts turned to the security of the codes being used, however, the same codes were in use all over the UK Maritime Establishment and the coded messages gave no indication of cargos or even the type of ship concerned. All ships used arbitrarily assigned code names and those names were independent of the transmission codes."

"The problem was finally cracked by analyzing the personnel with access to the combination of information required to select the proper ships. Only three clerks in the offices in Bristol could have assembled the necessary facts in the time available to spur action; Mr. Tristan Jones, The Honourable Wilburforce Penn and Shamus Casey. Each was put under observation, but no contact with possible enemy agents could be found."

"Mr. Jones was Welsh and spent most of his time with his extended family in the country. Penn had relatives who managed two bakeries in the small village of Avonmouth where he was a frequent visitor, and consumer. Casey was from Ireland and kept up constant and voluminous mail communications with his relatives across the Irish sea. One of these persons had to be sending data to foreign agents who signaled the raiders when to attack."

"My break came when I visited the Avonmouth bakeries. The two shops offered wide selections of pastries at wildly varying prices, all similar, but differing in details. A quick check with the local constable revealed that these prices changed almost daily, with no apparent reason or logic. This was the mechanism for passing information to the enemy agents."

"Holmes," I gasped. "You can't mean…"

"Yes Watson, it was the pie rates of Penn's aunts that told the tales."

This was written by "An Ill-dressed Vagabond."
It was first published on the Shamlockians' List on August 18th, 2005.

POPULAR MUSIC

Not content with despoiling Gilbert & Sullivan, Sherlockians continue to run rampant over the lyrics of popular music to this day. Indeed, I expect to see a Sherlockian pun set to a Rap beat any day now.

I'm An Old Cow Hand [SHPUN195]

As did Watson's Literary Agent, the famous Baker Street duo also paid a visit to America, concentrating on the great state of Texas.

On their return trip to England, Watson was remarking to Holmes about the many cowboy songs he had heard and so enjoyed.

"Without doubt, Holmes, my favorite tune has to be 'There's An Empty Bunk In The Cat House Tonight'."

"My good fellow," replied Holmes, "I believe you've had a bit too much Beaune again. The title is 'There's An Empty Cot In The Bunk House Tonight'."

This was written by "The Rascally Lascar."
It was first published on the Shamlockians' List on June 5th, 2005.

The Long Search [SHPUN099]

After these many years it is now possible to relate that my friend Sherlock Holmes, during his later retirement, spent a total of three years in search of a famous undercover photographer on the island of Cuba. The photographer, known only a "Mr. E," was employed by a very popular American magazine, which had sent him to the Caribbean isle to do a pictorial exposé on corruption in the sugar refining industry.

Holmes suspected from the start that "Mr. E" had met with foul play, and after three years of searching, his suspicions were confirmed when he finally discovered the body of the missing photographer buried under tons of refined sugar in a remote warehouse. Upon discovering the body, Holmes was reported to have exclaimed:

"Ah, sweet Mr. E of *Life* at last I've found you!"

This was written by "The Rascally Lascar" from a Suggestion by David Galerstein.
This was first published in Plugs & Dottles, Issue #109, October, 1987.
It was later published on the Hounds of the Internet List on February 17th, 2005.

A Goon and His gal [SHPUN293]

Singular, perhaps even outré, one might say. I speak of this strange circumstance of two Canonical characters, from widely disparate backgrounds, meeting and joining forces to offer entertainment on the music hall circuit.

Cast your thought back to Janet Tregellis. You will remember that she lost her new beau, the butler Brunton, when that fickle Don Juan snuffed it under the flagstone. Unhinged by the tragedy, the lorn lass ran off to the great cesspool to make for herself a new life. The bereft babe ended up pulling pints and quarts in a low dive in the East End.

Now shift your attention to the partner of Count Negrito Silvius, said no-count who was consigned to Wormwood Scrubs to do 10 to 20 after having been caught with the Mazarin Stone in his pocket. That left the Count's goon, his faithful but fatuous Sam Merton, to his own devices. He sought solace in that same disreputable dive in the East End as has the jaded Janet.

Picture, now, these two orphans of fickle fate after a few bumpers of the juice that sustains and cheers. They essay, in a desperate bid to allay their angst, a few choruses of "Roll me over in the Clover." When that met with approval from the discriminating patrons, the daunting duet next tried that moving melody, "Knees up Mother Brown." There followed wild applause, and the rest is history.

They moved, thanks to this critical acclaim, to the music halls of the West End, and their star turn was trumpeted on the hoarding as:

MERTON & TREGELLIS
IN
SAM 'N JANET EVENING

This was written by Frank Darlingtom.
It was first published in Plugs & Dottles, Issue #169, October, 1992

The Fakir Was A Faker [SHPUN201]

And then there is the little known incident in Sherlock Holmes's life, when suffering from Rheumatism in his later years, he purchased a leather strap from a Hindu fakir which, when worn around his neck, was supposed to banish his pain. After some years, the strap rotted and fell off, having done nothing for the pain. When questioned by his fidus Achates about this panacea, the Great Sleuth replied:

"The thong has ended, but the malady lingers on."

This was written by "The Rascally Lascar."
It was first published on the Shamlockians' List on August 5th, 2005.

The Adventure of the Mad Millionaire [SHPUN041]

"Good heavens, Holmes" I ejaculated flinging down the copy of *the Times* I had been reading, "There is a story here that surely must attract your attention."

"What is it old fellow," responded Holmes regarding me through a blue fug of pipe smoke.

"Elmer K Fludd, the eccentric American millionaire, has announced a plan to revitalize some of England's industries."

"Indeed, and what does he intend to do?"

"He is buying up disused cotton factories in Birmingham and Manchester, with the intention of importing large numbers of dogs from Bavaria to breed them."

"So the Mills will be Alive with the Hounds of Munich," observed Holmes (ducking swiftly as I hurled my boots at his head).

This was written by Richard Milne.
It was first published on the Hounds of the Internet List on January 12th, 2005

Music Hath Charm [SHPUN259]

While on their way to Covent Garden Theater one July evening, Holmes and Watson came upon what appeared to be a most tragic scene. A couple named Hill had been struck down by a Hansom cab whose horse had, for some strange reason, suddenly bolted. The accident had taken place just outside the concert hall, and as far as could be ascertained, the unfortunate couple were adjudged to be dead.

In the meantime, the concert had commenced, and the two,

resounding E flat major chords which began Beethoven's mighty *Eroica* could easily be heard from within the hall, the doors of which had been left open due to the oppressive July heat.

Then suddenly, as the strains of the first movement continued to fill the night air, both victims of the aforementioned accident began to stir, and within a few minutes, to the amazement of all, had risen to a sitting position.

"Look, Watson!" Holmes shouted. "The Hills are alive with the sound of music."

This was written by "The Rascally Lascar."
It was first published in Plugs & Dottles, Issue #053, February, 1983.

With Apologies To Rogers & Hammerstein [SHPUN192]

I had just returned to Baker Street one blustery November evening, when Holmes eagerly greeted me at the door.

"Ha, Watson, glad you're back. The European Secretary has just left, and it appears that the game is once again afoot."

"How's that?" I queried.

"It seems that a special diplomatic messenger, who was on a most delicate mission to France, has been found dead in his Paris hotel room. Cause of death has not yet been established. The body did not appear to have suffered any violence. However, the Paris gendarmerie are puzzled by the presence of a scorched patch of hair about the size of a sovereign on the messenger's head. At any rate, I leave for Paris tomorrow, and would appreciate your presence and medical expertise when I examine the body. Will you join me?"

"I wouldn't miss the opportunity, Holmes," I replied. "And I have already decided on a title for the case when I present it to the public following its dénouement."

"Really? And what's that?"

'Well, how does 'The Adventure of the Courier with the Singe on Top' sound?"

This was written by "The Rascally Lascar."
It was first published in Plugs & Dottles, Issue #40, January 1982
It was later published on the Shamlockians' List on June, 2nd, 2005

Interlude at Baker Street, #01 [SHPUN234]

It was a rainy, cold, blustery day in late November in the year 1889. Holmes and I were comfortably ensconced in our Baker Street lodgings, a cheery fire blazing in the grate. My friend had had no cases of interest for some weeks and sat moodily before the fire, puffing steadily on his old and oily black clay pipe. The dense clouds of acrid smoke, which arose from his odious shag, were beginning to produce nothing short of a lachrymatory effect, but I knew better than to complain to my friend. Besides, I would rather have him resort to excessive use of tobacco as an anodyne to boredom than that damnable narcotic he was wont at times to employ.

As the afternoon wore on, the intensity of the November storm increased and the rain beat against the windows with savage fury. A sudden gust of wind caused me to remark.

"I say, Holmes, have you ever noticed the strange sound the wind makes at times?"

"Strange? How's that, Watson?"

"Well, just now … that last gust … the wind actually cried and sobbed like a child in the chimney!"

Holmes smiled devilishly.

"The reason it sounded like that, my dear fellow, is because there is a child in the chimney."

"Come now, Holmes," I replied, "what do you really mean?"

"I mean just what I said – there is a child in the chimney — and a most obnoxious one at that! It is little Ikey Sykes, Mrs. Hudson's nephew. She left him here with me while she went to the market and you were out posting the mail. He refused to keep his grimy little mitts off my chemical equipment and tore up my research notes on how to make ethyl palpitate. So after numerous warnings, I shoved him up the chimney for punishment and safekeeping until our landlady returns *[This is not the first time Holmes resorted to this unique form of chastisement. See "The Adventure of the Ignoble Bachelor," Afghanistanzas, III (October, 1978)]*.

"Ha! I can't say that I blame you, Holmes. I've had problems with the nasty little blighter myself. I feel the punishment is both deserving and effective. But enough for Ikey."

"As you know, I am in the process of chronicling some of your heretofore unpublished cases. More specifically, I have in mind the strange case of Millard Fillmore who, having been inaugurated as president of the United States, stepped into the White House and was never more seen in this world. And then there's the Maggie Jiggs, the ship which is associated with the giant cat of Sinatra, a story for which the world is not yet prepared *[The American title for this case will be "What's New Pussycat?" – if and when it is published]*. And I felt that if it were not overstepping the bounds of modesty, I would enlighten the public concerning the atrocious conduct of Colonel Firewood in connection with the famous photo scandal at the Nonapparal Club

[Such clubs are known in the United States as nudist camps] in which, as a member, he took various pictures of fellow members in their most natural state and then sold them to Professor Moriarty for distribution to London porn peddlers."

"Now, in addition to these three, there is a fourth I would like to document at this time, but for which I have been unable to select an appropriate title. I thought you might be of some help in this area."

"I may be, Watson. To which case do you refer?"

"I had in mind the rather astonishing case of Major Kipperswaite. It is not only of interest from the standpoint of its bizarre features, but also because it is the only case among your many which still lacks a solution."

"Yes, Watson, the case continues to give me fits to this day … and the Major has been dead some six months now. I still insist that the cause of death was somehow related to the hypodermic needle and the curry."

Holmes was referring to the fact that the Major, a bachelor, was found seated before the dinner table, very much dead, with a case of curried mutton staring him in the face. The most astonishing and inexplicable feature, however, was the presence of a hypodermic needle resting on top of the mutton. Numerous tests to detect he presence of poison or drugs in Kipperswaite's body were all negative and no other signs of foul play could be found.

"Yes, Watson," Holmes continued, placing a fresh charge of shag in his pipe, "it is the most bewildering case of my entire career, but I still hope to provide the public with a solution some day. I'm afraid, however, that the final dénouement will require many hours of laborious cerebration."

"But you were wanting for a title. I have always maintained

that a title should be as descriptive of the pertinent facts within a case as possible. Let me see now ... yes ... yes ... I think I have it. Curry ... hypodermic needle – how about calling it 'The Case of the Curry with the Syringe on top'?"

"Excellent, Holmes, excellent!" I exclaimed. "In addition to being most descriptive, the title has somewhat of a musical ring to it. By Jove, you never cease to amaze me! Ah, but I believe Mrs. Hudson has returned. Time to extricate little Ikey from the chimney. And then, I believe something nutritious at Simpson's would be in order."

This was written by "The Rascally Lascar."
It was first published in Wheelwrightings, Vol. 02, Issue #03, January, 1980

The Brooding Bitch [SHPUN313]

During the early days of my residence in Baker Street, I was constantly surprised by the sheer variety of cases that were brought to Holmes' attention. I have mentioned elsewhere the odd mixture of clients that passed through our rooms, but this was nothing when compared to the different kinds of troubles with which they sought help. One of the strangest accompanied a stylish matron who was ushered in by Mrs. Hudson soon after the Lauristan Gardens case. She brought a beautifully coloured bitch on a leash and declared that she was at her wit's end.

The Lady introduced herself as one Mrs. Dalrymple, the wife of a Barrister who had taken the Queen's silk and maintained very stylish offices in The Inns of Court. Holmes took in the well-dressed lady and her canine accompaniment and politely inquired as to the source of her problem. She said that her own interests included breeding and showing dogs and that her companion was a recent purchase that she hoped would become a prize-winning entry in show competitions and a breeding addition to her kennel. Her problem was that the bitch seemed quite moody and she was afraid it would be unfit to show for this reason. Of course, Mrs. Dalrymple was worried that she had wasted her time and money. She had tried to make inquiries with the breeder from whom she had purchased the bitch, but they were out of business and she was worried that she would also have to look elsewhere for a show animal.

Holmes asked for details of the purchase and promised to look into the matter. As soon as she had left, he commented that the address given was one that had some associations with Professor Moriarty, whom he had discussed after our contact with the Professor's influence in the earlier case. I was asked to find a reputable Veterinarian to examine the bitch and Holmes left to make inquiries about the "kennel" operation.

I made arrangements to have a Veterinarian examine the bitch at the Dalrymple kennels and visited Mrs. Dalrymple to assure her that this was merely a precaution and not an indication of disaster. Upon my return to Baker Street, Holmes had returned and was looking quite puzzled. He said that the person who had bred the bitch was an innocent who had sold the entire litter of six puppies to an agent of the Professor. He had somehow bred the litter in a completely un-orthodox fashion that Holmes could not understand that involved introducing elements of the inheritance of a cantaloupe into the animals to obtain the beautiful colouration. I assured him that such 'mixing' of heritages was completely impossible, but he said that is what the breeder had maintained was the source of the litter's colours.

After the Veterinarian had examined the animal, we called on Mrs. Dalrymple to offer Holmes' conclusions. He said that he had looked into the breeder's past and found nothing to prevent showing the bitch or breeding her. The Veterinarian had carefully examined her and concluded that her moodiness was simply due to her youth and would disappear when she reached breeding age. Holmes said that Mrs. Dalrymple should not worry, the bitch was just a melon Collie baby.

This was blatantly stolen by "an Ill-dressed Vagabond" from a mailing by Peter Blau.
It was first published on the Shamlockians' List on October 24th, 2008, and, later in "Practice Notes," [Issue#17, 12/2009] and, again, in "Formulary, [#20, 12/2010].

The Star of Agra [SHPUN310]

In the first decade of the new Century, the venerable Alexander Holder of Holder & Stevenson of Threadneedle Street was approached in a private meeting by a portly figure he knew well. The new King had requested an "unofficial" appointment, which did not promise to be a welcome event to Mr. Holder.

The "unofficial" guest removed a folder from His jacket pocket and revealed an enormous blue sapphire. Mr. Holder instantly recognized it as the "Star of Agra," a gift to the Crown by a certain Rajah made shortly after the Sepoy Mutiny in an effort to keep his throne. It had never been put to any use among the Crown Jewels and was treated as an oddity rather than a functional piece of jewelry. In fact, the awkward setting, in which it appeared as a single, un-complimented stone, had precluded Her Majesty, the Queen Empress, from making any use whatsoever of the piece.

When asked what amount of money he would be willing to lend with the stone as security, Mr. Holder replied "Twenty Thousand Pounds, Sir."

His Royal guest was astounded and made a number of comments, few of which were appropriate to the "First Gentleman of Europe." The general tenor seemed to be that such a priceless piece should merit more brass than a paltry twenty thousand quid.

Mr. Holder retained his equilibrium and took the opportunity to comment on the troubles he had encountered over the affair of the "Beryl Coronet." He explained that such transactions fell outside the Normal Banking Practices and that any larger sum would require approval by the Board of Trustees, a most unlikely occurrence. His personal discretionary limit on loans as a Bank Official was limited to the proposed Twenty Thousand.

Again, his Royal visitor demurred, at length, and in several variations. He finally asked if Mr. Holder was unaware of to Whom he was speaking.

Mr. Holder replied, "When you wish to pawn a Star, it makes no difference who you are."

This was stolen by "an Ill-dressed Vagabond" from a mailing by Peter Blau.
It was first published on the Shamlockian's List on November 13th, 2007.

THE SPORTING LIFE

As was typical of Victorian gentlemen, Holmes and Watson shared a more than casual interest in sports, although it is clear the each had different sporting interests. Watson pursued the improvement of equine genetics and the geometry of solids on a plain, while Holmes was a devotee of the noble art. Further, both possibly, were practitioners of the ancient and honourable sport, but certainly not the Royal Game.

Another Beer Commercial [SHPUN005]

Shortly before the Great Detective's retirement, a group of New York City Detectives came to London to observe operations at Scotland Yard. During a particularly slow day they offered to instruct their London hosts in the great American game of baseball. Having only seven men at his disposal, Inspector Lestrade invited Holmes and Watson to fill in the missing spots.

Pitching for he New Yorkers was a crusty old beer-guzzling curmudgeon named Milton Phaymie. As was his usual custom, Phaymie got into the brew in no slight fashion prior to the game and proceeded to walk the first two batters who happened to be Holmes and Watson.

As he bent over to pick up the rosin bag prior to facing his third batter, a partially consumed bottle of beer fell out of his uniform onto the pitching mound. Holmes (on second base) eyed the bottle briefly and, bringing his astonishing ratiocinative powers to bear, yelled to first:

"Behold, Watson! ... 'Tis the beer that made Milt Phaymie walk us!"

This was written by "The Rascally Lascar".
This was first published in Plugs & Dottles, Issue #36, September, 1981.

Watson Takes A Dive [SHPUN015]

It was in the winter of '95 when Holmes was called upon to solve the mystery of the brutal murder of Lord Denis Throckmorton, Fifth Duke of Gumwitch.

On the evening of 18-February, Lord Throckmorton dined at his favorite club. Following dinner, he played a few hands of whist with friends, and then left for home ... a destination never realized. His garroted and terribly mutilated body was found on the West India Docks shortly before midnight.

Of course, the Great Fathomer was immediately asked by Lestrade to help in the investigation. With glass in hand, Holmes examined both the body and the surrounding area with punctilious exactitude.

"Watson!" he suddenly shouted, "I'll explain why later, but it's absolutely imperative for the solution of this case that I know the exact number of spaces between the dock's planking as measured from Sir. Denis's body to the end of said structure. Please count them if you will."

Watson, on all fours, eagerly threw himself into the task, counting aloud as he proceeded. "One, two, three ... seventeen ... twenty-two ... twenty-nine ...." SPLASH! A momentary silence hung upon the damp night air, and then—

"Damn it, Holmes, come help me out of this stinking Thames!"

"Watson," Holmes replied, "if I've told you once, I've told you a thousand times -- when you're out of slits, you're out of pier."

This was written by "The Rascally Lascar."

52

This was first published in Plugs & Dottles, Issue #63, December, 1983.
It was later published on the Hounds of the Internet List on December 17th, 2004.

Batter Up! [SHPUN257]

We read earlier of a visit by a group of New York City detectives to Scotland Yard and how they introduced their British hosts to the American game of baseball. I now learn that they played a second game the following day at Old Sholto park.

Separating the park from an adjoining pig farm was a rather rickety and dilapidated fence. First to bat for the Scotland Yard team was Inspector Lestrade, who hit a screamer down the right field sideline. The ball slammed into the corner of the fence and, in so doing, attracted the attention of an extremely huge boar, a resident of the adjoining farm. This porcine brute stuck his ugly snout through a hole in the fence, grabbed the ball in its mouth, and swallowed it whole.

As would be expected, an immediate rhubarb as to how the play should be scored resulted.

"Well, Holmes," remarked Watson to his companion as they sat in the stands, "I doubt if they'll be able to resolve this one."

"Oh, I don't know, Watson," Holmes replied. "The whole thing is very clear-cut to me."

"Really, Holmes, your forte is that of a detective – not a baseball official. But, since you appear to have an opinion concerning the problem that has called a halt to this game, I would like to hear it. How *would* you score that last play?"

"Elementary, my dear Watson. It was simply an inside the pork home run."

This was written by "The Rascally Lascar" from a suggestion by Gary List.

It was first published in Plugs & Dottles, Issue #050, November, 1982.

Golf and Watson [SHPUN119]

Holmes and Watson were playing a round of golf, when a funeral cortege passed by on the adjacent highway.

Watson immediately put down his club, removed his cap, and stood, head bowed, hand on heart, until the little procession had passed by.

Looking at him admiringly, Holmes said "That was very reverential of you, Watson."

"Least I could do, Holmes," came the reply.

"Mary and I would have been married a year tomorrow."

This was written by "Anonymous".

It was first published on the Hounds of the Internet List on February 26th, 2005

Better Safe Than Sorry [SHPUN126]

"Watson, I dare say Mrs. Hudson's cooking has been agreeing too well with you. I have noted a definite increase in your waistline, and recommend a bit more exercise."

"I agree, Holmes. In fact, as soon as I don another pair of pants I'm off to the links with my friend Anstruther for a game of golf."

"Excellent idea, my good fellow, but why two pair of pants?"

"Elementary, Holmes -- I might get a hole in one."

This was written by "The Rascally Lascar."
It was first published in Plugs & Dottles, Issue #130, July, 1989.
It was later published on the Shamlockians' List on March 3rd, 2005

Death In The Afternoon [SHPUN105]

'Twas in the summer of '96 that Holmes and I found ourselves in Madrid, having successfully brought to a conclusion the mystery of the Giant Armadillo of Zaragoza -- a case for which the world IS prepared, but is not worth telling. Before returning to London, we decided to attend the local bullfight that, on that day, was featuring the famous matador, Juan Carlos Arruza.

Arruza's performance was nothing short of electrifying. All eagerly awaited the Hour of Truth. Not three feet from the bull, Arruza raised on tiptoe and was about to thrust his estoque between the beast's shoulder blades, when the enraged animal made a sudden and unexpected charge at the famous matador, skewering him through the groin with its right horn. Arruza was dead before he reached the hospital.

"Well, Watson," my friend observed, "the breaks of the game as they say. This time, the bull wins -- and how he reminds one of a professional golfer."

"A professional golfer? Good Lord, Holmes, whatever do you mean?" I queried.

"Elementary, my good man! The bull got a hole in Juan, didn't he?"

This was written by "The Rascally Lascar" from a Suggestion by David Galerstein.

This was first published in Plugs & Dottles, Issue #116, May, 1988.

It was later published on the Hounds of the Internet List on February 20th , 2005

BOTH BARRELS

"Both Barrels" is meant to categorize tales with multiple puns. Some authors simply cannot restrain themselves and so, produce these "volleys" of assaults on our senses. There is probably no better way to start this section than to plunge right into the wacky world of multiple puns before readers have a chance to catch their balance. If this one makes sense to you, with its various Canonical references, then you are truly a lost cause and are well on your way to writing puns on your own, the final stage of this horrible addiction.

An Abbey Jest [SHPUN237]

It was a sunny summer in 1903 when I received a phone call from Holmes as I sat down to breakfast with my wife.

"Well, Watson, what do you say to a trip to Westminster Abbey?"

I glanced over at my wife who mouthed the question, "Holmes?" to me across the room.

I nodded and replied into the mouthpiece.

"You've never been church-going man, Holmes. What's happened at the Abbey?"

"They have a couple of dead musicians they can't identify. Apparently they and the police are so in the dark they called me."

"Really?"

"I thought considering the circumstances they might be able to use a physician as well as a detective. Would you care to meet me there?"

I glanced again at my sweet wife. She smiled and gave me a shooing motion with her delicate fingers.

"I can be there in a half hour."

"Excellent. See you there."

The Dean of the Abbey's long craggy face was pale as he led the two of us into a private crypt room where they'd stored the two bodies, both laid out side-by-side on a table covered in white sheets.

"The circumstances are these," he said quietly, as if he were concerned that someone might overhear though no one was about. "The Abbey is in need of a new bell-ringer. Our last died a week ago, and none of us here have proven to have the proper strength to pull the bells. We're thinking of updating the bell system to some mechanical one, but until then, we do need a ringer. So I placed an advertisement in the Times. Sadly, the two applicants we saw first both fell to their deaths from the bell tower as they auditioned."

"Good Lord," I said. "They weren't pushed—."

"Oh, no-no. They were merely clumsy the both of them. Apparently it runs in their family, as they are brothers."

"And you did not get their names?" asked Holmes.

"Well, they both came in together and were rather in a rush to get up to the tower. It was if they were in competition to see who could ring better than the other. I never had the chance to ask their names."

Holmes sighed impatiently. "In any event the lack of identity is why I'm here. Pray proceed with what occurred."

"Well, they raced up to the tower and the first began to ring the bell. And—well, perhaps you should take a look at him so you might see his rather unique condition—."

Holmes raised an eyebrow curiously and flipped back the sheet to the first body. Besides the obvious grisly state of a body that had fallen from great height, the victim's face had been bludgeoned.

"Good heavens," I cried. "What happened to his face?"

"More to the point, Watson, what happened to his arms?"

I moved my gaze to the man's appendages—or rather, where they should be. "Why—he has none! How did he propose to ring the bell?"

"He rang it with his head," answered the dean with a stoic expression. "Hence the condition of his face."

Holmes and I looked at each other, then back to the victim. It struck me as so amusing that I began to tremble with silent laughter, my eyes watering with my effort to hold silent.

Holmes glared at me and turned back to the dean. "So I take it he knocked himself senseless and stumbled to fall from the height of the belfry tower?"

The Dean nodded.

"Now what of the brother?" Holmes flipped back the second sheet. The second was a young man in rather hardy condition save for the injuries that caused his death.

"Well, horrified at his brother's death, he admitted he came up only to help his brother fulfill his dream of ringing the Abbey bells. And in his honor, he'd like to do it for him right there. I acquiesced of course, and the young man was doing well until the rope caught his feet and—down he went as well."

I started to tremble more. I fear I was about to burst out loud with raucous laughter when Holmes turned to the Dean and said, "Would you mind letting the two of us have a word alone for a moment?"

"Not at all," the Dean said, and left the room, closing the heavy oak door behind him.

Finally freed, I let out a peal of laughter.

"Watson, what the devil is wrong with you?" Holmes said in a harsh whisper.

"Holmes I'm so sorry, but while we may not know who this poor blighter is here." I pointed to the armless man. "We do know one thing."

"What's that?"

"His face surely rings a bell."

Holmes groaned. "Watson, this is no time for puns—."

"Oh, you don't understand, it gets worse, because this one—"

"Please, don't say it—"

"He's a dead ringer for his brother!"

This was written by Ann Margaret Lewis.
It was first published on the Shamlockians' List on August 24th, 2006.

Tetrademimonde [SHPUN267]

One evening shortly after events in The Greek Interpreter, Holmes and Watson were sharing their dinner hour with Mr. Mycroft Holmes. Sherlock felt it was appropriate to introduce Watson to his brother in a more informal fashion, so Mycroft was induced to desert his club for a meal at Simpsons. Over brandy, the diners were watching the pedestrian parade along the Strand when the clocks struck 10:00PM. As they watched, the nature of the traffic began to change and the ladies of the evening seemed to spring up from nowhere, to mix with the traffic from which family groups were rapidly disappearing.

Watson commented on the changing nature of the passing parade and he characterized it as "a jam of tarts."

Sherlock said that it seemed more like a "flourish of strumpets," whereupon, Watson replied that it seemed rather more a "volume of Trollops."

Mycroft said it was not a jam nor a flourish nor even a volume. He asserted it was obviously an "anthology of English pros."

This was adapted (stolen?) by "an Ill-Dressed Vagabond" from earlier pieces by several authors.
It was first published, in this form, on the Shamlockians' List on October 10th, 2006.

Everyone But The 'Dough Boy' [SHPUN179]

It was with considerable surprise that I received a telegram from Sherlock Holmes last Tuesday. After all, the man himself was sitting across from me in front of the fire, and the spoken word would have sufficed.

"Why not tell them of the Cornbread Horror," it read. "Strangest case I have ever handled."

Baker Street was like an oven that day, and I suspect it was this which had reminded him of the pastry shop affair, a case which I shall always think of as "The Adventure of the Devil's Food." Thieves had broken into the bakeshop owned by Miss Sarah Lee.

Surprised by her, in the act of cleaning the dough out of the cash box, the villains had plunged Miss Lee into a large mixing vat containing a blend of confectioner's sugar and butter.

Holmes was outraged by the crime. "Women are never to be entirely frosted!" he cried.

"But I know the mastermind behind this coffeecake ring, and I intend to teach her a lesson."

"Her?"

"Indeed! The crime was obviously cooked up by Captain Crocker's wayward sister, Elizabeth."

"You don't mean...."

"That's right, Watson, this was the work of Betty Crocker!"

This was written by Rosemary Michaud.
It was first published in Plugs & Dottles, Issue #231, December 1997.
It was later published on the Shamlockians' List on May 3rd, 2005.

Foot-Loose and Fancy-Free [SHPUN245]

"Unfortunate, most unfortunate, and more so because the whole matter was easily predictable," I overheard Holmes mutter as he slowly lowered the evening paper with a long-drawn sigh. Turning to me across the table, he announced that our old friend, the tobacconist, had suffered a serious accident that morning. Holmes passed the paper to me for perusal, and I read with sorrow of the poor chap's fall near the tracks leading to Charing Cross Station and the subsequent severing of his left foot above the ankle by a passing train.

"What a shame," I cried, "to have an affliction of this type added to his existing handicap!" Holmes and I were both aware that our friend had lost his right foot some years ago as a result of frostbite and had since made good use of an artificial limb. During the conversation that ensued, I chanced to remark upon the tobacconist's notable penchant to interlard his discourse with those old, familiar maxims—*Rome wasn't built ..., a stitch in time ..., turn the other cheek..., a penny saved is ....* "Holmes," I said, "the man was a veritable treasury of folk sayings."

"It was his inordinate use of those damnable maxims and proverbs that led to his undoing," Holmes replied with what I considered unnecessary heat. "You certainly are aware, Watson, that the mind's repeated acceptance of any statement is bound to result eventually in a subconscious response. You may rest assured that it was one of his oft repeated and despicable old saws that cut off his remaining foot—if you'll pardon the pun.

"And a puny pun it is, Sir," I shouted, jumping to my feet, "but no more puny than your puerile effort to forge a tasteless connection between our friend's delightful apothegms and his lamentable accident! Holmes, you owe me an explanation for this unseemly reasoning!" Having thus expressed myself, I fell back into my chair.

"My dear Watson, you may have my sincere apology for the pun – although I must confess that I thought it rather first-rate when compared to my original temptation to use a play on words involving a loss of footing – but, as to my thesis of mental connection which you have termed unseemly reasoning, I invite you to consider one incontrovertible fact which I shall now state: -- if our friendly purveyor of the noxious weed had not, throughout years of habitual practice, become so addicted to a certain aphorism, he would never have *put his best foot forward!*"

This was written by "Howard E. Burr".
This was first published in Plugs & Dottles, Issue #43, April, 1982.

If At First You Don't Succeed... [SHPUN030]

"I say, Holmes, have I ever told you about my old friend Killaby?" Watson was in one of his more garrulous moods. Holmes decidedly was not.

"I seem to have been spared," replied Holmes.

"Dr. J. Rodon Killaby," Watson went on, undeterred. "We were in school together. Quite a brilliant fellow. Very shy, so he went into research rather than practice. Not much money in that, but he made a promising beginning. And then, all went sour. He spent six years seeking a cure for the common cold. Nothing came of it, but his expenses were nothing to *sneeze* at."

"Then he moved to the Congo with some theories for curing jungle rot through a serum made from aphids which live exclusively on the leaves of the Kapoona bush. After five years in this forsaken place, he had nothing to show for his efforts but the worst feet imaginable, and the poor chap was near bankruptcy."

"Then, fortune smiled. One morning, as he checked the Kapoona grove, he found that overnight there had been an immigration of an entirely new strain of aphids. Back to his jungle laboratory he took them, concocted a new batch of serum, injected himself, and in a matter of days he had toes again!"

"Bravo!" said Holmes, stifling a yawn.

"Quite so," replied Watson. "Now the fellow is back in England, prosperous as you please."

"I prefer the brilliant deduction to the lucky find, Watson," said Holmes. "Nonetheless, I am impressed. The story you have told is the finest example of how just one lucky day can give a fellow a new lice on leaf."

This was written by "The Rascally Lascar".
This was first published in Plugs & Dottles, Issue #190, July, 1994.
It was later published on the Hounds of the Internet List on January 1st, 2005

Breathing May Be Hazardous to Your Health [SHPUN033]

'Twas a blustery evening in early January. Watson was absent from Baker Street, having been summoned out on an emergency call shortly after dinner. Awaiting the good doctor's return, Holmes was ensconced before a cheery fire, avidly reading a paper in *the Italian Journal of Chemistry* by the famous Naples chemist, Guido Rodino. Within an hour, Watson's familiar step was heard upon the stair.

"Ha, Watson, so you have returned," remarked Holmes. "I trust you were able to be of some assistance to your patient."

"Quite so," came the reply. "'Twas a relatively simple matter.

The fellow was a glassblower. While at work, it seems he inhaled at the wrong time and ended up with a pane in his stomach."

AN ADDED EXTRA

"I say, Holmes, isn't that Lady Frances Carfax going into the chemist's shop? I wonder why?"

"Probably wants something for her coffin spell."

This was written by "The Rascally Lascar".
This was first published in Plugs & Dottles, Issue #194, November, 1994.
It was later published on the Hounds of the Internet List on January 4th, 2005

Comparative Anatomy, Primitive [SHPUN067]

At the beginning of HOUN, Dr. Mortimer told Holmes how he and Sir Charles Baskerville would discuss the comparative anatomies of the Hottentot and the Bushman.

It is not generally known that they also compared the anatomies of the Eskimo and the Eunuch.

After due consideration, they concluded that whilst the Eskimo was a frigid midget with a rigid digit, the Eunuch was a massive vassal with a passive tassel.

This was written by "Anonymous."
It has never been published before.

The Spanish Question [SHPUN091]

It was a cold, foggy day and we had received a visit from the Spanish Ambassador who was ushered into our presence by Mrs. Hudson. With his usual courtesy Holmes bade the neatly moustachioed representative of his country welcome, seated him in a comfortable chair and handed him a large brandy. Senor de Cadiz glanced at me suspiciously.

"Oh don't mind old Watson, he is the soul of discretion in all matters," said Holmes, "why do you wish to consult with me?"

"You have read, no doubt, of the troubles assailing the King of Spain and his family?" said the ambassador, after a long sip from his glass.

"Of course, it was in the *Times* this morning," I burst out.

"Quite so," said the ambassador a little irritated, I thought, at my interruption. "The unhappy state of my country – the rebels attacking the Escorial, the King and his family forced to jump down a sewer to escape - all except his cousin, a prince nicknamed 'Squarepeg'."

"It would be difficult for a Squarepeg to fit in a round hole," observed Holmes.

"But it is the fate of the monarchy of Spain that I wish to talk to you about," wailed the ambassador, "What is to be done?"

"At the moment," said Holmes, "very little?"

"Why Senor?"

"Because I fear the reign in Spain has fallen mainly down the drain."

This was written by Richard Milne.
It was first published on the Hounds of the Internet List on February 11th, 2005

Sherlock Holmes And The GI Microorganism Murder
[SHPUN208]

It was in the spring of the year 1894 that all London was interested, and the fashionable world dismayed, by the murder of the Honourable Edward Coli under most unusual and inexplicable circumstances. On the evening of 14-April, Edward Coli was found shot to death at the entrance of the St. *Pancreas* Hotel from which he had just emerged after a dinner of *sweetbreads* and kippers.

Three of the killers were seen running from the hotel immediately after the shots were fired.

My good old gumshoe fidus Achates, Sherlock Holmes, was immediately asked by the Yard to bring his *digestive* powers to bear on the case. It was my friend's immediate *gut* reaction that the murderers must have had some *gall* to gun down an individual in such a heavily populated section of London.

It wasn't long before Holmes ferreted out the murderers -- a Sam Monella, Carl Perfringens, and a female born-again-Christian minister known only as Pastor Ella.

The three miscreants were brought before the Assizes, and executed the next day by a firing squad using antibiotic-loaded darts.

I would like to add an *appendix* to this tale, but I simply don't have the *intestinal fartitude* to do it.

This was written by "The Rascally Lascar".
It was first published on the Shamlockians' List on September 6th, 2005.

The Case of the Cold Shoulder... [SHPUN125]

"Anything in the papers, Watson?" asked Holmes as his familiar visage emerged from the blue fug of pipe tobacco he had been enjoying on this rather warm August morning.

"Not much," I said. "A couple of street urchins arrested for letting off fireworks in the public lavatories at Kew Gardens."

"Just a flash in the pan. Anything else?"

"A couple of stand-over men arrested in a billiard hall at the Rotherhithe..."

"Mere bagatelle, Watson... is there no crime?"

"There's this Holmes ... 'Cold Air Experiment Goes Awry. Audience frozen to the marrow'."

"What's that about?" enquired Holmes eagerly.

"A young man named Samuel Toose, who had inherited an ice-works and refrigeration equipment factory in Birmingham, attempted to demonstrate an experimental machine that can chill air in closed public spaces to a large audience at the Albert Hall last night. Unfortunately, the machine was too efficient and many in the audience were overcome with cold. It appears the young man may be charged with committing a public nuisance." I put the paper down on the arm of the chair."

"Never mind," said Holmes, "once he has paid his debt to society at least he will have a ready made advertising slogan."

"What would that be, Holmes?"

"Toose Company freezes a crowd"

This was written by Richard Milne.
It was has never been published before.

GENERAL CATEGORY

Most Sherlockian puns cannot easily be assigned to some grouping. In fact, the majority of these efforts simply defy categorization. No amount of parsing and paring can ease the stress induced by these assaults upon reason. One simply has to accept them as they are.

Phillimore's Revenge [SHPUN243

Sherlock Holmes, sporting an extremely short haircut, was once again on the beach, hurling stones at terns. It's vile temper aroused by Holmes's missiles, the largest bird in the flock decided to exact retribution in the way birds favor most. This avian bombardier scored a direct hit on the Great Detective's noggin. Definitely enraged, and realizing that most terns are extremely jealous of their city dwelling cousins, Holmes took revenge by loudly exclaiming to Watson:

"A bird in the Strand has worse doo in the butch!"

This was written by Brad Keefauver, "James Phillimore".
This was first published in Plugs & Dottles, Issue #33, May, 1981.

The Problem Of the Sore Bridge [SHPUN072]

It was in the fall of '87 that Holmes and I were privileged to hear the great piano virtuoso, Hans Von Steinroden, play at St. James Hall. I probably should not use the word "privileged," because it was the only concert in Steinroden's career that was not marked by excellence.

As we later learned, the famed pianist was in a most uncomfortable way the evening of the concert due to a new set of extremely ill fitting dentures. The teeth had been so poorly made that Steinroden could only close his mouth with the greatest of pain.

Discussing the concert one evening after we had learned of the problem, Holmes remarked:

"You can say what you like, Watson, about those false teeth, but Steinroden's Bach was definitely worse than his bite."

This was written by "The Rascally Lascar."
This was first published in Plugs & Dottles, Issue #97, October, 1986.
It was later published on the Hounds of the Internet List on February 2nd, 2005

Panic of 1893 [SHPUN307]

When the Panic of 1893 hit Great Britain, my cousin, Bertram Watson, actually lost his entire business one day in less than a minute: somebody jumped from a window and landed on his pushcart. But, that's another story.

This tale concerns Pierre Vernet, an uncle of Holmes. Holmes still shakes his head in disbelief when he tells this story. He was a wealthy Parisian who derived his total income from his real estate dealings. He depended entirely on his tenants and their monthly rents to keep him solvent.

Unfortunately, this French realtor was not the most benevolent of landlords. He often let conditions of his houses and apartments go to rot. He was reluctant to make repairs, and he rarely did anything to benefit his renters or enhance the value of his properties.

Conditions worsened and worsened, and eventually his tenants had had enough. They got together and decided that until repairs were made, they were not going to pay their rents.

The owner was distraught; eventually he ran out of all his savings, and he had no recourse but to kill himself. He paced the boulevards of Paris trying to decide how to do it. He was bankrupt, his tenants would not pay, and life seemed hopeless. He decided to jump into the river.

As he jumped, two of his friends came by and shouted to him to come out of the river. Things could not be that bad. Certainly he had something to live for. But try as they might, they could not convince him to swim to the riverbank.

"None of my tenants have paid me. I won't come out!" he shouted. And he drowned, not having had enough rents to come out of the Seine.

This was written by "Anonymous" and adapted by Dave Milner.

A Brief Course in Economics [SHPUN301]

As the police led "Killer" Evans into the police van, Holmes and Watson returned to Nathan Garrideb's house for a spot of liquid refreshment. Although aching from his recent wound, Watson was curious about the case and his friend's methods in solving it.

"My dear Holmes," pleaded the doctor, "won't you tell me how you knew that the counterfeiting press was hidden in the basement?"

"Ah," replied Holmes with a sigh, "I confess that I was not certain of the exact location of the press. But had I been the ideal reasoner you profess me to be, I might have known it."

"But how?"

"By the laws of Economics, Watson. You see, I ought to have remembered that the counterfeiting business is a cellar's market."

This was written by the Rosemary Michaud.
It was first published in Plugs & Dottles, #210, March, 1996.

Watson Wins one! [SHPUN298]

"I hope, my dear Watson, that you have had some success in fathoming the cause of the mystery malady that has so regularly befallen most of the members of the cast of the Christy Minstrels as they prepare to go on stage."

"Good that you ask, Holmes. The case is closed, and I am in the process of penning an article for *The Lancet* detailing its singular solution. The cause of the mass fainting during preparations for the show proved to be the miasma from the burning of corks over an alcohol flame – a process undertaken to provide makeup material for the blackface actors. The resulting toxic fumes brought down Mr. Bones, the Interlocutor and other key members of the cast."

"Well done! I do hope that you will not indulge in any romantic embroidering of this straightforward tale. I can easily imagine you calling it 'Watson's Wobblies' or some such."

"Not a bit of it. I plan to title the article, and the disorder, simply; PMS – Pre Minstrel Syndrome."

This was written by Frank Darlington
It was first published in Plugs & Dottles, #181, October, 1993.

The Tarlton Murders [SHPUN295]

From time to time in our early years together at Baker Street, Holmes would fill in some of the time he spent waiting for clients to turn up by telling me of his early cases. As I was still recruiting my health, these interludes served to prevent my wasting my meager funds at Billiards or at the Track.

During an earlier discussion the affair I recorded as 'The Musgrave Ritual,' Holmes mentioned 'The Tarlton Murders,' another early case he had dealt with. One day when he was waxing expansive, I asked him to tell me about that very early case.

"It wasn't properly a case, you see," Holmes remarked. "I was reading in the *Times* of the deaths of an entire family, one Charles Tarlton, his wife and their four children, due to poor ventilation of their fireplace when I remarked some details that seemed to me to be suspicious. I mentioned these to then Sergeant Lestrade and suggested he find answers to one or two questions."

"What details were those, Holmes?" I enquired.

"It seems that a distant cousin, one Daniel Tarlton, made all the funeral arrangements for the family which was practically indigent. His only concern, however, seemed to be that proper death certificates be made out on all the family members, even the twin infants. Further, he posted an elaborate announcement of the tragedy in several Newspapers."

"What questions did you ask the good Lestrade to answer?" I asked.

"I suggested that the exact relationship of Mr. Tarlton to the deceased family be ascertained and that any other relatives be identified."

"Did any such relatives turn up?" I asked.

"Indeed yes," replied Holmes. "There was an elderly recluse who was more closely related to the deceased family than to Mr. Daniel Tarlton. In fact, his will left his entire estate to the dead Charles Tarlton with the rest of his family being his heirs. With the death of these people, Mr. Daniel Tarlton was now the sole heir to a considerable fortune. It became apparent that the 'blocked' fireplace should be investigated further and, of course, it proved to have been tampered with during a 'free cleaning' offered by a chimney sweep who was later shown to be a servant of Dan Tarlton in disguise."

"So, the fact of the murders was revealed only by the existence of an unsuspected will?" I commented.

"Yes," said Holmes, "the will was a dead giveaway."

This was written by the "an Ill-dressed Vagabond" to a suggestion by Ann Margaret Lewis, "The Vatican Cameo."
It was first published on the Shamlockians' List on October 17th, 2006.
It was later published in The Gaslight Gazette; Vol. 12, Issue #11, November, 2006.

The Impatient Patient [SHPUN311]

Dr. Watson maintained an office several times during his association with Holmes, most notably during "The Great Hiatus," after Holmes disappeared at The Reichenbach Falls. Such an undertaking required major changes from the idyllic routine of a retired Army Surgeon. Office Hours had to be established and kept, patients had to be visited regularly and a staff had to be hired and paid. Of course a suitable suite of offices had also to be hired and maintained. This required at the very least, an Examining Room or two, an Office and a Patient Waiting Room, with a receptionist or, possibly, a Nurse-receptionist to aid in surgeries and other treatments.

In any case, such an establishment was needed to insulate the Doctor from new arrivals while treating and examining patients or counseling relatives, parents and caregivers. In addition, the Doctor was usually kept separate from the billing and payment aspects of the practice since such matters were not really a gentlemanly pursuit, and were best left up to the Doctor's 'Office staff.' Further, the presence of a female at examinations and treatments of the fairer sex was indispensable.

It was into just such a scene on one late Autumn day in 1892 that a frantic man charged, saying "I am in terrible trouble. I must see the Doctor immediately!"

He squirmed and wiggled and paced and complained. He kept insisting that his case was dire. The receptionist tried and tried to calm him, saying that the doctor was engaged with another patient, but the man kept insisting he was in dire straits. Finally, the girl had to give up and told him she would speak to the Doctor. At this the man subsided a bit, muttering about the serious nature of his affliction.

The receptionist consulted the Nurse who was bandaging a patient Dr. Watson had just treated and the Nurse agreed to speak to the patient. She went to the Waiting Room and asked the patient to describe his symptoms, but he would have none of her help and insisted on seeing the Doctor at once. Defeated, she returned to the Treatment rooms and gently knocked on the door to the room where the Doctor was examining another patient.

In a quiet conference, she explained the problem with the impatient patient to the Doctor who agreed to speak to the man in a moment. He went to the Waiting Room to speak to the patient, who immediately burst into full complaint form:

"Doctor, Doctor!" he cried. "I'm shrinking! I'm wasting away to nothing! My weight has dropped ten pounds since yesterday and I've lost a full two inches in height! What can I do?

Dr. Watson said "Please calm yourself. You shall just have to be a little patient until I can get to you".

This was stolen by "an Ill-dressed Vagabond" from a mailing by Peter Blau.
It was first published on the Shamlockian's List on November 25th, 2007.

Inspectors-at-Law [SHPUN312]

"Holmes," I ejaculated as the familiar lean figure entered our Baker Street rooms. It was not quite ten o'clock in the morning and I was only half way through the Times agony column.

"I thought you would be all day giving evidence in court," I said.

"So did I Watson," replied Holmes with a sigh. "But when I arrived at the Old Bailey the court usher buttonholed me and asked me to come into the court. There I found Inspectors Gregson, Lestrade and Athelney Jones standing in a little clump in the room."

"You mean group, Holmes," I suggested mildly.

"No I think 'clump' expresses it well enough. They were staring at the Judges bench and seated there was a baby wearing a judges wig."

"Good Heavens, Holmes" I said "What did it mean?"

"I solved it in a few seconds of course. It was just one of those little things sent to try us."

This was written by Richard Milne.
It was first published on the Shamlockians' List on December 18th, 2007.
It appeared in The Gaslight Gazette, [Vol. XIV, #01-02, 01-02/2008]

Another Famous British Tradition [SHPUN294]

'Twas toward the latter portion of the year 1888 when a virtual epidemic of strong-arm robberies struck the City of London. The prime victims of these attacks were the Underground Transport System employees, who were consistently being relieved of the day's receipts as they took them to the bank.

"Well, Watson," remarked Holmes one evening as he read yet another article on the subject in the day's paper. "I see that the Underground employees are now being escorted to the bank each day by our City Policemen."

"Yes indeed, Holmes," replied Watson. "'Tis a ritual which will no doubt become known as the guarding of the change."

This was written by "The Rascally Lascar."
It was first published in Plugs & Dottles, Issue #171, December, 1992

A 'Corny' Conclusion [SHPUN289]

One day in the famous Baker Street sitting room, Holmes was regaling Watson with the details of the Dundas separation case.

"Ah yes, Watson, that was a strange case indeed, but not nearly so strange as its sequel," remarked Holmes.

"Whatever do you mean?" asked Watson.

"Well, just last week Mr. And Mrs. Dundas happened to be dining in the same restaurant. When he saw his estranged wife, Mr. Dundas became deranged and attempted to beat her to death with an ear of cooked corn."

"Good heavens, Holmes! I hope he was stopped in time."

"Oh, yes. He was arrested on the spot for a salt and buttery with intent to kill."

This was written by William Ballew.
It was first published in Plugs & Dottles, Issue #157, October, 1991.

A Fishy Story [SHPUN136]

And then there was the time Mrs. Hudson entered a fish-cooking contest in London's fashionable West End. Recipes were numerous, but were finally narrowed down to two by the judges. One of these was that of our long-suffering landlady, the other a creation by a Henrietta Pike of Bermondsey. Deciding on a winner was most difficult, both entries being of near equal merit, but the judges finally awarded first place honors to Mrs. Pike because of the special glaze she had applied to her piscatorial creation.

Mrs. Hudson was, of course, disappointed for not having won. As the first place prize was awarded to the winner, she soulfully remarked to Holmes and Watson:--

"Alas, there but for the glaze of cod go I!"

This was written by "The Rascally Lascar."
(Dangling Prussian Amateur Press Association #3, Feb. 1992)

The Kipper Caper [SHPUN230]

It was in the summer of '95 that the great Baker Street Gumshoe was called in to investigate the murder of Thaddeus Cuthwaite, Managing Director of London's Kippered Herring Canning Corporation. A nark named Ned informed Holmes that it might be to his advantage to interview a certain Victor Sexauer, an employee at said canning factory.

Entering the lobby of the establishment, Holmes approached the receptionist and enquired, "Pardon me, madam, but do you have a Sexauer here?"

"Sex hour?" she retorted, "Mister, we don't even get a coffee break in this place!"

This was written by "The Rascally lascar."
It was first published on the Shamlockians' List on August 15th, 2006.

Anstruther's New Undertaking [SHPUN286]

"Tell me, Watson," remarked Holmes one May evening, "is it true that your old colleague Anstruther has given up the practice of Medicine and gone into the undertaking business?"

"'Tis indeed true," replied Watson, "and a most unfortunate decision, I'm afraid. There's another undertaking establishment in the same neighborhood as Anstruther's, and since it's offering lower rates it's getting most of the business. Poor Anstruther is not doing well at all."

"Well, Watson," said Holmes, "considering the business he's in, I guess you could say Anstruther has *stiff* competition."

This was written by "The Rascally Lascar."
It was first published in Plugs & Dottles, Issue #152, May, 1991.

Holmes Said It First [SHPUN281]

Sometime after the conclusion of the Von Bork affair, Holmes and I were summoned to Downing Street, doubtless for another mission. There had been a Zeppelin raid the night before our interview, and a bomb had exploded quite nearby. We suffered no major damage, but our ears were still ringing when we set out in the morning. Knowing Holmes had certain views on transportation, I pointed to the cab rank and shouted, "Shall we take a good old hansom, or one of these modern motor cars?"

Holmes turned to me, pointed to his mouth , and mimed: "Watson, read my lips – no new taxis."

This was written by David R. McCallister.
It was first published in Plugs & Dottles, Issue #144, September, 1990.

Soup's on — But Not for Long [SHPUN280]

"Well, Watson, what do you say we dine out tonight?"

Holmes's sudden query interrupted the brown study into which I had fallen one late afternoon in August. It had been a quiet, pleasant day with moderate temperatures, and the thought of a stroll through London's streets, with a good restaurant our destination, sounded most appealing.

"A capital idea, Holmes," I replied. "How about trying that new Chinese restaurant in The Strand?"

"I would not recommend it," said my friend.

"Oh? For what reason, may I ask?"

"I dined there yesterday with a client, and was forced to return my soup."

"And what did you tell the waiter?"

"I told him that it had been tried and found Won Ton."

This was stolen by "The Rascally Lascar," from Art Moger's *The Complete Pun Book*.
It was first published in Plugs & Dottles, Issue #143, August, 1990.

Art in the Blood Is Not Necessarily Transmitted [SHPUN279]

"The stupidity, Watson, of the average London citizen never ceases to amaze me."

These words from my friend Sherlock Holmes greeted me one June morning as I descended to breakfast, the day following Holmes's successful conclusion to the Tinkerbell Club Scandal.

"Our fellow citizens stupid, Holmes ... how's that?" I asked.

"The *Morning Herald* has it all here. A chap in Bermondsey, whose father was an art collector, recently sold a French Impressionist painting from his sire's collection for £25. 'Tis obvious he knew absolutely nothing about art, for the painting was auctioned yesterday at Christie's for the amazing sum of £500,000.

"Not surprising, Holmes," I replied. "It's just a beautiful affirmation of the old saw – a fool and his Monet are soon parted."

This was written by G. Earle Hamerstrand.
It was first published in Plugs & Dottles, Issue #141, June, 1990.

Elixer Vitae Leporidae [SHPUN276]

It was in the summer of '05 that I made one of my infrequent visits to the South Downs in order to spend a few days with my old friend Sherlock Holmes. The man whose exploits I had the privilege of chronicling for some twenty years had retired two years earlier, and when I had last visited him was spending a good portion of his leisure time in the serious pursuit of apiculture. It was with some surprise, then, that upon arriving I found my friend emerging from a small enclosure at the rear of his cottage. Contained within the wired area were some fifteen to twenty large, white domestic rabbits. Holmes was carrying one of the animals that appeared rather sick.

"My dear Holmes, good to see you again," I greeted him. "It appears that you have added rabbits to your pastime of beekeeping."

"Yes, Watson. I've discovered that the local gentry are rather fond of rabbit stew and related dishes, and have gone into the business of providing them with the desired product. It helps a bit with the income. But I'm afraid this poor fellow will go before his time. Do you have any suggestions?" Holmes handed me the sickly creature that certainly appeared to be on its last legs.

"I believe I might be able to help," I replied, "if you would be so good as to fetch my medical bag from the wagonette in front of the cottage."

Holmes was back in a minute. Filling a 10cc syringe from one of the many bottles in my collection, I injected the rabbit subcutaneously and returned it to the enclosure. For a minute it remained absolutely still, unmoving, its eyes nearly closed. Then suddenly, it bounded up with amazing vigor and began racing round and round within the confines of the pen.

"Good heavens, Watson, that's incredible!" Holmes exclaimed. "What was that stuff? I must keep some on hand for future emergencies."

"Hair restorer," I replied.

This was written by "The Rascally Lascar."
It was first published in Plugs & Dottles, Issue #131, August, 1989.

Upon returning to Baker Street one foggy December evening, Holmes found Watson deep in thought, pacing the floor of their sitting room.

"I see you have adopted my methods, Watson," remarked Holmes.

"Eh, what ... Holmes?" mumbled Watson, half roused from his preoccupation.

"You have obviously been pacing the floor for some time, Watson, as the accumulation of cigarette stubs in the ashtray near the umbrella stand and in the one across the room on the deal table amply testifies. And the air in the room is poisonous."

"My problem is extraordinary, Holmes. Never have I seen or heard anything like it. I am completely baffled."

"It is a medical problem, Watson?"

"Yes, and it is unique*. Even the Harley Street specialists whom I have consulted confess themselves totally at a loss to explain it."

"What exactly **is** the problem?"

"A lady came to me three weeks ago. She complained of urinating pennies! I was, of course, astounded. I examined her thoroughly, but I could find neither the cause of her extraordinary complaint nor any evidence of physical illness or harm. I instructed her to go home and rest for several days. Last week she returned and informed me that her condition had worsened; she was urinating shillings! Again, I examined her, found no evidence of harm, and counseled complete bed rest. Today she appeared again in a state of extreme agitation and told

me she was now urinating guineas! Examination indicated not
the slightest physical evidence of disease or trauma, and I could
only offer the same ineffectual advice: complete bed rest. I am
afraid, Holmes, that unless I can find the cause of this
phenomenon very soon, her mind will become unbalanced."

"The problem is elementary and no cause for alarm, Watson.
It is clear from the evidence that the lady is just going through
her change."

*This syndrome is not as unique as Watson states. A similar
case in the United States, involving Ida P. Nichols, can be found
documented in *The New England Journal of Urology*, Vol. #08,
Issue #06, pp 14-20, 1928 -- ed.

This was written by Gordon R. Speck.
It was first published in Plugs & Dottles, Issue #135, December,
1989.

The Psilly Psychic Psyndrome [SHPUN275]

"Damnable, crazy woman!" Watson's angry words echoed
through the stairwell as he ascended the well-worn seventeen
steps to the familiar sitting room in Baker Street. His words had
not gone unheard by Holmes who greeted his companion as he
stormed into the room.

"Watson! What seems to be the trouble, my good man?"

"The trouble, Holmes, is one Euspasia Paladino."

"The famous Italian spiritualist?"

"The *crazy* Italian Spiritualist would be more like it. When I
delivered my account of the Eugenia Rounder case to Dr. Doyle
the other day, a discussion of departed family members arose. I
related to Doyle how I have never forgiven myself for not having

been closer to my late brother, whose tragic life you will no doubt recall you once deduced from a careful examination of his watch. Dr. Doyle, being an authority on psychic phenomena, suggested I attempt to contact my brother through a spiritualist.

"I thus made an appointment with the Paladino woman who is currently holding séances here in London. No sooner had I sat down and explained to her my desire to attempt contact with my dear, departed brother, when she broke into a fit of uncontrollable, hysterical laughter which persisted despite my efforts to quiet her. Finally, my patience ran out. I backhanded the crazy crone across the side of her face and walked out."

"A rather violent demonstration on your part," remarked Holmes. "Don't you think you overreacted to the situation?"

"Not at all, Holmes," was Watson's rejoinder, "my mother taught me always to strike a happy medium."

This was written by The Rascally Lascar.
It was first published in Plugs & Dottles, Issue #128, May, 1989.

The Exorcist [SHPUN308]

Although Holmes denied any interest in matters of the supernatural, there were several occasions when such events intruded on our existence in Baker Street. I do not propose to explain everyday events as deriving from supernatural causes, but there are times when adequate, mundane explanations escape me. One such event occurred just before my marriage, shortly after the St. Simon affair. An older man appeared on our doorstep one morning demanding that Mrs. Hudson "Take me at once to Mr. Sherlock Holmes! I'm being haunted!"

Since the man's comments were easily heard by neighbors all along Baker Street, Holmes had no hesitation in asking our landlady to show the gentleman up. Once settled, our visitor identified himself as Josiah Scrimshaw, a retired 'lending agent,' which Holmes and I both interpreted as a pawnbroker. Mr. Scrimshaw said that he had recently purchased a detached villa in Pimlico and began settling into his new home. This required a larger staff than he was accustomed to employ, so he had advertised for a housekeeper/cook to supplement his valet, who would assume the duties of a butler.

After interviewing several candidates, he had employed a widow with a grown son and daughter who could assume the duties of a stable hand and a maid; "quite a bargain," as he commented. This staff seemed adequate to his needs and the household began to settle into a comfortable routine when his troubles began. Noises and misplaced articles escalated quickly into a variety of creaks, groan and moans and damaged and lost furnishings. His own bedchamber had been upset, with bedding strewn about, clothing thrown into the fireplace (fortunately unlit) and toilet articles smashed and scattered.

Neighbors had hinted at some sort of dark past for the villa, citing tales of everything from alchemy to the white slavery trade, but all that local records showed was that the previous owner had defaulted on the mortgage and the lender had taken the property for sale to cover the unpaid loan. The servants became increasingly agitated and demanded something be done, so Mr. Scrimshaw had made contact with the local rector. After some discussion, the priest had recommended the services of a colleague who specialized in exorcisms, feeling that the problems might lie in the property itself rather than the persons inhabiting the house.

After a number of ceremonies were conducted, the divine had pronounced the property to be "Cleansed" and had declared that the problems should cease. Mr. Scrimshaw agreed that things seemed to be quieter, but he had received a bill for ten Guineas from the exorcist, which he refused to pay as being "much to high." After a few days, the noises had started up again and he wanted Holmes to investigate the situation.

Holmes agreed to visit the villa that afternoon and assured Mr. Scrimshaw that he would "look into the matter." When we arrived at the given address at 4:00 PM, we were admitted and told that the Master would be with us presently. However, the butler returned in a few moments saying that Mr. Scrimshaw had locked himself in his study and didn't answer the door. When we had forced our way in, there was nobody and all the windows were closed and latched. Mr. Scrimshaw had disappeared!

Holmes examined the room thoroughly and then recommended that the butler call the police and inform them that Mr. Scrimshaw was missing. His only comment was "He who doesn't pay his exorcist should expect to be repossessed."

This was written by "an Ill-dressed Vagabond."
It was first published on the Shamlockians' List on April 30th, 2007.

A Case of Identity [SHPUN274]

"I say, Watson," remarked Holmes, "did you read my manuscript relating to the case of the blanched soldier? I do believe in your absence I have penned a compelling narrative that will appeal to the popular taste."

Watson, still subdued from Holmes's rebuke of his having taken a wife, turned to the detective and said, "But was it necessary to call in that cowardly army chaplain, Colonel Saunders?"

Holmes rose to his full height, grinned unnaturally, and replied: "A case of mistaken identity, Watson. Your "Colonel" Sir James Saunders is a noted dermatologist, not a chicken friar."

This was written by Carolyn Low.

It was first published in Plugs & Dottles, Issue #127, April, 1989.

Adrift at Sea without a Bic to Flick [SHPUN273]

It was in the Summer of '85 that Holmes and Watson found themselves returning to England from France, having spent the previous two weeks in the quaint town of Lons-le-Saunier where the Great Detective had solved the mystery surrounding the death of Rene-Nicolas de Maupeou, Comte de Maurepas. A jealous paramour, Holmes discovered, had poisoned the Comte's Brie. Too sordid for the *Strand Magazine*, the details of the case were published by Watson in *Le Monde* in 1890 under the title, "la Adventure du Fromage Toxique."

Midway across the Channel, the steamer carrying the famous sleuth and his Boswell capsized in high seas. Fortunately, the two found the safety of a lifeboat, and began calmly to await rescue. But, being the inveterate smoker that he was, Holmes was soon longing for a cigarette, his and Watson's having been wet through before they discovered the lifeboat. Suddenly, the cargo from the capsized boat began to drift by, one item of which was a sealed case of cigarettes. Holmes soon had it aboard. "Now, Watson, we will have a relaxing smoke," he remarked with joy.

"Holmes, I hate to say this," put in Watson, "but we have no matches."

"No matches?" Holmes put his fingertips together and lapsed into deep thought. A moment later he exclaimed: "The problem is solved, Watson!" He then proceeded to break open the crate and remove a package of the smokes. Tearing it open, he extracted one cigarette and tossed it overboard. "There we are, my good fellow," he promptly announced.

"How in God's Name does that help?" queried Watson.

"Elementary, my Boswell," replied Holmes, "our lifeboat is now a cigarette lighter."

This was created by "The Rascally Lascar" from a suggestion by Dave Galerstein.
It was first published in Plugs & Dottles, Issue #119, August, 1988.

Throw the Switch [SHPUN271]

Holmes and Watson sat on either side of a cheery fire on a blustery March evening, the two engaged in a lively discussion of Penology with emphasis on the subject of the death penalty.

"I see, Holmes," remarked Watson, "where our American cousins have come up with a rather novel way of dispatching society's evildoers. The electric chair appears to be a most efficient device for this purpose."

"Ah yes, the chair, Watson – definitely a piece of Period Furniture, I would say."

"Period Furniture, Holmes – how's that?"

"Well, my good fellow, it does put an end to a sentence, doesn't it?"

This was created by "The Rascally Lascar."
It was first published in Plugs & Dottles, Issue #114, March, 1988.

Just Follow Your Nose [SHPUN270]

It was a cold, gray day in the early Spring of '95 that Holmes's attention was first drawn to the spate of wine thefts from country estates in the West of England. Wine cellars were being systematically looted of their rarer vintages, and the owners, although they from time to time saw them, had been unable either to stop the thieves or later to identify them. It was now, in mid-October that, as a result of Holmes's deductions, we found ourselves huddled together in the Duke of Holderness's wine cellar, awaiting the arrival of the band of rogues.

It was toward the early hours of the morning that our vigil was at last rewarded with the sound of muffled footsteps upon the stairs, followed by the shaded glow of a dark lantern. My involuntary start brought an urgently whispered "Not a sound, Watson," from Holmes. The thieves, of whom there were four, conferred quietly for a moment, and then moved off in the direction of a cask of rare Amontillado that was the pride of the Duke's cellar. Presently, they reappeared at the foot of the stairs and started up, carrying the cask. "Good Heavens, Holmes," I said, "we must do something – that wine is priceless."

"Steady, Watson," Holmes replied as he reached into the commodious pocket of his Inverness, drawing forth a small animal that he proceeded to toss on the direction of the parting thieves. The skunk, for such it proved to be, took immediate umbrage at such rude treatment by reacting in the way of its kind. The thieves, upon being sprayed, dropped the cask and fled.

"Well, Watson, we seem to have prevented the burglary, and we should surely be able to identify the members of the ring in the morning if we but follow our noses."

"Holmes," I cried, overcome with admiration, "However did you think of such a novel solution?"

"Elementary," he replied. "I simply followed the advice of an old proverb."

"Old proverb, Holmes?"

"Of course, dear fellow – A stench in time saves wine."

This was created by the Chuck Neblock.
It was first published in Plugs & Dottles, Issue #111, December, 1987.

The Big Sleep [SHPUN269]

It was in the summer of '88 that Holmes and I were called to the town of Isherwood in Dartmoor to solve the strange case of the disappearance of Lady Bromley's prosthesis. This case was a trying and exhausting one, lasting no less than three weeks, and consuming at least eighteen hours each day. Upon the successful conclusion of matters, Holmes and I gladly returned to our Baker Street lodgings.

Being completely done in by the events of the last three weeks, I headed straight for my room, collapsed in my bed and slept an incredible eighteen hours straight through.

Upon arising, thoroughly refreshed, I recalled that I had for some time been meaning to replace the wick in my bedroom lamp. Knowing that Holmes kept a fresh supply, I proceeded to our sitting room to obtain one.

"Ah, Watson," Holmes remarked as I entered, "you have certainly had a long and, I trust, restful sleep?"

"Very restful indeed," I replied. "I say, I believe you have a supply of new lamp wicks in your desk. Might I please have one for my bedroom lamp."

"No, you may not, Watson." Holmes's reply, needless to say, left me almost speechless.

"I don't understand, Holmes. I simply asked you for a new

wick for my lamp. Why on earth do you refuse my request?"

"Elementary, Watson ... as everyone knows, there is no wick for the rested."

This was created by "The Rascally Lascar."
It was first published in Plugs & Dottles, Issue # 095, August, 1986.

Where There's Smoke, There's a Clue [SHPUN265]

It was on one of the most tragic days in recent memory that Mr. Sherwood Finsparkler brought his troubles to our doorstep at 221b Baker Street. The headlines of all the evening papers were shouting of the giant blaze that had been in the process of destroying the Toxler Marina on the South bank of the Thames. Toxler Marina was quite an exclusive network of docks that held the big boats of most of London's rich and nautical, Finsparkler included, and its burning put an end to some of the most fabulous privately owned sailing vessels of our time. At 8:00 that evening, when Sherwood Finsparkler called on us, I had just finished reading the account of the fire in the *Times*.

Finsparkler was a robust, active-looking fellow, but this image was somewhat lessened by the bandages wrapped around his muscular arms and by the slight traces of soot on portions of his face and clothing. Sherlock Holmes ushered him in and immediately began to question him.

"So what did Lestrade have to say about the matter?" Holmes asked.

"My word, Holmes," I exclaimed, surprised at the strangeness of his first question to the bandaged man. "How did you know Mr. Finsparkler has been to see Inspector Lestrade? He has barely said a word since arriving here."

"As usual, Watson, you have missed the obvious," Holmes chastised me. "The bandages, the soot-smearing ... surely it is plain that earlier today Mr. Finsparkler was by yacht-land scarred."

This was written by "Anonymous."
It was first published in Plugs & Dottles, Issue #070, July, 1984.

A Simple matter of Hirsuteness [SHPUN262]

The uncanny observation of the seemingly insignificant by Sherlock Holmes has always amazed me.   With March approaching, I am reminded of the case involving Lord Flutebeetle and his son Thaddeus.

It was early evening on the twelfth of March, a Saturday to be exact, when Holmes and I were called to the estate of Lord Flutebeetle.   When we arrived, we found Inspector Lestrade in command.   He briefed us thoroughly about the crime. Thaddeus' piggy bank had been broken into and his savings stolen.   To his credit, Lestrade had narrowed the guilty party down to one of two female employees – the *femme de chambre* or the cook, both of whom denied the theft.

At this point, Holmes requested that the two ladies be brought to the library.   They arrived and stood before us by the window. Without interrogation, Holmes asked that they both remove their headwear.   The cook did so first by removing her cook's cap, from which a lovely flow of blonde hair fell to her shoulders.   However, when the chambermaid took off her bonnet, everyone, save Holmes, was aghast to see that the young lass had hair shorn to the scalp.   Turning abruptly away and lighting his pipe, Holmes remarked: "Lestrade, arrest the cook! She is the thief!" Indeed, she subsequently confessed.

No doubt you can sympathize with me, for I couldn't fathom how Holmes had managed this merely by having the two women remove their head coverings. When we returned to Baker Street, I inquired as to how he had discerned the guilty one.

"Watson," Holmes began, as he picked up his violin, "the crime of breaking young Thaddeus' piggy bank was certainly not horrifying. It was, however, heart-rending. It was obvious to me that the cook must have been the thief when I perceived that the chambermaid was the most dis-tressed."

This was written by Tom Simpson.
It was first published in Plugs & Dottles, Issue #066, March, 1984.

Moriarty's Redemption [SHPUN261]

For many years after "The Adventure of the Empty House," my friend Sherlock Holmes suffered occasional periods of depression. They would occur during sharp breaks in the weather and predominantly in the early months of the year. During these dark periods Holmes would seldom speak to me save for necessary communication. His activity would also drop, which was a trait I had never witnessed during our early years together.

There finally came a time in late March. The day had started beautifully, with the sun shining and Spring at our doorstep. However, by mid-afternoon, dark skies prevailed and the wind began to howl about our windows. Holmes, who had been reading the week's newspapers, was noticeably on edge. He shifted about incessantly. Casting his papers aside, he rose and went to the mantle. He lit his pipe, only to put it out immediately. The violin was next. After playing a short portion of "The Edinburgh Cannonball," he discarded it and went to the window to gaze outside. Several minutes elapsed before he startled me by turning about briskly and, in a sobbing voice I had never heard before, crying out: "I tried to save him, Watson – truly, I tried to save him."

You can well imagine the shock I felt and the hideous, unwarranted thoughts that crossed my mind. I should have known better than to doubt the intentions of this great man. I persuaded him to sit down and relax. I provided some tea and encouraged him to break with himself – to use me as a confessional.

Alas, he did so. His misery he linked to that climactic incident at Reichenbach Falls. Holmes proceeded to relate to me all the details of that fateful day. Moriarty had attacked him. The enemy was a fiend. He bit, swore and scratched at Holmes as the two grappled at the precipice. At length, Holmes's tolerance wore out. He went after his adversary with a vengeance, causing him to back up. Knowing full well of his intent, Holmes dealt Moriarty a blow that sent him reeling over the edge. Immediately my friend realized what he had done and dove to save him. It was too late. The demon had fallen, leaving only his left shoe in the hands of Sherlock Holmes.

The Great Detective was crying hysterically when he finished. No doubt he felt better by confiding in me, and I endeavored to further alleviate his feelings of guilt by remarking: "Holmes ... trouble yourself no more. You did at least save his sole."

This was written by Tom Simpson.
It was first published in Plugs & Dottles, Issue #062, November, 1983.

Blessed Are the Poor [SHPUN260]

"You know, Holmes, I had a most unusual experience this afternoon."

These words from his faithful companion roused Sherlock Holmes from a rather pleasant reverie one blustery March evening as the two sat before their usual cheery fire.

"Indeed, Watson. Well, pray enlighten me concerning this *outré* event. My mind craves stimulation of late."

"Yes, of course. Well, I was returning from a patient in the Tottenham Court Road about two O'clock when I was approached by the seediest beggar I've ever seen. But in spite of his filth and the unmistakable odour of gin on his breath, I was moved to compassion and offered him fifteen shillings."

"Most generous of you, old fellow. Do proceed."

"I thought so too, Holmes, but – and you won't believe this – when I went to hand him the money, the ungrateful wretch told me that if I couldn't donate at least a thousand pounds to his cause I should forget the matter entirely. The damnable *outrecuidance* of the man was beyond comprehension. I put him down as one whose mind had snapped, and went on my way. Really, Holmes, why do the authorities permit lunatics like this to roam the streets of London?"

"A lunatic, Watson? I think not. This man knew exactly what he was doing."

"Come now, Holmes, certainly you jest."

"No, Watson, I do not. 'Tis most elementary. Your beggar friend was simply putting all his begs in one ask it."

This was written by "The Rascally Lascar."
It was first published in Plugs & Dottles, Issue #054, March, 1983.

More High Jinks in Cornwall [SHPUN229]

After the Great War, I saw Holmes only at long intervals.

His retirement in Sussex was more complete every day and my own ill health kept me close to home. One summer, I visited him for a few weeks and time seemed to slip back to the old days in Baker Street, but without the constant stream of clients at the door. The more leisurely pace suited my own inclinations and Holmes was able to busy himself with his bees and his writings and still enjoy occasional company. Our daily contacts were undemanding and we were probably more comfortable together than we had ever been.

One day a cable arrived from Cornwall. A new Chief constable was in office, but the memory of Holmes' earlier services was still kept by the constabulary. A series of baffling robberies at society weekends had the local officers in a quandary. The individual crimes were all marked by seemingly impossible elements; valuables were taken from rooms with no access except through sleeping quarters, locks were bypassed, hidden compartments rifled and all the indications of a cat burglar at large were in evidence.

Since the tales of my literary agent's brother-in-law had appeared, society burglars were on everyone's mind. The fact that entertainment at all these affairs included a "Gentleman's Cricket Challenge Team" along with the usual raff and skaff of musical comedy troops, performing midgets giving séances and a tempestuous coloratura and her "manager" kept all eyes looking for a "Raffles" among the guests.

Holmes was reluctant to leave the observations of his hives and, of course, I was not up to the strenuous activity that a trip to Cornwall would require. After some consideration of the problem, he wired the Chief Constable to take the midgets into custody and to search their gear thoroughly. This was met with disbelief, but an effort was finally mounted and their current accommodations were visited by a sergeant and two constables. To everyone's surprise, the police were overpowered, bound and gagged and locked in a cellar to be found only the next day.

It was obvious to the police that Holmes had been right in "fingering" the troop, but all managed to escape and none of the loot was found. Further, Holmes was incensed when the story hit the gutter press and the next day's newspapers appeared with the headlines "Small Mediums at Large!"

This was written by "An Ill-dressed Vagabond" from a suggestion by Ann Margaret Lewis.
It was first published on the Shamlockians' List on August 14th, 2006.
It was later published in The Gaslight Gazette, V12, Issue #09, September, 2006.

The Hesitant Patient [SHPUN256]

According to my notes, it was late august in 1893 when Mr. Evarius Klenmore made a sudden entrance at my Kensington Consulting room. Hand pressed tightly to a dark spot on his trouser leg, Klenmore hobbled past my manservant, shouted my name and proceeded to make a nuisance of himself.

"My leg!" he shouted. "It's cut open from the knee to…"

"Let me look at it," I told him sternly. "Quiet, please."

"Stitch it shut!" he demanded as I looked the leg over.

"It's merely a surface wound," I told him. "Stitches won't be necessary."

"But I'm bleeding to death!" Klenmore screeched, grabbing my collar threateningly. "Stitch it up!"

Freeing myself from his grasp, I found a needle and thread on a nearby table. But my medical integrity was not to be besmirched: I handed Evarius Klenmore the needle and thread.

"Suture self!" I told him.

This was written by an anonymous contributor.
This was first published in Plugs & Dottles, Issue #49, October, 1982.

The Adventure of the Disillusioned Diamond Miner [SHPUN253]

"I say Holmes, this cannot be true," I said, as I flung my copy of the *Times* down for the second time this week. "There's an article here that claims if Cecil Rhodes is found guilty of any illegalities by that Parliamentary Committee investigating the Jamieson Affair, he will take his relatives and go and live in the Capital of Italy and give his money to the Vatican. What a loss to the Empire."

"If he is found responsible I would have thought it an obvious act on his part," observed Holmes exuding a cloud of blue grey smoke from his pipe.

"Why Holmes?" I asked.

"Because all Rhodes lead to Rome."

This was written by Richard Milne.
This has not been published before.

Simpson's on the Strand [SHPUN250]

One evening after successful conclusion of a case, Holmes and I were celebrating with a festive meal at Simpson's when the Headwaiter, Mr. Charles, approached and asked our indulgence. He said that he had heard of Holmes' knack at solving problems and hoped that he would lend his expertise to a problem that had occurred in the restaurant.

Holmes had enjoyed his veal cutlets and felt well satisfied so he asked Mr. Charles to explain.

It seemed that the restaurant had recently hired a new head chef and the wearer of the cordon bleu was all that he had been expected to be. His sauces were exquisite and his soufflés were unmatched. He was adding touches of continental elegance to the menu, but, all the while preserving the core of solid British competence for which Simpson's had always been noted. It seems he even knew how to prepare roast beef and Yorkshire pudding that one could swear to have been brought fresh from the Dales.

The problem occurred with the introduction of a new German dish, Hassenpfeffer. Each serving had been sent back by irate customers who claimed it was either too hot or too cold or too sour or not sour enough. Every complaint was different but each serving resulted in a complaint.

Holmes listened politely and then assured Mr. Charles that there was nothing to worry about. This was simply a coincidence. He explained:

"Don't worry. Your chef is merely having a bad hare day."

This was written by "An Ill-Dressed Vagabond."
It was first published on The Shamlockians' List on September 9th, 2006.

Touché! [SHPUN249]

A recent accident in London involved the collision of a small sports car and a van at the corner of Baker and Oxford streets. Neither driver was injured, but a heated exchange of words between the two rapidly ensued as they surveyed the damage to their respective vehicles. The driver of the sports car was especially abusive and soon worked himself into a murderous frenzy. Losing complete control of himself, he broke the antenna off the van and, with a single thrust, speared its driver clean through the throat. He then made good his escape.

"Well, Watson," remarked Holmes, "this man's assassin may have gotten away, but the cause of death is most obvious."

"No doubt about it, Holmes," replied Watson. "Even a nonmedical person can see that his man died from van aerial disease."

This was written by "The Rascally Lascar" from a suggestion by Gary List (Colonel Moran).
This was first published in Plugs & Dottles, Issue #48, September, 1982.

Das Geheimnis der Zwei Professoren[1] [SHPUN246]

Without doubt, the most bizarre case my friend Mr. Sherlock Holmes was ever called upon to investigate was that involving the noted German geneticist, Dr. Klaus Friedrick von Spitzenschlagen. Spitzy, as he was known to his students, was found dead at the base of a sixty-foot cliff that was a short distance from his laboratory. Foul play was suspected and Holmes was summoned by the *Polizei*[2]. A day's journey brought us to the little town of Knackwurst, the site of the professor's laboratory. We had just made our introductions to the German authorities and were being advised of the details of the case, when who should walk into the police station but the dead man himself!

"Gentlemen, gentlemen, fear not ... relax ... *ich kann alles erklaren*[3]," the professor shouted.

The story he told was incredible. It seems his genetic researches had led him to the discovery that he could make an exact replica of himself. The details of the process he refused to divulge. This deutero- or dopple-Spitzenschlagen was indistinguishable from its original except in one detail. The original Spitzy was mild-mannered and prided himself on never employing foul or abusive language. His double, however, due to some genetic aberration, had a mouth as foul as the Augean stables. Spitzy(1) could not and would not countenance this disgusting behavior. The two met on the cliff one evening and the professor, as he freely admitted to us, pushed his foul-mouthed double to his death.

With this pronouncement, the *Polizeibeamte*[4] in charge intoned, "Dr.Klaus Friedrich von Spitzenschlagen(1), I arrest you for the murder of Dr. Klaus Friedrich von Spitzenschlagen(2)!"

"*Bitte, bitte*[5]," broke in Holmes. "I believe a charge of murder is indefensible. I would suggest a lesser charge."

"And what might that be?" barked the German officer with Teutonic vehemence.

"*Einfach, mein Herr*[6]," replied Holmes. "This man is guilty on only one count – namely, that of making an obscene clone fall."

1. The Mystery of the Two Professors
2. Police.
3. I can explain everything
4. Police Officer
5. Please, please
6. Elementary, sir

This was written by Brad Keefauver.
This was first published in Plugs & Dottles, Issue #45, June, 1982.

The Case of the Screaming Greek [SHPUN001]

'Twas in the summer of '88 that Holmes and Watson found themselves in the ancient Greek city of Athens, the famous detective having been summoned there by the government regarding a matter of the highest international importance.

Having settled matters to everyone's satisfaction, Holmes and his faithful Boswell decided to take in some of Athens' famous historical sites. Unfortunately, their visit to the Parthenon was less than anticipated due to an extensive renovation project going on at the time. The site was crowded with numerous workers and construction equipment. Work was obviously not proceeding according to the wishes of the person in charge, a tall, swarthy Greek who kept screaming at the workers at the top of his lungs in a futile attempt to get them to do things correctly.

The shouting continued for some thirty minutes, but eventually ceased (much to the delight of the workers) when the boss-man's voice finally gave out, fading to an inaudible whisper.

Having observed the entire proceeding with some interest, Holmes pointed at the voiceless Greek and remarked:

"Behold, Watson, the hoarse foreman of the Acropolis!"

This was written by "The Rascally Lascar".
This was first published in The Dangling Prussian Amateur Press Assn., Issue #5, April, 1992.
It was later published on the Hounds of the Internet List on August 25th, 2002.

The Caseophile's Soiree [SHPUN003]

"People may make fun of our British grub, Watson, but

there's no getting around it when it comes to our famous Stilton and Cheddar cheeses. Would you not agree?"

"Absolutely, Holmes, and let's not forget that caseophilic delight which is the pride of Scotland."

"Scotland? I wasn't aware it was noted for any type of cheese."

"Certainly, my good fellow, you've heard of Loch Ness Muenster."

This was written by "The Rascally Lascar".
This was first published in Plugs & Dottles, Issue #78, March, 1985.
It was later published on the Hounds of the Internet List on December 3rd, 2004

A Violin End [SHPUN263]

The two men had worked their way carefully down a trail more suitable for goats than the frock coated pair who had come out from London, in thin hope, to find a clue to the tragic disappearance.

Dr. Watson and Mycroft Holmes gazed at the foreboding heights of Reichenbach Falls.

"To plummet from that cliff to these crags, locked in a death's embrace with that fiend, Moriarty, leaves no room to hope your brother has survived," said Dr. Watson.

"Not so, my dear Watson," was the reply. "Look here, my brother has left us a most reassuring message."

Mycroft Holmes pointed to the violin, readily recognizable as the one on which the Great Detective played so often when thinking out the problems of difficult cases. It was battered, the strings were gone, and it was stained with gore as though used as a weapon in a desperate battle.

Watson shuddered. "You say there's a message from Holmes in this? How can you find such a sight reassuring?"

"Elementary, my dear Watson. My brother wishes us to know that, like this violin, from which he has removed the strings, he is bloody, but unbowed."

This was written by Jack Kavanagh.
It was first published in Alfred Hitchcock Mystery Magazine, Volume 28, #05, May, 1984.
It was later published in Plugs & Dottles, Issue #068, May, 1984.

Dinner at Simpson's [SHPUN004]

While dining at Simpson's one evening, Sherlock Holmes opted for the more traditional steak & kidney pie (real British Grub!), while his good old fidus Achates went for roasted wild rabbit.

Halfway through the meal, Watson asked, "Would you care for a taste of my rabbit, Holmes?"

"No thank you," replied the famous sleuth, "you know I am not one for splitting hares."

This was written by "The Rascally Lascar".
It was first published on the Hounds of the Internet List on December 4th, 2004

An Ursine Three Course Dinner [SHPUN006]

"I say, Holmes, I see in the paper where there was some

excitement at the Birmingham Zoo the other night. A huge bear escaped from its cage and proceeded to kill three of the zoo's other animals -- a skunk, a bird of prey, and a lion."

"Does it say whether the bear ate its kills?"

"For sure! The report says that it swallowed all three ... hawk, lion, and stinker."

This was written by "The Rascally Lascar".
This was first published in Plugs & Dottles, Issue #140, May, 1990.
It was later published on the Hounds of the Internet List on December 6th, 2004

Nothing False about Watson [SHPUN007]

"So, Watson, tell me -- do you have any stocks or bonds?"

"None whatever, Holmes."

"What about debentures?"

"No, I have all my original teeth."

This was written by "The Rascally Lascar".
It was first published on the Hounds of the Internet List on December 7th, 2004

The Man Who Feared Christmas [SHPUN009]

"I read here, Holmes, of a fellow in Bermondsey who has a strange and inexplicable fear of Christmas. What could be the cause of such strange behavior?"

"Psychiatry is not my field, Watson, so I can't answer your question. But the chap of whom you speak can't help but bring to mind one of Britain's leading playwrights."

"A playwright?"

"Yes, Watson, this Bermondsey fellow is obviously another Noel Coward."

This was written by "The Rascally Lascar".
This was first published in Plugs & Dottles, Issue #87, December, 1985.
It was later published on the Hounds of the Internet List on December 10th, 2004

The Case Of The Great Cover-up [SHPUN010]

'Twas in the winter of '87 when someone proceeded, on two consecutive nights, to break into the London Museum and cover all pieces of nude sculpture with bed sheets.

"Certainly, Holmes," I remarked, "this case doesn't warrant your esteemed powers. 'Tis simply the work of some prankster, or some madman whose sensibilities are offended when he views the human body in puris naturalibus."

"No, Watson, I'm afraid you're wrong. These are mighty deep waters, and I will not rest until I have ferreted out this evildoer and see him before the next assizes."

"But on what grounds?" I asked.

"Elementary, my good fellow -- when apprehended, this individual will be charged with statuary drape."

This was written by "The Rascally Lascar."
This was first published in Plugs & Dottles, Issue #57, June, 1983.
It was later published on the Hounds of the Internet List on

December 11th, 2004

The Behemoth of the Thames [SHPUN012]

It was first seen by a charwoman named Potter as she crossed the Vauxhall Bridge one morning on her way to work. But no one believed her. Too much gin, they said. But two days later, it was spotted again, this time by a clergyman and a constable. There could be no doubt about it now -- a monster lurked in the Thames!

Some were terrified, but most took a gleeful pride in the fact that Loch Ness had nothing on London. But unlike the monster to the north, the Thames monster was finally captured by the Royal Navy and a team of biologists. However, the huge beast (5 tons!) succumbed to the shock of capture and, for the sake of charity, was processed into sausage for distribution to the poor.

"You know, Watson, this whole strange affair reminds me of a story by Charles Dickens," remarked Holmes one evening.

"A story by Dickens? How do you figure that? Dickens wrote nothing about monsters to my knowledge."

"True, my good fellow, but surely you recall the beginning of *A Tale of Two Cities*: 'It was the beast of Thames, it was the wurst of Thames...'."

This was written by "The Rascally Lascar."
This was first published in Plugs & Dottles, Issue #59, August, 1983.
It was later published on the Hounds of the Internet List on December 13th, 2004

A Simple Case of Detailing [SHPUN013]

He was one of those mixed breeds -- a veritable canine ollapodrida — a mongrel among mongrels. When not roaming the streets, he lived with Mrs. Parker in the Bloomsbury Road.

Max, as he was called, had an insatiable craving for mutton chops, and when she could afford them, Mrs. Parker would provide Max with his favorite delicacy. But such times were too infrequent to satisfy Max's lust for the chop, and it was then that he resorted to the thievery of London's butcher shops to maintain his tasty habit, thus presenting Sherlock Holmes with his most humorous case.

Max was very successful with his butcher shop raids until he picked on the shop of Mr. Allardyce, a man who had a pathological hatred of dogs. One evening, Allardyce caught Max red-handed (pawed?), and proceeded to lop off poor Max's tail with a meat cleaver.

Max went ululating back to Bloomsbury Road, and the next day Mrs. Parker engaged Holmes to ferret out Max's maimer. Holmes had no trouble in tracing the detailing to Allardyce, but shortly thereafter, Mrs. Parker succumbed to dropsy, and Max disappeared from the streets of London.

"You know, Watson," remarked Holmes, "knowing Max's insatiable lust for mutton chops and Allardyce's hatred for Max's species, it was absolutely inevitable that things happened as they did."

"For sure, Holmes," replied Watson, "the final outcome *was* inevitable -- much like Max's tail."

"Max's tail? How's that, Watson?"

"Elementary, Holmes, it was bound to a cur."

This was written by "The Rascally Lascar."
This was first published in Plugs & Dottles, Issue #60, September, 1983.
It was later published on the Hounds of the Internet List on December 14th, 2004

Watson and the Higher Mathematics [SHPUN016]

"Having trouble, old man?" queried the Great Sleuth one evening.

"I hate to admit it, Holmes, but I am. I offered to help Mrs. Hudson's nephew with his spherical trigonometry, but I'm afraid I've bitten off a wee bit too much. My early training was in regular trigonometry that was relatively simple. You know -- the sum of the angles of a triangle is 180 degrees, there can be but one right angle ... stuff like that. But good Lord, I read here that the sum of the angles of a spherical triangle can total anywhere from 180 to 540 degrees, and that said triangles may have up to three right angles! I am completely and hopelessly confused!"

"Well, Watson, you know that you ARE getting older."

"And what has that to do with it?"

"My dear man, you are certainly familiar with the old adage which states that you can't teach an old dog new trigs."

This was written by "The Rascally Lascar".
This was first published in Plugs & Dottles, Issue #64, January, 1984.
It was later published on the Hounds of the Internet List on December 18th, 2004.

Watson's Patient Gets The Point [SHPUN019]

"Well, Watson," remarked Holmes one blustery December evening, "may I be so bold as to ask if you've kept abreast of the latest advances in your field?"

"So glad you ask, Holmes. I am happy to report that I have

recently completed a course in acupuncture, taught by the famous German authority on the practice, Herr Doctor Hermann Rodenschlagger, and have had occasion to employ the procedure on a patient just this afternoon."

"And the result?"

"Well, Holmes, I don't mean to brag, but I feel it was a jab well done!"

This was written by "The Rascally Lascar".
This was first published in Plugs & Dottles, Issue #214, July, 1996.
It was later published on the Hounds of the Internet List on December 21st, 2004

A Skin Deep Case [SHPUN021]

"Holmes, is it true that you've been investigating that Polish tattoo artist, Casimir Rodanski, in the Upper Kennington Road?"

"Yes, my good fellow, I've been surreptitiously observing the no good rascal for the last two weeks."

"For whatever reason, Holmes?"

"Elementary, Watson -- the fellow obviously has designs on his customers."

This was written by "The Rascally Lascar."
This was first published in Plugs & Dottles, Issue #209, February, 1996.
It was later published on the Hounds of the Internet List on December 23rd, 2004

No Use Crying Over Spilled Wine [SHPUN022]

During his late retirement years, Sherlock Holmes was
visited by his old fidus Achates. Entering the great sleuth's
cottage in Ruden Lane on the South Downs, Watson found his
friend deeply engrossed in one of Sax Rohmer's "Fu Manchu"
novels.

"Ha, Watson, you come at a critical moment in my reading,"
remarked Holmes – "Nayland Smith's friend and colleague has
just spilled a whole bottle of sherry over Smith's new carpet."

"Heavens, Holmes, what does the doctor do?"

"Nothing, my good fellow, he just lets out a Petrie whine."

This was written by "The Rascally Lascar".
This was first published in Plugs & Dottles, Issue #212, May,
1996.
It was later published on the Hounds of the Internet List on
December 24th, 2004

Up The Creek... [SHPUN023]

One foggy evening, Holmes and Watson found it necessary
to cross the Thames by boat. Having secured a small dory,
Watson manned the oars, and the intrepid duo set out to cross the
famed river. Although short in distance, the trip was an arduous
one since the currents were numerous and strong.

In midstream, Watson sneezed, and his reflexes caused him
to lose both oars. He and Holmes were at the mercy of the
currents! Soon, however, they heard the steady pulling of a
strong set of oars, and glimpsed a boat with three figures aboard
moving across their bow.

Through the pea-soup fog, Watson was just able to make out

the name of the craft —"The Rodina."

Watson jumped up and shouted, "Hello! Hello!"

The sound of the rowing stopped, and a deep voice answered: "Halloo, kin I help yer?"

"We are helpless, can you throw us one of your oars?"

An angry reply boomed back through the Stygian gloom.

"Hey, guv'nor, watch your language. These ain't 'ores. One's me wife, and the other's me sister!"

This was written by "The Rascally Lascar."
This was first published in Plugs & Dottles, Issue #213, June, 1996.
It was later published on the Hounds of the Internet List on December 25th, 2004.

Watson Learns Another New Technique [SHPUN024]

We have recently seen how Watson went in for a bit of alternative medicine by studying the method of acupuncture under the famous German practitioner Herr Hermann Rodenschlagger. Wishing to master yet another new technique, he next took a course in chiropractic from the Canadian specialist in that field, Dr. Kristoffer Bodin. Fortunately, Watson soon had his first patient -- Sherlock Holmes himself, who had thrown his back out while carrying in a huge load of British Grub ingredients from the local market for Mrs. Hudson.

While working over the subluxations in the great detective's spine, the good doctor remarked: "I do believe, Holmes, it's going to rain."

"However do you know that?" queried his friend.

"I can feel it in your bones," returned Watson.

This was written by "The Rascally Lascar."
This was first published in Plugs & Dottles, Issue #215, August, 1996.
It was later published on the Hounds of the Internet List on December 26th, 2004

Xmas Story -- 2 Days Late [SHPUN025]

The ill-fated convict ship, *Gloria Scott*, did set sail from Falmouth on October 8, 1855, as recounted by Old Trevor to Holmes, but he neglected to inform us of the following episode.

Since the Christmas season was approaching, and the ship was certain to be at sea during the holidays, the captain -- a Swedish fellow named Lars Rooden -- ordered a goodly store of holiday cheer and decorations of the nature of a Yule-log, evergreens, boughs of holly, etc..., for the enjoyment of the officers' mess. When he got to the quay, however, he spied the deck hands wrongly stowing the decorations in a neighboring ship.

"Ahoy," Lars shouted to the stevedores, "you're treeing up the wrong barque!"

This was written by "The Rascally Lascar."
This was first published in Plugs & Dottles, Issue #195, December, 1994.
It was later published on the Hounds of the Internet List on December 27th, 2004.

Fetch! [SHPUN026]

In a follow-up to the famous Baskerville case, Holmes was informing Watson one bitterly cold December evening of some of the heretofore unknown facts concerning the infamous Hound of Hell.

"Yes, Watson, Mrs. Stapleton swears that the hound was not only the most vicious of animals, but one of the smartest. According to wife Beryl, the beast had been instilled with incredible retrieving abilities by the famed Canadian canine trainer, Christopher Weatherwax, grandfather of the American, Rod Weatherwax, the trainer, in turn, of America's beloved Lassie. Would you believe that Stapleton's dog could retrieve an object from five miles away?"

"Sounds rather far-fetched to me," replied Watson.

This was written by "The Rascally Lascar."
This was first published in Plugs & Dottles, Issue #184, January, 1994.
It was later published on the Hounds of the Internet List on December 28th, 2004.

And Then There Were Two [SHPUN027]

"I say, Watson, there's good news here from Prague in the *Evening Standard*. Those Capek Siamese twins have undergone successful surgery under the skillful hands of the country's famed neonatal surgeon, Dr. Ladislav Rodanacek."

"Really, Holmes?" replied Watson with a twinkle in his eye. "Reminds me of our request of the waiter at Simpson's last night."

"Whatever do you mean, my good fellow?"

"Separate Czechs, Holmes, separate Czechs!"

This was written by "The Rascally Lascar."
This was first published in Plugs & Dottles, Issue #185,

February, 1994.
It was later published on the Hounds of the Internet List on December 29th, 2004.

And Did He Bounce? [SHPUN028]

Sherlock Holmes and his faithful amanuensis were enjoying their postprandial cigars before a warming hearth, following one of Mrs. Hudson's delicious British Grub dinners of mutton jowls with Rodinaise sauce.

"Well, Watson," said Holmes, "I see where the Yard has secretly incarcerated that diminutive and villainous criminal from Prague, Karel Capec."

"Yes, Holmes," rejoined the good doctor, "I wonder where one could cache a small Czech?"

This was written by "Rev. Dr. Benton Wood."
This was first published in Plugs & Dottles, Issue #186, March, 1994.
It was later published on the Hounds of the Internet List on December 30st , 2004

The Bermondsey Cannibal Caper [SHPUN233]

The ycar of '89 saw my friend Mr. Sherlock Holmes engaged in some of the most sinister and bizarre cases of his long and illustrious career. Many of these will probably never see publication due to the highly sensitive nature of the circumstances with which they were surrounded and the lofty social status of the personages involved. However, one event of this notable year received so much publicity at the time that there was no keeping any of the sordid and sensational details from the public. I refer to the gruesome and sanguinary case of Charlie Watts, "The Cannibal of Bermondsey," a title bestowed upon him by the London press. The case was notable in view of both its lurid aspects and the fact that it was one of the few problems that Holmes solved without ever leaving the confines of Baker Street. In addition, it illustrated so beautifully my companion's amazing ability to coruscate as a detective in spite of the enigmatic nature and the paucity of evidence presented him.

It all began one dull, foggy morning in late November, a miserable day made even more so by a cold drizzle of rain. Holmes and I had just finished our rashers and eggs and had settled down to our morning pipes when Mrs. Hudson ushered in a somewhat wet and chilled Inspector Lestrade.

"Ha! Lestrade! Come in, come in. Move up to the fire there and warm yourself. Could I interest you in a little breakfast?"

Holmes's overly solicitous (almost saponaceous) attitude was obviously prompted by the anticipation that the Scotland Yard Inspector had come with a problem that had his department stymied.

"I'll get right to the point, Mr. Holmes.," Lestrade began, ignoring the offer for breakfast. "My superiors have requested that I consult with you in view of your extensive knowledge of poisons. The department, I must admit, has before it the strangest and most confounding case in its history."

"Pray continue. You have my curiosity aroused already," replied Holmes, at the same time sending a dense cloud of blue-gray smoke ceiling ward.

"Well, these are the facts as we have them. At about five o'clock this morning, a factory labourer named Albert Higgins was on his way to work in the borough of Bermondsey. As he made his way down Pike Street he noticed that the door to Number 15 was wide open. The residence is, or I should say was, occupied by a dockhand by the name of Charlie Watts.

From the doorway Mr. Higgins could see the kitchen stove and a large pot from which steam was slowly rising. Sensing that something might be amiss because of the open door, he tried to raise someone within. He received no answer, and thus decided to enter the residence—a decision that the poor fellow now probably regrets in view of the state of shock he's in. What he saw in that kitchen would shake any man.

"Higgins' terrifying screams brought a local constable to the scene and, subsequently, a contingent from my department. I swear, Mr. Holmes, I have seen all manner of hideous sights during my career with the Yard, but I was certainly not prepared for what met my eyes at Number 15, Pike Street early this morning.

"I'll try to describe the scene as best I can. Lying on the floor of the kitchen was the body of a Roman Catholic priest later identified as a Father Joseph from the local parish. He had apparently been killed by a savage blow to the base of the skull. The sight of this would make any man shudder, but the other mayhem to which his body had been subjected was almost more than I could stand." Lestrade wiped his brow with a nervous hand and proceeded with his account.

"Dear God, I can still see it! Both of the victim's arms had been hacked off at the elbows with a meat cleaver, which we found beside the body. And now comes the most horrifying part of all – one would have to see it to believe it. Mr. Holmes, one of those arms was found in the pot of boiling water atop the stove and the other, the partial remains of which had been boiled until cooked through, was found on a large platter on the table over which was slumped the body of Charlie Watts.

"My God!" I exclaimed.

"Yes. And the implications of the scene were horribly obvious; Watts had murdered the priest and then had proceeded to engage in an act of cannibalism!"

Those last words of the Inspector engulfed me in a wave of nausea and, in spite of his cold and calculating nature, it was apparent that Holmes was shaken by the account of which he had just heard. Lestrade continued.

"How the priest came to be in that madman's house we'll probably never know. A thorough examination of Watts' body failed to reveal any marks of violence. On the table beside that gruesome platter we found a small vial containing what appears to be a mixture of dried herbs, possibly for use – God, I shudder to think of it! – as seasoning. It could, however, be of a poisonous nature, and in view of Watts' state of mind there is a distinct possibility that after consuming his ghoulish meal he partook of the contents of the vial in an act of suicide. I have brought the vial with me and my department would be most grateful if you would analyze its contents and determine if they are indeed poisonous."

Holmes took the vial which Lestrade handed him, removed the lid and cautiously sniffed the multicoloured mixture.

"Definitely an herbal seasoning mixture; any good *chef de cuisine* would recognize it," he remarked. "I have, incidentally, written a trifling monograph on the subject wherein I identify some one hundred and fifty herbs used in the culinary arts and for the treatment of various ailments. No, this did not kill Mr. Watts ... but ... I know what did."

This last statement, spoken with such plerophory, brought Lestrade and myself out of our chairs.

"Really, Holmes," I exclaimed, "I find this no time for joking."

"I assure you, my dear Watson, that I do not jest. The cause of death is most obvious when you consider the evidence."

"It's elementary, my dear Lestrade .. elementary. Everything hinges on the fact that Watt's victim was a Roman Catholic priest. From this one can't help but deduce that Charlie Watts died from eating improperly cooked food."

"Improperly cooked food!?"

"Absolutely! You see, Mr. Watts had a friar and he went and boiled him."

This was written by "The Rascally Lascar."
It was first published in Wheelwrightings, Vol. 03, Issue #02, September, 1980.

The Old Shikari-Bengal Tiger Caper [SHPUN232]

The Name of Colonel Sebastian Moran is certainly not an Unfamiliar one to the student of the Holmes Canon. As Moriarty's chief of staff, this "second most dangerous man in London" was responsible for two attempts on Holmes's life, a much more successful one on that of the Honourable Ronald Adair, and, according to Holmes, was the mastermind behind the death of Mrs. Stewart, of lauder, in 1887.

As we learned in EMPT, Professor Moriarty kept Moran liberally supplied with money, "and used him in only one or two very high-class jobs, which no ordinary criminal could have undertaken." Just how much devilry Moran was engaged in in addition to that involving Holmes, Ronald Adair and Mrs. Stewart will probably never be known. One other nefarious deed of the Colonel, however, *was* known to the Master. It involved the kidnapping and death, in 1886, of the son of the wealthy Czechoslovakian industrialist Jaroslav Hasek, the details of which were related by Holmes to Watson one evening shortly after the Colonel's capture.

"It was the most remarkable case, Watson," Holmes began. "To this day, the facts of the matter have been kept in the highest secrecy, with only myself, the Hasek family and the two individuals hired by Mr. Hasek to pursue Moran privy to just what occurred. And what I tell you tonight must go no further."

"You may trust me, to be sure, Holmes," Watson replied.

"In briefest form, Watson, Moran, no doubt under the direction of Moriarty, kidnapped the seven-year-old son of Jaroslav Hasek, demanding a huge ransom for the safe return of the child. The usual death threats were made to the father should he attempt to contact the authorities, and taking these seriously, as well as wishing private revenge on the abductor of his son, Hasek hired two of his friends, noted for their hunting prowess (much like Moran's), to hopefully locate the boy, return him unharmed, and assassinate the culprit of the dastardly deed.

"Moran, fearing detection if he remained in Czechoslovakia, made for a remote village in central India where he had spent some time previously in the pursuit of big game. Unfortunately, however, the young Hasek came down with a severe calenture and, due to the lack of immediate medical treatment, succumbed within forty-eight hours.

"By now, because of some careless slips on Moran's part, Hasek's hired gunmen had managed to trace him to that remote Indian village. He had barely finished burying the kidnapped boy's body when he was confronted by his pursuers. They demanded at gunpoint that Moran produce Hasek's son. The Colonel, needless to say, was in a panic. His mind sought frantically for an explanation. If he said nothing, his captors would assume that he had killed the boy, and any pleas for mercy would be useless."

"Moran the recalled seeing two huge Bengal tigers, one male and the other female, on the outskirts of the village early that morning. In an instant, his story was fabricated. Hasek's men demanded to know where the boy was. Moran then proceeded to remorsefully tell them that one of two large Bengal tigers had killed and eaten the lad as he was permitted some brief exercise that morning.

"Not thoroughly believing Moran's story, his captors insisted that they search for the male tiger, the one which Moran claimed had killed Hasek's son. This they did, and fortuitously found the beast after about an hour's hunt. Asked again if he was sure it was the male tiger that had killed the boy, Moran replied in the affirmative, whereupon the animal was immediately shot by one of Hasek's men.

"This, Watson, was done, you have no doubt surmised, for the sole purpose of determining the truthfulness of Moran's story. The tiger was thus gutted, and a search made of its digestive tract for the remains of the unfortunate lad. None, of course, were found. But so intent were Hasek's men in their examination that Moran managed to escape.

"An incredible story, Holmes," Watson remarked.

"Yes, my good fellow, it is. And it also contains within it the quintessence of one of life's basic maxims."

"A basic maxim? And what might that be, Holmes?"

"Never, Watson—never trust a Moriartian henchman when he tells you that the Czech is in the male!"

This was written by The Rascally Lascar.
It was first published in Wheelwrightings, Vol. 09, Issue #02, September, 1986.

Keen-Eyed Watson [SHPUN029]

While Holmes and Watson were enjoying a rare holiday in the Highlands. They began to reminisce about cases the Master had recently brought to a successful conclusion.

"I must say, Holmes," Watson began, "I've got to hand it to you for the quick manner in which you apprehended Glenn, the glabrous, globose, albeit glamorous, Gloucester glove pilferer."

"'Twas nothing, old friend," replied Holmes, "compared to your astute powers of observation at Lady Rodinia's masquerade ball, when you picked out the good guise from the bad."

This was written by "Rev. Dr. Benton Wood."
This was first published in Plugs & Dottles, Issue #187, April, 1994.
It was later published on the Hounds of the Internet List on December 31st, 2004.

The Moth And The Flame [SHPUN031]

It was on the second day of the new year in '96 that Holmes and Watson were invited down below to Mrs. Hudson's quarters to celebrate the second birthday of her nephew, Christopher Rooding, who was visiting with his parents from Canada.

The sitting-room table abounded with gaily wrapped presents, and held a delicious looking cake on which burned two wax tapers. As the presents were frantically being opened by the excited two-year-old, a moth, attracted by the tapers on the cake, flew into one, singeing the rear portion of its body. And unable to resist its fascination for the flame, it proceeded to re-peat the process by flying through the flame of the second candle, leading this time to its unfortunate destruction.

Having observed this lepidopteral cremation, Holmes remarked: "There, my good people, is a prime example of burning your end at both candles!"

This was written by "The Rascally Lascar."
This was first published in Plugs & Dottles, Issue #193, October, 1994.
It was later published on the Hounds of the Internet List on January 2nd, 2005.

Gee, an Honest Lawyer! [SHPUN035]

It is not well known, but, prior to calling in Sherlock Holmes, Neil Gibson's first attempt to free Grace Dunbar was a bit heavy handed.

As might be expected of the American "Gold King," he set about to persuade the justices of Winchester to bend the Anglo-Saxon common law in favor of his potential paramour with "arguments of a golden hue." He therefore sent his minion Bates to Joyce Cummings' chambers with a generous bribe in hand, expecting success (after all, it worked in the Senate).

Gibson was frustrated, however, when the rising young barrister's response to the offer was:

"Absolutely not! The attempt would be fatal, for it has long been established that Britannia does not waive the rules!"

PS: Did Grace become a Gibson Girl?

This was written by "The Rascally Lascar."
This was first published in Plugs & Dottles, Issue #192, September, 1994.
It was later published on the Hounds of the Internet List on January 6th, 2005.

The Tall & the Short of It [SHPUN036]

Sherlock Holmes had finally cracked the case of the

mysterious locked-door robberies, having correctly deduced that the perpetrators were Gregor the Great and Wee Willie the Midget, performers with the Circus Rodan. These two had prowled the streets of London after dark, looking for open first-floor windows, which residents had supposed were too far above street level to require locking against the risk of unlawful entry. Into these open windows, Gregor would boost the midget, and the rest, as they say, was criminal history.

As the giant and his tiny cohort were led away by the police, Watson remarked upon the irony that it was the very difference in their heights that led them to their partnership in a life of crime.

"Yes, Watson," replied Holmes, "but where they're going, one Assize fits all.'

This was written by "The Rascally Lascar."
This was first published in Plugs & Dottles, Issue #216, September, 1996.
It was later published on the Hounds of the Internet List on January 7th, 2005.

The Adventure of the Intermittent Island... [SHPUN039]

I had risen late after a hard night at the club, and having come downstairs found Holmes clad in his blue/purple/mouse coloured dressing gown in the act of skewering a telegram into his impressive collection of jack-knifed correspondence.

"A new case Holmes?"

"Indeed, Watson, you progress ... and so you should after all these years," said my companion with his usual touch of the acerbic. "A telegram from the President of the United States no less requesting my professional services."

"Shall I pack?" I asked, eagerly anticipating a chance to extend my knowledge of women to a fourth, and possibly, fifth continent.

"No I have solved the puzzle. It appears there is an island off the coast of Alaska that keeps appearing and disappearing..."

"You mean...!" I gasped.

"Exactly ...it is an optical Aleutian."

This was written by Richard Milne.
It was first published on the Hounds of the Internet List on January 10th, 2005.

The Adventure of the Boulevard Assassin [SHPUN040]

"So Holmes," I observed as we sat in the spring sunshine in a street café in Paris, drinking coffee and eating rolls the morning after the night's adventures, "another successful case for me to write up and publish when I need a few shillings."

"I doubt if Huret will feel the steel blade of French justice, however", said Holmes, sadly.

"But surely the evidence is enough to convict him ten times over," I exclaimed.

"So it might appear, Watson. But you remember how he attempted to evade capture by the police by jumping off the left bank into the river?"

"Certainly. But he was easily captured and will still stand trial."

"Yes but I fear the verdict will be 'Guilty but in Seine'."

This was written by Richard Milne.
It was first published on the Hounds of the Internet List on January 11th, 2005.

The Adventure of the Missing Scotch [SHPUN042]

"Holmes," I said as we sat in the dining car of the Flying Kipper returning to London, enjoying a postprandial port and cigar. "How did you know that Young Donald Mount-Stewart was behind the theft of his uncle's reserve malt Scotch?"

"It was obvious that who ever had stolen the casks had to have inside assistance. While it might have been any employee of the distillery it was apparent to me who was behind the theft as soon as we entered the distillery office and learned young Donald was Sir Lachlan Mount-Stewart's sole relative. He is a weak character and was unable to resist the temptation to taste some of the stock as it was removed."

"So you knew he was guilty how…"

"By the nip in the heir" observed Holmes.

This was written by Richard Milne.
It was first published on the Hounds of the Internet List on January 13th, 2005.

The Deadly Throne of King Mambuto [SHPUN247]

While on a tour of British possessions in South Africa in the year '88, Holmes and Watson were called upon to investigate the death of one of the local native chieftains. A cursory examination by the Great Fathomer was all that was necessary to show that the chief's untimely demise was purely accidental.

It seem King Mabuto, as he was known to his followers, was

given a throne by his wife on the fifth anniversary of his reign. Since it was a most uncomfortable piece of furniture, the King abhorred sitting on it, and finally, much to his wife's dismay, decided to remove it from his living quarters and store it atop the rafters of his grass shack. A few days thereafter, a violent windstorm struck the area, and while the King slept below, the throne was dislodged by the force of the storm and fell upon him, killing him instantly.

"How tragic!" remarked Watson upon hearing the account from Holmes's lips.

"Yes, Watson, so true. And it proves one thing so dramatically."

"Which is?"

"Elementary, Watson – people in grass houses shouldn't stow thrones."

This was written by Dr. Neil Taylor.
This was first published in Plugs & Dottles, Issue #46, July, 1982.

The Adventure of the Incompetent Engineer [SHPUN043]

"But how did you know that young Hoskins was the man behind the collapse of London Bridge?" I asked as that unhappy young man was lead away by a couple of stout constables.

"It was elementary in itself," said Holmes with a pitying smile at my obtuseness, "Young Hoskins is a man with addicted to puns and an incompetent engineer. I merely asked him what his bridge building experience was and he fell into my punning trap."

"I heard him mention he had built the Forth Bridge in

Scotland."

"Indeed and when I asked when he had built it, he answered 'After the first three fell down'."

This was written by Richard Milne.
It was first published on the Hounds of the Internet List on January 14th, 2005.

The Adventure of the Oriental Banker [SHPUN044]

"So", hissed the director of the failed Shanghai Rice Development Bank, Tso Fu, "you think you have beaten me Mr. Holmes, but there is nothing you can do to prevent from filing for bankruptcy and starting again. Besides, I have many thousands of people in debt to me. They purchased the rice plants on credit."

"You are right, Tso Fu. No doubt you will extort every penny at crushing interest rates," said Holmes.

"Of course," smiled the banker. "I shall resume my luxurious existence with the delectable Lotus Blossom and there's not a thing you can do."

"It is a pity that these wronged people can't send you to gaol," said Holmes, "but sadly never in the field of human misery have so many owed so much to Tso Fu."

This was written by Richard Milne.
It was first published on the Hounds of the Internet List on January 15th, 2005.

Monkey Business [SHPUN045]

As was their habit, Holmes and Watson were taking an evening stroll though Regents Park when they were approached by a keeper, and told to watch out for an ape that had escaped from its cage in the nearby London Zoo.

Sending Watson back to 221b to warn Mrs. Hudson, Holmes at once involved himself in the search for the missing animal.

Within the hour he was back at 221b, telling Watson he had found the ape in the Marylebone Library.

"Whatever was he doing there?" asked Watson.

"He was sitting quietly at a table," replied Holmes, with the Bible and Darwin's *Origin of Species* open in front of him."

"He was trying to find out whether he was his brother's keeper, or his keeper's brother."

This was written by "Anonymous."
It was first published on the Hounds of the Internet List on January 15th, 2005.

Mayhem At Allardyce's [SHPUN046]

Holmes and Watson had just finished a breakfast of scrapple and kippers one January morning. Holmes was engrossed in the *Morning Post*, while Watson was trying to decide where the pain from his Maiwand wound would be that day.

"I say, Watson," remarked the famous gumshoe, "did you hear about the accident at Allardyce's shop?"

"No, my good fellow, what happened?"

"According to the paper here, a costermonger's donkey went wild and crashed through our good butcher's shop window."

"Amazing, Holmes! I guess you could say that that animal

was a real ass in the pane."

This was written by "The Rascally Lascar."
This was first published in Plugs & Dottles, Issue #189, June, 1994.
It was later published on the Hounds of the Internet List on January 16th, 2005.

The Best Buns In Town [SHPUN049]

'Twas one of those wild, tempestuous evenings in mid January, with the elements lashing at our windows and little brats screaming in our chimney. Holmes and I were comfortably ensconced before a cheery fire with our pipes and port, having just finished one of Mrs. Hudson's famous suppers -- a delicious Cornish pasty, washed down with ample amounts of a robust Beaujolais. Holmes was languidly leafing through an old copy of the *Police Gazette*, while I was lasciviously slobbering over the pages of the latest catalog from Victoria's Secret.

"Holmes," said I, breaking the silence, "have you heard about the problem Rooden's Bakery in Blandsford is having?"

"I'm afraid not, my good fellow. Do elucidate."

"Well, it's a very popular bakery in the area. It features not only the finest baked goods*, but also fresh lemons and limes which Rooden obtains from his brother Jonas, a citrus importer of some means. As an added convenience for his customers, Rooden decided to squeeze the juice from his lemons and limes and sell the product in handy three and six ounce bottles. But as soon as the authorities heard of this, they informed him that the juice operation was illegal and would not be tolerated. Have you ever heard of anything so silly, Holmes?"

"I don't find it at all silly, Watson. The authorities are simply acting in accordance with one of the oldest of maxims."

"Maxim! What maxim?" I queried.

"Elementary, Watson -- bakers can't be juicers."

*Baker Rooden was noted for his buns -- bath buns, that is ....
not buns of steel.

This was written by "The Rascally Lascar."
This was first published in Plugs & Dottles, Issue #72,
September, 1984.
It was later published on the Hounds of the Internet List on
January 18th, 2005.

And an Order of Hash Browns [SHPUN051]

Holmes and Watson were planning their itinerary for a trip to
the United States, and were listing the various cities and persons
they wished to visit.

"We must certainly stop in Peoria," remarked Holmes. "I
understand it's the home of that sham Sherlockian and general
all-around nutbar and agitator, "The Rascally Lascar."

"Quite true," replied Watson. "And after Peoria, we might try
Hammond, Indiana. It's the egg capital of the world, you
know."

"Egg capital, Watson, how's that?"

"Well, Holmes, anytime you're in a restaurant you always
hear people ordering Hammond eggs."

This was written by Newton Williams.
This was first published in Plugs & Dottles, Issue #74,
November, 1984.
It was later published on the Hounds of the Internet List on

January 19th, 2005.

Holmes Suggests a Specialist [SHPUN052]

'Twas a beastly cold day in late January when I returned to our Baker Street quarters from visiting a patient, and found a note from Holmes:

"Gone to Allardyce's," it read, "back shortly." It was not long before I heard my friend's familiar tread upon the stairs.

"So, Holmes," I remarked when he entered our sitting-room, "you are back from Allardyce's. Surely, you weren't practicing your harpooning again?"

"No, Watson," came the reply, "not this time, but a pig, at least the flesh from its bones, *is* involved. To be brief, a rather strange theft has occurred at the good butcher's. At one o'clock today, a stranger entered the shop and, when Allardyce had his back turned, stole a sausage."

"'A' sausage?"

"Yes, Watson, just one. Strange, is it not? Why not take several while you're at it? As insignificant as the theft is, Allardyce wants the culprit apprehended and the sausage returned. After considering all facets of the case, I decided the matter was beyond my powers, and recommended that Allardyce contact Professor Rooten Tooten-Thorpe of the Oxford University Anthropology Department."

"An anthropologist, Holmes? What the devil for?"

"Dear fellow," replied my friend, "can you think of anyone more qualified to investigate a case of a missing link?"

This was written by "The Rascally Lascar."
This was first published in Plugs & Dottles, Issue #75, December, 1984.

It was later published on the Hounds of the Internet List on January 20th, 2005.

A Strange Transformation [SHPUN053]

"Good heavens, Holmes, here are some very strange goings on."

My comment was prompted by an article in the *Daily Gazette*.

"And what might that be, Watson?" my friend responded.

"Well, it seems a dairy farmer in Kent awoke the other morning and found, to his utter (pun intended) amazement, that his best milk producer had lost her normal black and white coloration and had turned completely purple! What could cause such a thing?"

"'Tis most obvious, my good fellow."

"Well, it's not obvious to me, Holmes. Please explain."

"Elementary, Watson, she herded through the grapevine."

This was written by "The Rascally Lascar."
This was first published in Plugs & Dottles, Issue #77, February, 1985.
It was later published on the Hounds of the Internet List on January 21st, 2005.

A Brilliant Diagnosis [SHPUN054]

Thaddeus Twickham was the most frugal of souls. Thus, when he found that his chimney and fireplace were badly in need of replacement, he sought the services of the cheapest stonemason available. The lowest bidder was a Japanese mason named Okubo Toshimichi. An agreement was signed, and in three weeks the work was completed.

The original chimney supported a lightning rod which, in order to save money, Twickham decided to reinstall himself. He gained access to his roof by way of a ladder, and was leaning on the chimney for support when the whole structure gave way with a deafening roar -- Twickham, bricks, and mortar ending up in the street below.

It was shortly thereafter that Holmes and Watson, out for a brief stroll, came upon the ghastly scene. Watson quickly made his way through the rubble and began examining poor Mr. Twickham.

"Is he badly hurt?" Holmes inquired.

"It looks like nothing too serious, Holmes, but when this unfortunate fellow comes to, I'm going to recommend that he take two aspirin, drink plenty of chicken soup, and get lots of bed rest."

"And why's that, Watson?"

"Elementary, Holmes -- this man has obviously come down with the Asian flue."

This was written by "The Rascally Lascar."
This was first published in Plugs & Dottles, Issue #79, April, 1985.
It was later published on the Hounds of the Internet List on January 22nd, 2005.

A Canonical Chuckle [SHPUN056]

One hot Summer's evening, whilst enjoying a pre-prandial whiskey and soda, Watson told Holmes -

"After my rounds today, I dropped in to the Alpha Inn for a quick half pint, and the landlord told me that his pretty little barmaid had taken maternity leave."

"That's right," Holmes replied, "The silly girl pulled the wrong knob, and got stout!"

This was written by "Anonymous."
It has never been published.

One Bad Pun Deserves Another [SHPUN057]

"Watson, you won't believe this, but remember that French madam we were discussing yesterday?"

"How could I forget?"

"For sure! Well, get this -- I hear that she has decided to write her autobiography, and will do so, believe it or not, in the form of an epic poem!"

"Good heavens, Holmes, that certainly won't help matters."

"How's that, my good fellow?"

"Because, Holmes, in doing so she will simply be going from bed to verse."

This was written by "The Rascally Lascar."
This was first published in Plugs & Dottles, Issue #80, May, 1985.
It was later published on the Hounds of the Internet List on January 24th, 2005.

Victorian UFO [SHPUN058]

"Holmes, here is a story in the paper which reminds me of the Dundas separation case and the husband who wound up each meal by throwing his false teeth at his wife."

"And what, Watson, might that be?"

"Well, it seems a fellow in the West End got into a row with his wife yesterday, and in a fit of rage hurled a copy of the *Canterbury Tales* at her. She managed to duck in time, and the tome sailed out the window, striking a passerby but inflicting little injury."

"Most interesting, my good fellow. I believe that you'll find this to be the first recorded case of a flying Chaucer in London."

This was written by "The Rascally Lascar."
This was first published in Plugs & Dottles, Issue #85, October, 1985.
It was later published on the Hounds of the Internet List on January 25th, 2005.

Retirement Blues [SHPUN059]

During his declining years, Dr.Watson found himself a place in a nice nursing home in Eastbourne.

On his first day there, he was sitting on the verandah, with a nurse by his side, when he started to keel over to his right. The nurse put her hand on his shoulder, and gently pushed him upright.

A little while later, he started to keel over to his left, and the nurse put her arm around him, and once again pulled him upright.

A few days later, he was visited by his old friend, Sherlock Holmes, who asked how he found his new quarters.

"Oh, it's very comfortable Holmes," he replied.

"Only thing is, they won't let you fart on the verandah."

This was written by "Anonymous."
It has never been published.

Biblical Love [SHPUN060]

One evening, Watson and Holmes were enjoying a glass of cognac and a cigar after enjoying one of Mrs. Hudson's newly acquired recipes, creamed scrapple on toast.

Watson was deeply engrossed in an article in *The Evening Standard*. Finally he spoke.

"Holmes, it says here that archeologists studying ancient athletic practices believe that tennis dates back to the time of the Pharaohs. It even adds that several biblical scholars agree with them and bring forth the preposterous notion that Joseph was the first great tennis player in recorded history. Such rubbish!"

Holmes replied, "To the contrary, my good fellow! You are, I am certain, aware that he served in Pharaoh's court!"

This was written by David J. Milner.
It was first published on the Hounds of the Internet List on January 25th, 2005.

They Were the Footprints of a Small Child [SHPUN062]

Many Sherlockian scholars do not accept the Master's account of his wanderings during the so-called Great Hiatus. Recently discovered documents now prove conclusively that he was not in Tibet, etc., but on a secret government mission to the crown colony of Hong Kong.

During his stay there, the Great Sleuth had the good fortune to meet his Oriental counterpart, the famous Charlie Chan. At their first meeting, Mr. Chan related to Holmes that a thief had broken into his woodshed the previous two nights and had made off with a considerable quantity of its contents. Chan suspected a youngster because of the many small footprints outside the shed. Holmes thus suggested that they stake out the structure that evening.

The two hid behind some thick bushes, when long about two o'clock a huge black form loomed out of the shadows and made its way to the shed. Our two friends could not believe their eyes when the creature emerged moments later with an armload of wood. For there stood a large bear--a bear in every respect, except that it had the feet of a small child!

"Incredible!" remarked Sherlock Holmes.

"Ah-So!" replied Charlie.

And as the strange beast began to leave the premises with its loot, Holmes shouted:--

"HALT! Go no further, boyfoot bear with teak of Chan!"

This was written by "The Rascally Lascar."
This was first published in Plugs & Dottles, Issue #82, July, 1985.
It was later published on the Hounds of the Internet List on January 27th, 2005.

The Dancing Doctor [SHPUN063]

During one of their encounters, Lestrade asked Holmes "Is it true that Watson is taking dancing lessons ?"

"That is correct, Lestrade," replied Holmes. "At present he is practicing some Spanish dances, and is coming along nicely. You should see him dance the fandango, with his fan in one hand, and his dango in the other."

This was written by "Anonymous."
It has never been published.

A Truly Cannon(ical) Tale [SHPUN064]

It was in the spring of '95 that Holmes and I were called to the little Surrey town of Esher to solve a rather delicate matter for the late Lady Bromley-Acton. A country fair was in progress at the time, and Holmes and I decided to take in the festivities before returning to London.

The fair's feature attraction was The Great Zucchini--the Human Cannonball. Hawkers told how The Great Zucchini would be shot from a cannon and safely land in a net two hundred and fifty feet down range. Holmes and I took our places in the stands. The Human Cannonball soon appeared amidst great fanfare, climbed a ladder to the mouth of the cannon, and slowly disappeared inside.

The next we knew, there was a thunderous roar from the cannon (the powder charge obviously just for effect), and The Great Zucchini flew from the cannon's mouth like an arrow, most likely propelled by a huge spring. That day, however, was to be Zucchini's last. 'Twas obvious that the spring has lost some of its original tension, for the performer slammed into the ground with a sickening thud some fifty feet short of the net, dead as a doornail.

"How perfectly horrible!" I remarked to Holmes.

"To be sure, Watson," my friend replied. "Where will they ever find another man of his caliber?"

This was written by "The Rascally Lascar."
This was first published in Plugs & Dottles, Issue #83, August, 1985.
It was later published on the Hounds of the Internet List on January 28th, 2005.

This One Should Be Given The Pitch [SHPUN066]

It was a Mrs. Beecham whom our landlady ushered into our rooms one late January morning. "And how might I be of help?" Holmes inquired after we had made the proper introductions.

"Well, Mr. Holmes," she replied, "the matter is such a trifling one, I hesitate to bother you, but I've become so frustrated and angered, and have received no help elsewhere, that I thought you might look into the problem if you had a spare moment."

"Unfortunately, that is ALL I have at the moment. Pray, go on."

"I recently purchased a piano from a family that was moving to America. It was badly in need of tuning, so I hired a tuner to correct the situation. I had to be away during his visit, but left his fee with the charwoman with instructions to pay him when he finished the job. Much to my disappointment, when I returned home I found the instrument to still be way out of tune. I, therefore, contacted the tuner, a Mr. Oppernokety, and asked him to come back and tune the piano to my satisfaction. This he refused to do, and has repeatedly done so each time I've contacted him. What would you suggest I do, Mr. Holmes?"

"You have done all you can, Mrs. Beecham. Permit me and Dr. Watson to look into the matter." Our client left, and Holmes and I hastened to the address of the tuner, which she had provided.

"Mr. Oppernokety?" Holmes queried.

"I understand that you recently tuned a piano for a Mrs. Beecham, that she is unsatisfied with the job, and that you steadfastly refused to retune the instrument to her liking. Is that correct?"

"Yes, it is."

"And would you be so kind as to explain the reason for your refusal?"

"Certainly. As everyone knows, sir, Oppernokety only tunes once."

This was written by "The Rascally Lascar."
This was first published in Plugs & Dottles, Issue #84, September, 1985.
It was later published on the Hounds of the Internet List on January 29th, 2005.

In Retirement [SHPUN069]

I had called upon my friend Sherlock Holmes at his retirement cottage on the South Downs early in the year 1912, and found him engaged in a heated discussion with a rugged faced chap who I later learned was a brick layer named Timothy Rooden. The discussion soon ended with Rooden leaving in a huff and muttering under his breath.

"What was that all about?" I asked my friend.

"Rooden has just completed building that little brick structure to your right in which I plan to store my honey*. When I refused to pay him for the job he became rather nasty, and we came to words, as you have no doubt just heard."

"Good Lord, Holmes," I exclaimed, "I don't blame the man for his anger. Why ever have you refused to pay him? You have always been a honourable person."

"You don't have all the facts, my dear fellow. I have checked into Mr. Rooden's background, and have discovered he's an active member of The United Grand Lodge of England."

"What the devil does that have to do with you not paying him for the brick work?"

"Elementary, Watson--the man is obviously a Freemason!"

*The material made from nectar by bees....NOT some London East End bimbo.

This was written by "The Rascally Lascar."
This was first published in Plugs & Dottles, Issue #89, February, 1986.
It was later published on the Hounds of the Internet List on January 31st, 2005.

The House Watcher [SHPUN070]

It was in the summer of '95 that Sherlock Homes was contacted by a Mr. Jonas Buster of London's fashionable West End. Mr. Buster had become increasingly suspicious of a strange dark haired individual who, every day for three weeks, had stationed himself across the street from our client's residence and then proceeded to stare intently at the house, some times for hours.

The case was not without interest to Holmes, and within a few days he had managed, by way of his many contacts, to identify the stranger as a Greek olive grower by the name of Aristotle Yutakis.

Wishing to see this mysterious person in the flesh, Holmes and I proceeded the next day from our Baker Street lodgings to the Buster residence on Park Lane. Sure enough, as we approached the address, there was our Greek friend staring intently at the residence of our client.

"Behold, Watson," Holmes exclaimed, "there is Aristotle contemplating the home of Buster!"

This was written by "The Rascally Lascar" from a suggestion by David Galerstein.
This was first published in Plugs & Dottles, Issue #93, June, 1986.
It was later published on the Hounds of the Internet List on February 1st, 2005

Lestrade's Garden Thief [SHPUN071]

During one of his visits to 221b, Inspector Lestrade described an incident which had occurred a few days previously, at his home in the suburbs.

"I caught a man in my back garden, trying to steal my rhubarb!" he declared.

"What did you do ?" asked Holmes.

"I took him into custardy." replied Lestrade.

This was written by "Anonymous."
It was first published on the Hounds of the Internet List on February 1st, 2005.

Wiggins and the Board Schools [SHPUN073]

Have you ever wondered what became of Wiggins, the leader of Sherlock Holmes' useful little bunch of street Arabs - (SIGN and STUD) - when he became too old for Holmes' employment?

He was one of the many boys who escaped the net of the Board Schools, those "beacons of the future," as Holmes called them, (NAVA) and the "School Board Man," the ogre whose job it was to seek out the parents of children who played truant, and try to coerce them into seeing that their unwilling offspring put in a more than occasional appearance at the new-fangled seats of learning. Along with many of his ilk, he was to live to regret his sad lack of formal education.

One day, during the early 1890's, he visited 221B to tell Holmes and Watson the result of his application for the position of junior footman in the London establishment of Lady Brackwell (CHAS).

He had managed to scrounge a reasonably presentable whistle and flute (suit) and a pair of daisy roots (boots), and, armed with a character reference from the Great Detective, Wiggins was interviewed by her Ladyship's steward, who told him that he stood a good chance of obtaining the position. However, the final decision would be made by her Ladyship, who would interview him on the following day.

According to Wiggins, her Ladyship began by telling him he would be required to wear tight-fitting livery, and asked him to remove his jacket and shirt, so that she could examine the muscular development of his chest and arms.

This done, she went on to say that the uniform included long stockings, and asked him to roll up his trouser legs so that she could examine his calf muscles.

Then she said "That seems quite satisfactory. Now let me see your testimonials."

As Wiggins said to Holmes, "If I'd been an educated chap, Mr. 'Olmes, I would have got that job."

This was written by "Anonymous."
This was first published in News from the Diggings, March, 1998.
It was later published on the Hounds of the Internet List on February 2nd, 2005.

Speaking Of Billy [SHPUN074]

Having attained the age of pubescence, Billy, the chasseur of Baker Street, was escorted by Holmes and Watson one evening on a walking tour of London's seamier districts. As they approached a certain address famous for catering to those who chose an alternate lifestyle, they were hailed by an effeminate male voice asking them to come up for a good time.

Holmes turned to Watson and said:

"Promise him anything, but give him our page."

This was written by "The Rascally Lascar" from a suggestion by Dave Milner.
It was first published on the Hounds of the Internet List on February 3rd, 2005

As the Bishop Said to the Actress [SHPUN075]

"I say, Watson," said Holmes, "Mrs. Hudson told me that her niece fell in love while traveling on the London Underground."

"She says the girl married beneath her station."

This was written by "Anonymous."
This was never published before.

A Fine Cup Of Tea [SHPUN077]

Holmes and Watson were seated before the breakfast table one morning, about to enjoy for the first time the latest drink sensation in England -- a new tea brewed from the leaves of a unique plant found only on the South Pacific Island of Moorzy. In addition to the tea itself, the leaves from this Moorzy plant were found to be a special delicacy of the Australian koala bear, whose main diet was previously thought to consist solely of eucalyptus leaves. The brew there from had thus become known as koala tea.

Watson proceeded to pour a cup of the new brew, noted that considerable bits of leaves had carried over into his cup, and remarked to Holmes that he was going to ask Mrs. Hudson for a strainer.

"Not on your life, my good fellow!" remarked the famed sleuth.

"But, Holmes, I can't drink the tea like it is .... besides, what the devil do you have against the use of a strainer?"

"Surely, Watson," replied Holmes, "you must know that the koala tea of Moorzy is not strained."

This was written by "The Rascally Lascar."
This was first published in Plugs & Dottles, Issue #99, December, 1986.
It was later published on the Hounds of the Internet List on February 4th, 2005

Watson's Practice [SHPUN079]

In his surgery one day, Watson was sounding the chest of a young girl.

As he applied his stethoscope to her chest, he said encouragingly "Big breaths", and she replied

"Yeth, and I'm only thirteen."

This was written by "Anonymous."
This was never published before.

A Bird In The Hand... [SHPUN081]

I had called upon my friend Sherlock Holmes at his cottage on the South Downs shortly after his retirement, and found him bent over the table examining a small bird which lay upon a towel, and which appeared quite dead.

"Ha, Watson, you come at just the right time," he exclaimed. "As a medical man this should be of interest to you. This unfortunate creature made the mistake of flying into the side of my cottage just shortly before you arrived."

"Is it dead?" asked I.

"No," my good fellow, "just stunned, and I'm about to attempt to revive it using a method suggested to me by my neighbor, Dr. Christopher Finch, a noted ornithologist. I have here a small vial of petrol, and using this tiny pipette I will introduce a few drops of the liquid into the bird's mouth. There we are ... and now let's see if the creature revives."

We had not long to wait before the bird began fluttering its wings. Soon it was on its feet, and suddenly it took off and began flying wildly about the room.

"Amazing, Holmes ..." I began to say, when the bird suddenly stiffened and fell to the floor with a sickening thud.

"Surely it's dead this time," I remarked.

"No, Watson," replied Holmes, "just out of gas."

This was written by "The Rascally Lascar."
This was first published in Plugs & Dottles, Issue #96, September, 1986.
It was later published on the Hounds of the Internet List on February 6th, 2005.

A Short, Short Christmas Story [SHPUN082]

"Well, Holmes, Mrs. Hudson sure has taken a liking to that stray kitten she found on the beach during her visit to Brighton."

"Yes, Watson. And in view of where she found him and the festive season just past, I think she should name him Sandy Claws."

This was written by "The Rascally Lascar."
This was first published in Plugs & Dottles, Issue #100, January, 1987.
It was later published on the Hounds of the Internet List on February 7th, 2005.

Gloussement de Canon [SHPUN086]

Upon his return from Paris, whence Holmes had gone, at the invitation of the French Government, to track down Huret, the boulevard assassin (GOLD), the detective was regaling Watson with stories of his time spent in the French capital.

"I was walking along the banks of the Seine, when I came upon a group of people who were watching an unfortunate cat, struggling for it's life in the river."

"It came up once, and the group counted 'Un.' A second time, and they counted 'Deux',
and a third time, when they counted 'Trois'."

"What happened then ?" asked Watson.

"Quatre cinque" replied Holmes, with a grin.

This was written by "Anonymous."
It was first published on the Hounds of the Internet List on February 8th, 2005.

Two All-Beef Patties, Lettuce, Pickles... [SHPUN087]

We all know how Holmes, when he entered the Pearly Gates with Watson, was able to identify Adam and Eve from among the multitudes. Elementary, they were the only two people without navels.

In the meantime, that great hamburger mascot, Ronald McDonald, had passed on (probably from too many trans-fatty acids) and had entered the Heavenly throng. As they strolled the paths of eternal paradise one day, Watson remarked to his friend:

"Well, Holmes, you have a real challenge today,"

"How's that, Watson?"

"Well, the way you identified Adam and Eve was simple, but I understand that Ronald McDonald of hamburger fame has recently joined us. However will you be able to identify him?"

"Elementary again, my good fellow, he will be the only person with the sesame seed buns."

154

This was written by "The Rascally Lascar."
This was first published in Plugs & Dottles, Issue #108, September, 1987.
It was later published on the Hounds of the Internet List on February 9th, 2005.

Geometry by Moriarty [SHPUN088]

During his term in the chair of mathematics at a minor university, Moriarty was asked by one of his students to give a practical demonstration of Pythagorus' Theorem.

After some thought, he told the following story:

"A Red Indian Chief had three squaws, each of them pregnant.

The first one slept on a bed of buffalo hides, and she gave birth to a son.

The second slept on a bed of deer hides, and she, too, brought forth a son.

The third slept on a bed of hippopotamus hides, and she brought forth twin sons.

Which proves that the squaw on the hippopotamus is equal to the sons of the squaws on the other two hides."

This was written by "Anonymous."
This has never been published before.

The Teepee/Wigwam Syndrome [SHPUN089]

"What are you perusing there, Watson?"

These words from my friend Sherlock Holmes broke my

concentration one evening as I read with some interest and article by Sigmund Freud in the latest issue of *Die Zeitscrift fur Abnorme Psychologie*.

"'Tis most interesting, Holmes. The learned Dr. Freud writes here of a case involving an American Indian who is obsessed with the feeling on alternate days that he is a teepee and then a wigwam. One day he's a teepee, the next a wigwam. How's that for strange? Freud is at a complete loss as to the cause of the condition."

"That is surprising, Watson, in view of Dr. Freud's expertise in the field of psychology. Why, the cause of the Indian's problem is nothing short of elementary."

"Really? And what might that be, pray tell?"

"'Tis quite evident, Watson, that the fellow in question is simply too tense."

This was written by "The Rascally Lascar."
This was first published in Plugs & Dottles, Issue #104, May, 1987.
It was later published on the Hounds of the Internet List on February 10th, 2005.

Critic's Choice [SHPUN094]

I descended to breakfast one morning in March to find my friend Sherlock Holmes engrossed in the morning paper. The previous evening we had attended a concert by the Berlin Philharmonic at St. James's Hall. Holmes had come away most impressed by maestro Von Dahlingstein's treatment of Tchaikovsky's Fifth Symphony —"nothing short of electrifying," according to Holmes.

Before I could wish Holmes good morning, he slammed

down the paper in disgust, shouting: "Neville Brookings is an incompetent idiot, Watson!"

"Who is Neville Brookings?" I queried.

"He supposedly is a music critic for the *Morning Herald*, but when he writes that Von Dahlingstein's rendering of Tchaikovsky's Fifth was clinical and without feeling, he proves to me that he's a musical ignoramus!"

"Surely, Holmes, the man must possess some expertise in the field."

"No, Watson, he does not! From his comments regarding last night's performance at St. James's, it is quite obvious that he doesn't know his brass from his oboe!"

This was written by "The Rascally Lascar."
This was first published in Plugs & Dottles, Issue #102, March, 1987.
It was later published on the Hounds of the Internet List on February 13th, 2005.

Touché! [SHPUN095]

"Good Lord, Watson, the moral fiber of British society is becoming extremely frayed!"

These words from my friend jolted me from a deep chocolate brown study into which I had fallen one evening.

"How's that, Holmes?" I asked, having roused myself.

"I read in the paper here that a group of admirers of that disgusting rogue, Oscar Wilde, have formed a fencing club in the West End of our fair city. And this, while Wilde still resides in Reading Gaol as a result of his sordid liaison with Lord Alfred

Douglas."

"Disgusting, Holmes, to be sure," I replied. "And does this fencing club have a name yet?"

"As a matter of fact they do, Watson, they're known as 'The Gay Blades'."

This was written by "The Rascally Lascar."
This was first published in Plugs & Dottles, Issue #103, April, 1987.
It was later published on the Hounds of the Internet List on February 14th, 2005.

Any Church in a Storm [SHPUN096]

"Some excitement in our town last night, Watson," remarked Holmes one morning as the two sat at breakfast.

"How so?" queried the good doctor.

"Well, as you are no doubt aware, the Ronder Circus is in town, and one of its brown bears escaped its cage and began chasing some poor soul through the streets of our fair city. The pursued, seeing that he was quickly losing the race, finally sought refuge by running
into St. Monica's Church in the Edgeware Road."

"Good heavens, Holmes, that certainly didn't show much upbringing on the fellow's part."

"I'm afraid I don't follow you, Watson...."

"Surely, Holmes, no decent individual would run into a church with a bear behind!"

This was written by "The Rascally Lascar."

This was first published in Plugs & Dottles, Issue #106, July, 1987.
It was later published on the Hounds of the Internet List on February 15th, 2005.

Ding Dong Bell, Watson's In The Well [SHPUN098]

Sherlock Holmes began to worry. His faithful chronicler had left that morning to attend a patient in the country, and had yet to return by six o'clock. But finally, the familiar footsteps of the Good Doctor were heard upon the stair. Seconds later, a tired and bedraggled Watson, his right arm in a sling, entered the familiar sitting-room.

"Watson!" exclaimed Holmes, "whatever has happened to you?"

"Well, I'm almost ashamed to admit it, but as I was making my way to my patient's cottage in a remote area of the countryside, I spied an old abandoned well. With the curiosity of a child, I tried to peer into the accursed thing, lost my balance, and fell in. Fortunately, it was not very deep, and my cries for help soon brought aid. Unfortunately, however, the fall resulted in a broken arm, which has taken the better part of the day to treat and set."

Holmes chuckled merrily upon hearing Watson's sad account. "Let this be a lesson to you, old fellow," he remarked. "In the future, you should concentrate on tending to the sick ... and leave the well alone."

This was written by "The Rascally Lascar" from a Suggestion by Edward B. Bagley.
This was first published in Plugs & Dottles, Issue #107, August, 1987.
It was later published on the Hounds of the Internet List on February 16th, 2005.

Westward Ho Ho Ho! [SHPUN103]

The Mormons allowed John Ferrier to ride in their wagons with them just after they rescued him from the Great Alkali Plain, but after he had been with them for a while and had put on some weight, they made him get out and walk. The benches in the wagons were narrow and the westward-bound pilgrims had imposed a strict limit of 18 inches of seat space per person for those riding in the wagons. Those taking up more space were not even allowed to start on the journey, for there was, they said,

"No West for the rear-y."

This was written by Karen Murdock "May Blunder."
It was later published on the Hounds of the Internet List on February 18th, 2005.

Naturally [SHPUN101]

One evening, after dining on Mrs. Watson's delicious grouse soufflé, Holmes and Watson were enjoying a post-prandial cigar and brandy while scanning the day's newspapers.

"Holmes, it says here in the *Times* that the world famous naturalist, Kristofer Dahlenwicd has taken up residence in The Great Grimpen Mire where he intends to spend the next five years studying the area. Perhaps we should pay him a visit and discuss what we saw there."

"To the contrary, Watson. We'd only be in his way. As a naturalist with a specialty in marsh ecosystems, he'll be swamped with work."

This was written by David Milner.
It was first published on the Hounds of the Internet List on February 17th, 2005.
It was later published in the Gaslight Gazette, V11, #03,

03/2005.

The Telltale Odor [SHPUN104]

The good Dr. Watson, returning rather late one evening to Baker Street, was queried by Holmes:

"A bit late I see, Watson."

"Late? Well, I guess I am."

"And from the distinct odor of beer on your breath, my amazing detective powers tell me that the reason for your tardiness is that you stopped off at the local pub on your way home and had a pint or two. Not so?"

"Absolutely wrong, Holmes," replied Watson. "I stopped off at Simpson's for an order of frogs' legs. What you smell are the hops."

This was written by "The Rascally Lascar."
This was first published in Plugs & Dottles, Issue #113, February, 1988.
It was later published on the Hounds of the Internet List on February 19th, 2005.

Holmes and Watson's Tent [SHPUN106]

Sherlock Holmes read in a newspaper that there lived, amongst a great herd of bison on the fertile plains in America, an Indian who was a phenomenal tracker of footprints, perhaps the best in the world. Sensing a possible new monograph, Holmes enticed Dr. Watson to accompany him on a trip to visit this genius. Once there, Holmes and the Indian got into a dispute about some arcane facet of the art. There seemed to be no way to settle the issue, so an elder suggested that the two retire to Holmes's and Watson's tent and stay there, without food or sleep, until they could settle the issue.

The pair retreated to the tent and the murmur of conversation could be heard. To provide them with some sustenance, every hour Watson took them a pot of tea. Holmes, to keep his mind clear, eschewed even that, but his Indian friend welcomed it.

Hours and hours later, Holmes emerged, exhausted. Apparently they had been unable to reach an agreement. Within a few minutes, he was partaking of a hearty dish of pemmican when a cry was heard, and the elder rushed over to Holmes to inform him that his adversary had suddenly died. Holmes, anticipating a call for his services, reached for his magnifying glass. But the elder held up his hand:

"No need, Great White Tracker. No crime. Him drown in tepee."

This was written by Don Dillistone.
It was first published on the Hounds of the Internet List on February 20th, 2005.

On the Beach [SHPUN107]

Holmes and Watson were enjoying the sunshine, sitting in hired deckchairs on the beach at Eastbourne.

"It looks nice out." said Watson.

"It does," replied Holmes, "I think I'll take mine out as well."

This was written by "Anonymous".
This was previously unpublished.

Hasenpfeffer On Parade [SHPUN093]

While out for a country stroll one day, Holmes and Watson espied some thirty rabbits walking backwards in single file.

"Good Lord, Holmes, what does that mean?" queried Watson.

"Elementary," replied the great sleuth, "'tis nothing but a receding hare line."

This was written by "The Rascally Lascar."
This was first published in Plugs & Dottles, Issue #30, March, 1981.
This was again published in Plugs & Dottles, Issue #101, February, 1987.
It was later published on the Hounds of the Internet List on February 12th, 2005.

Interlude at Baker Street #7 [SHPUN241]

'Twas a blustery and bitterly cold evening in early January. Holmes and I had just finished a steaming platter of Bangers and mash, made as only our Dear Mrs. Hudson could. Having ensconced ourselves on either side of a cheery fire, Holmes became engrossed in the *Evening Standard*, while I fell to musing about my experiences of women which extended over many nations and three separate continents.

"Here's an interesting piece, Watson," remarked Holmes, breaking into my thoughts. "It seems that the Maharajah of a remote Indian province decreed last year that there would be no more killing of wild animals. Soon the country was overrun by man-eating tigers, panthers and the like. Hundreds of the natives were killed by the wild beasts, with the result that last week they revolted against their leader. Their efforts seem to have been successful, for at last report the Maharajah was said to have fled the province in fear of his life."

"Well, if the story is true, Holmes," I replied, "it's definitely a first."

"A first, my dear fellow? How's that?"

"Elementary, Holmes. It's obviously the first time in history that a reign was called on account of the game."

This was written by "The Rascally Lascar."
This was first published in Wheelwrightings, Vol. 12, Issue #03, January, 1990.

Heh, What Did You Say? [SHPUN122]

"Well, Watson, you've finally done it! I've been telling you for a year now to do something about your hearing problem. You have ignored my entreaties, and as a result it now appears that you, and possibly myself as well, will be slapped with a nice libel suit." Holmes's voice displayed considerable irritation as he tossed aside the latest issue of *The Strand*.

"Libel suit? Whatever are you talking about?"

"I refer to the latest *Strand* wherein appears your account of the Sir Christopher Reading affair. In giving you the details of this case, I stated to you quite plainly that Sir Christopher was a unique and important individual -- UNIQUE and IMPORTANT, Watson! But because of your partial deafness, which you refuse to do anything about, your account in *the Strand* states that Sir Christopher was a 'eunuch and impotent individual'."

"Watson, I believe we may be in deep doo-doo!"

This was written by "The Rascally Lascar" from a suggestion by Howard E. Burr.
It was first published in Plugs & Dottles, Issue #125, February, 1989.

One Smart Dog [SHPUN123]

"Watson," remarked Holmes one evening, shortly after the two had settled together in Baker Street, "that bull pup of yours has to go. His constant yapping is driving me to distraction. And besides, he's the dumbest cur I've ever known!"

"Dumb, Holmes? I don't know about that. Why just five minutes ago he was in my bedroom pouring over *The Evening Standard*."

This was written by "The Rascally Lascar."
It was first published in Plugs & Dottles, Issue #126, March, 1989.

Unsafe Sex [SHPUN124]

"Ah, here is an item of interest, Holmes."

"How's that, my good fellow?"

"I read here that the rather notorious adventuress, Lillie Langtry, has had an accident which resulted in a broken leg."

"Does the report say how it happened?"

"No. But knowing Lillie's reputation as a Grande Horizontale, she probably did it sliding down a barrister."

This was written by "The Rascally Lascar."
It was first published in Plugs & Dottles, Issue #129, June, 1989.

Parlez-Vous Francais? [SHPUN127]

One blustery March evening, as the Baker Street Duo sat before a cheery fire, Watson chanced to ask Holmes about his recent trip to the Continent.

"Did you learn any French during your travels?" he queried.

"As a matter of fact, I did," came the reply. "I learned the curious expression which describes the effects of a bomb blast in a French kitchen."

"Surely, you must be joking," said a doubting Watson. "What could such an expression be?"

"Elementaire, mon cher Watson! Elle est 'linoleum blownapart'."

This was written by "The Rascally Lascar" from a suggestion by Howard Einbinder.
It was first published in Plugs & Dottles, Issue #134, November, 1989.
It was later published on the Shamlockians' List on March 4th, 2005.

And A Hearing Problem As Well! [SHPUN129]

Shortly after the retirement of my friend Sherlock Holmes, I decided to specialize in the field of ophthalmology, and in a few years had a rather lucrative practice at No. 114 Harley Street.

You can imagine my surprise, when one day a patient was ushered into my examination room who turned out to be a distant cousin of the King of Bohemia, that monarch who figured so crucially in the Irene Adler affair.

My patient, a Count von Ormstein, complained of poor sight in his left eye, and the cause of his problem was readily apparent upon examination.

"Count von Ormstein," I said, "you have a cataract."

"No, doctor," replied my patient with Teutonic indignity, "I drive a Mercedes-Benz!"

This was written by "The Rascally Lascar."
It was first published in Plugs & Dottles, Issue #136, January, 1990.
It was later published on the Shamlockians' List on March 6th, 2005.
It was later published in The Gaslight Gazette; V11, #06, 10/2005.

Say Cheese! [SHPUN132]

"How's your friend Doyle doing, Watson?"

"He's been very busy with his researches into psychic phenomena, and has recently had a discouraging setback. He had taken his camera and flash powder to a séance with the purpose of photographing an apparition should one appear. Luck was with him, the ectoplasmic trans-formation allowed a picture to be taken. But when the plate was developed, Doyle discovered that it was way underexposed and completely blank."

"Ah, too bad, my good fellow," replied Holmes, "it appears that the spirit was willing but the flash was weak."

This was written by "The Rascally Lascar."
It was first published in Plugs & Dottles, Issue #139, April, 1990.
It was later published on the Shamlockians' List on March 9th, 2005.

De Gustibus Non Est Disputandum [SHPUN134]

It was a wild, tempestuous, child-sobbing-in-the-chimney evening in January. With a cheery fire in the grate. Holmes was engrossed in *The Evening Standard*, while I was pruriently perusing Volume 1 of the Marquis de Sade's *Les 120 Journees du Sodome*.

"Here's a sad tale, Watson," remarked Holmes, interrupting my lubricious thoughts. "A Methodist missionary from Birmingham is reported to have been captured by cannibals deep in the Congo and eaten by the savages."

"Indeed tragic," I replied, "but there is at least one bright side to the story."

"Good heavens, Watson, pray tell how!"

"Well, the natives at least got a taste of religion."

This was written by "The Rascally Lascar."
It was first published in Plugs & Dottles, Issue #146, November, 1990.
It was later published on the Shamlockians' List on March 12th, 2005.

Anstruther's New Undertaking [SHPUN137]

"Tell me, Watson, is it true that your old colleague Anstruther has given up the practice of medicine and gone into the undertaking business?"

"True," replied Watson, "and a most unfortunate decision, I'm afraid. There's another undertaking establishment in the same neighborhood, and since it's offering lower rates it's getting most of the business. Poor Anstruther is not doing at all well."

"Well, considering the business he's in, I guess you could say that Anstruther has STIFF competition."

This was written by "The Rascally Lascar."

It was first published in Plugs & Dottles, Issue #152, May, 1991. It was later published on the Shamlockians' List on March 15th, 2005.

Seek And Ye Shall Find [SHPUN138]

My friend Sherlock Holmes was very busy in November of 1889 doing undercover work for the London police in connection with an international smuggling ring. Following the successful breakup of the ring and the conviction of all involved, Holmes was finally able to discuss the details of the case with me.

"Yes, Watson, this was one clever bunch of smugglers. They came up with the ingenious idea of employing a number of nursemaids as a cover for their operation. But, after much diligent work, we finally apprehended the scoundrels. And locating the contraband was no easy matter. I tell you, Watson, we virtually had to search every crook and nanny."

This was written by "The Rascally Lascar" from a suggestion by William Ballew.
It was first published in Plugs & Dottles, Issue #158, November, 1991.
It was later published on the Shamlockians' List on March 17th, 2005.

A Canine Left/Leaves Behind In The Strand [SHPUN139]

Strolling down the Strand one day, Holmes and Watson spotted an angry chap across the street who was attempting to walk his dog — a pit bull, which definitely had other ideas. The dog was refusing to walk, sitting back on its butt and bracing its feet. Only by dragging the animal by the leash could the owner move him. After pulling the dog in this fashion for some twenty feet, the owner gave up, dropped the leash, and walked away.

"I wonder why he did that?" queried Watson.

"I guess he realized," replied Holmes, "that he was simply creating a bottomless pit."

This was written by "The Rascally Lascar".
It was first published in Plugs & Dottles, Issue #162, March, 1992.
It was later published on the Shamlockians' List on March 19th, 2005.

A Unique Undertaking [SHPUN141]

"I say, Holmes, I see in the *Times* that the undertaking firm of Morse, Wayne and Company has come up with a novel way of entombment. The body of the deceased is encased in a translucent resin, much as nature preserves fossils."

"Most interesting, Watson. And if our American cousins wouldn't take offense, I would suggest that they call these unique tombs the amber graves of Wayne."

This was written by "The Rascally Lascar."
It was first published in Plugs & Dottles, Issue #165, June, 1992.
It was later published on the Shamlockians' List on March 22nd, 2005.

Terror in The W. C. [SHPUN142]

"Heavens, Holmes, I see here in the *Evening Standard* that some woman, who is said to be the grandmother of Jack the Ripper, has been knifing victims in many of London's public lavatories."

"Yes, Watson, the citizenry is, of course, quite concerned, and I'm sure we will soon be hearing from our old friend Inspector Lestrade with a petition for help in solving the case."

"No doubt, Holmes, and when I present the story to the public following its successful conclusion, I shall title it, 'The Case of the Old Woman Who Shivved in a Loo'."

This was written by "The Rascally Lascar."
It was first published in Plugs & Dottles, Issue #166, July, 1992.
It was later published on the Shamlockians' List on March 23rd, 2005.

Bet You Can't Eat Just One! [SHPUN143]

Never mentioned by Dr. Watson in his Holmesian chronicles was Bayh's Pub on Oxford Street, owned and operated by Henry Bayh, grandfather of the famous US Senator. The pub was one of Watson's favorite haunts, not only because of its fine ale, but also for its excellent food, personally prepared by the owner.

While lifting a few pints one March evening, the good doctor was asked by the owner to try a plate of his new homemade fried snacks. Upon sampling the new creation, Watson enthusiastically remarked:

"Good chips, Mr. Bayh!"

This was written by "The Rascally Lascar."
It was first published in Plugs & Dottles, Issue #170, November, 1992.
It was later published on the Shamlockians' List on March 25th, 2005.

Interlude at Baker Street #4 [SHPUN239]

During my long and memorable association with Mr. Sherlock Holmes, I never once failed to be amazed by his extraordinary powers of deductive reasoning. No matter how bizarre or *outré* the case, he was, with but few exceptions, always able to come up with a solution, while the efforts of the official police frequently ended in a cul-de-sac. In this regard I am especially reminded of the murder of Matthew Crowder.

I remember it was a blustery evening in late November. Holmes was comfortably ensconced before the fire cross-indexing his extensive records of crime. I had just sat down with a copy of the *Evening Standard* and had hardly finished reading my first article when there was a knock on the door and Mrs. Hudson announced our old friend Inspector Lestrade.

"Ha, Lestrade, come in, come in," cried Holmes. "Move up to the fire here and take off the chill."

"Thank you, Mr. Holmes, don't mind if I do," replied Lestrade, removing his heavy overcoat and advancing toward the fire.

"So, Lestrade, is your visit of a social nature, or might Watson and I be of some assistance to you in a police matter?"

"Well, we did have a little problem thrown in our laps this morning which I'm sure we'll eventually solve, but I thought you'd like to hear the details. I understand you've been wanting for mental stimulation as of late, so I have decided to make you privy to information regarding our latest case."

"Most kind of you, Lestrade," replied Holmes, a devilishly condescending smile slowly breaking upon his face. "Pray proceed with the facts."

Lestrade lit a cigarette, moved closer to the fire and provided us with the following account.

"Early this morning, we were called to Number 16, Harley Street by the landlady of the residence, a Mrs. Eliza Wigmore. As is her usual custom, Mrs. Wigmore had brewed her morning tea and had taken a pot to the rooms of her only tenant, a retired banker by the name of Matthew Crowder. After several unsuccessful attempts to rouse her boarder, she admitted herself to his rooms. The sitting-room showed signs of a struggle, and on the floor by the fireplace lay Crowder's body, a wicked looking knife deeply imbedded in his chest. He was, needless to say, quite dead."

"Upon questioning, Mrs. Wigmore related that Crowder had had two visitors the previous evening. About eight o'clock she admitted a tall stately gentleman attired in the most opulent manner with a top hat, silk scarf, and a luxurious astrakhan overcoat. She showed him the stairs to Crowder's second floor rooms and then went back to her own apartment. Approximately half an hour later she happened to glance out the window and saw this first visitor standing on the sidewalk. After several minutes, he managed to hail a hansom and was soon whisked away."

"Shortly thereafter, a second visitor arrived and asked to see Crowder. Unlike the first gentleman, visitor number two was a stout, florid-faced individual with a black bushy mustache. According to the landlady, he was dressed in a most seedy and slovenly fashion and smelled strongly of alcohol. She directed him to Crowder's rooms and then retired for the evening. She slept soundly and had no idea that anything was amiss until she entered the unfortunate man's rooms next morning."

"One question, if I may," broke in Holmes.

"Yes?"

"Was the front door locked this morning?"

"Mrs. Wigmore assures us that it was. The lock is such that the door is automatically secured when one leaves and pulls it shut."

"Good. This means that the murderer has to be one of the two visitors and not someone who entered much later in the evening."

"Yes, we naturally came to the same conclusion. I'm afraid the case may prove to be a most difficult one. Even if we are able to locate both individuals who visited Crowder last night we must still determine which one is the murderer."

"There's no need to locate both of them," remarked Holmes, as he reached for his cherrywood pipe.

"And why not?" queried Lestrade, in a tone which showed some irritation.

"Because, from the information which you have provided it is most obvious which of the two visitors killed Crowder."

"Really, Mr. Holmes, I've had a long and trying day. I feel this is no time for jokes." It was obvious that Lestrade's irritation with Holmes was slowly mounting.

"I assure you, my dear Lestrade, that I do not jest. It has long been an axiom of mine that appearances, as far as they relate to the criminal and the noncriminal, must be taken, if you will excuse a little Latin, *cum grano salis*. This case, however, proves the exception. There is no doubt in my mind that visitor number one is the murderer."

"And how the devil do you figure that?" barked Lestrade.

"His accoutrements, dear fellow, his accoutrements!"

"Accoutrements?"

"Yes. The top hat ... the silk scarf ... the expensive

astrakhan overcoat. Don't you see it? The man was obviously dressed to kill."

This was written by "The Rascally Lascar" from a suggestion by Marion Parker.
This was first published in Wheelwrightings, Vol. 04, Issue #02, September, 1981

Is There a Doctor In The House? [SHPUN145]

'Twas in the latter days of March in '95 that the good Dr. Watson was called out to a noted gambling casino in London's fashionable West End to attend to an apparent heart attack victim. The weather had turned vicious, and when Watson failed to return to Baker Street after two hours, Holmes became concerned about his friend's well-being.

Another hour passed, and the great sleuth could wait no longer. He phoned the casino and asked that Dr. Watson be paged.

"Sorry," was the reply, "the house does not make doctor calls."

This was written by "The Rascally Lascar."
It was first published in Plugs & Dottles, Issue #196, January, 1995.
It was later published on the Shamlockians' List on March 28th, 2005.

The Odiferous Defense [SHPUN146]

The prosecution of Josiah Amberley for the alleged asphyxiation of his adulterous wife and her lover at The Haven was being billed in the tabloid press as "The Trial of the 19th Century". Much of the legal maneuvering was lost amid the lurid details of the seductive youth and beauty of the wife, and the insidious chess playing of the Lothario medico.

Both sides seemed to be "playing to the gallery" as it were. At one point: in the course of testimony, one of the police officers offered that during his investigation, he could smell gas in the alleged death chamber. However, under the clever cross-examination of the "dream team" of solicitors and barristers for the defense, Cummings, McCallister & McFarlane, he admitted that his imagined smell of gas was certainly covered up by the overwhelming smell of new paint, so that any positive identification was questionable.

In the summing up, the point was made...

"If you can't smell the gas, you gotta acquit his ass."

A verdict of not guilty followed from the jury of 12 angry men.

This was written by David R. McCallister.
It was first published on the Shamlockians' List on March 30th, 2005.

A Real Parisian Fashion [SHPUN147]

While Mrs. Hudson served supper to her two Baker Street lodgers one evening, Holmes remarked about the fine angora wool sweater she was wearing.

"Yes, Mr. Holmes," she replied, "it was a Christmas gift from a friend in France. As you probably know, the angora breed of rabbit originated in France in about 1723, and the wool for this sweater, I'm told, came from rabbits bred and raised right in the heart of Paris in the hutch back of Notre Dame."

This was written by "The Rascally Lascar."
It was first published in Plugs & Dottles, Issue #197, February,

1995.
It was later published on the Shamlockians' List on March 31st, 2005.

A Collective Conundrum [SHPUN148]

"Godfrey, my love, you lawyers are so wise, so filled with all sorts of knowledge. Would you mind awfully if I ask you a little question?"

"Certainly not, my dishy little diva. Ask away, Irene, my sweet, and I shall do my very best to answer your query."

"Well, I was wondering. If you speak of one goose as a goose, whatever do you call two of them?"

"Sexual harassment."

This was written by Frank Darlington.
It was first published in Plugs & Dottles, Issue #196, January, 1995.
It was later published on the Shamlockians' List on April 1st, 2005.

Art in the Blood [SHPUN150]

"I say, Holmes, being the descendant of a famous French artist, have you read of this Lautrec fellow? It seems he's been having a hard time breaking into the ranks of the famous."

"'Tis no wonder, Watson, this Lautrec was born Toulouse."

This was written by "The Rascally Lascar."
It was first published in Plugs & Dottles, Issue #200, May, 1995.
It was later published on the Shamlockians' List on April 4th, 2005.

<u>Holmes Bites The Bullet</u> [SHPUN151]

Sherlock Holmes had spent a sleepless night due to a painfully abscessed tooth, and was about to leave for the local dentist's to have the pesky molar extracted.

Remarked Watson: "I wouldn't worry about it at all, Holmes. With the recent discovery of novocain, tooth extractions are absolutely painless."

"True, Watson, but I intend to forgo the novocain."

"Good heavens, man, why?"

"Because, my good fellow, I want to transcend dental medication."

This was written by "The Rascally Lascar."
It was first published in Plugs & Dottles, Issue #206, November, 1995.
It was later published on the Shamlockians' List on April 6th, 2005.

<u>Music Hath Charms(Sometimes)</u> [SHPUN153]

"Will you be going to the violin concert at Albert Hall, Holmes? The noted Emanuel Figgs is performing, you know."

"Well, I hesitate to go, to be honest. The program is definitely not Figgs' métier. The whole concert consists of romantic compositions, when it's an undisputed fact that Figgs' specialty is Bach, Handel, and Vivaldi, the masters of the baroque genre. Nevertheless, I suppose I will go."

As Holmes had predicted, the concert was a disaster. As he and Watson strolled back from Albert Hall, he turned to his friend and a said:

"You see, Watson, the concert was a perfect example of the old adage — if it ain't baroque, don't Figgs it."

This was written by Rosemary Michaud.
It was first published in Plugs & Dottles, Issue #203 August, 1995.
It was later published on the Shamlockians' List on April 8th, 2005.

The Sultan's Souvenir [SHPUN154]

The conical felt cap with its long black tassel had long ago been a presentation to Holmes from the Sultan of Turkey — a bit of baksheesh for having solved the Curious Case of the Conspicuously Concupisible Concubine. It had long served its purpose as a smoking cap for the World's Greatest Smoker. Now, shapeless and moth-eaten, Holmes had consigned it to the dustbin, but Mrs. Hudson, the canny Caledonian, had rescued it and returned it to its accustomed peg.

Holmes, waxing wrathful on seeing it returned, called upon Watson to question the landlady about this seemingly subservient action on her part. And this was the poor soul's apologetic response:

"I didn't mean any harm, sir. You see, it's just that ... I've grown accustomed to his fez."

This was written by Frank Darlington.
It was first published in Plugs & Dottles, Issue #167, August, 1992.
It was later published on the Shamlockians' List on April 10th, 2005.

Was It Crosby, the Banker? [SHPUN156]

One beautiful spring morning, the silence of Baker Street was shattered by the sound of a terrible accident outside 221. An unfortunate citizen had been struck by a runaway hansom. Dr. Watson was soon on the scene, and with the help of Holmes and a few bystanders, had the victim carried inside.

Watson's examination showed that the unfortunate pedestrian was suffering from a broken leg, but the fracture was an absolutely clean one. Reaching into his medical bag, the good doctor produced a small, squat jar from which he proceeded to extract a repulsive red leech.

"Surely, Watson, you're not going to apply that creature to this poor fellow's leg?" queried Holmes.

"And why not, may I ask?"

"Well, my good fellow," was Holmes's reply, "you certainly recall the old saw:

'Never give an even break a sucker'."

This was written by "The Rascally Lascar."
It was first published in Plugs & Dottles, Issue #164, May, 1992. It was later published on the Shamlockians' List on April 11th, 2005.

Her Majesty's Hairdresser [SHPUN157]

Sherlock Holmes and his faithful companion, Watson, were enjoying a postprandial cigar and brandy after dining on one of Mrs. Hudson's famous Haggis ala Modes.

"Look here, Holmes, the *Evening Standard* reports that Her Majesty has a new hairdresser. She has employed the famous French Salon owner Kristoff Rodinne to tend to her tresses. The Queen's spokesman, when asked why the Frenchman was hired, could only say that he had a certain something about him."

"Well, Watson, I guess that could be called, 'je ne sais coif'."

This was written by David Milner.
It was first published on the Shamlockians' List on April 12th, 2005.

They Failed To See Eye To Eye [SHPUN158]

"I say, Watson," remarked Holmes one bright and cheery morning as he perused the *Daily Chronicle*, "are you aware that a new medical building is being constructed in Cavendish Square? It will be occupied solely by ophthalmologists and, according to the paper, some of the best in England."

"Yes, Holmes, my agent, Dr. Doyle, informed me of such the other day. But, according to Doyle, the building's construction is being opposed by many owners of nearby businesses. They claim it will be a site for sore eyes."

This was written by "The Rascally Lascar."
It was first published in Plugs & Dottles, Issue #201, June, 1995.
It was later published on the Shamlockians' List on April 12th, 2005.

A Tibetan Housewife's Lament [SHPUN160]

One evening, years after his famous hiatus, Holmes was relating to Watson some of his experiences while in the land of Tibet.

"Yes, Watson, I was most fortunate to be taken in by a friendly and kind Tibetan family who provided me with the necessities of life for some three months. The mother of the family was the hardest of workers, never ceasing in her labors from sunrise to sunset. It was obviously a most strenuous routine, for you could constantly hear her lamenting, 'Oh, my baking yak!'"

This was written by "The Rascally Lascar."
It was first published in Plugs & Dottles, Issue #175, April, 1993.
It was later published on the Shamlockians' List on April 14th, 2005.

Addendum to CROO [SHPUN163]

During his inspection of the scene of the crime in CROO, this conversation took place between Watson and Holmes; -

Watson – "Then what was the beast?"

Holmes -- "Ah, if I could give it a name it might go a long way towards solving the case. On the whole, it was probably some creature of the weasel and stoat tribe...."

Not included was the following exchange: -

Watson – "Tell me, Holmes, what's the difference between a weasel and a stoat?"

Holmes – "Well, Watson, a weasel is weasilly distinguished, and a stoat's stoatally different."

This was written by "Anonymous".
It was first published on the Shamlockians' List on April 14th, 2005

Make Mine With Everything [SHPUN164]

It was shortly after the business of the six Napoleons that Sherlock Holmes became fascinated with the life and times of the little Corsican who became the famous emperor of France. One evening, reading one of the many tomes dealing with the French general, Holmes suddenly remarked:

"Here's an interesting fact, Watson. Did you know that Napoleon had a fondness for hot dogs?"

"Heavens, no, Holmes! What evidence is there to that effect?"

"Well, it says here in this biography that before the Battle of Waterloo Napoleon mustered his Franks."

This was written by "The Rascally Lascar."
It was first published in Plugs & Dottles, Issue #183, December, 1993.
It was later published on the Shamlockians' List on April 16th, 2005.

Plastic Fish [SHPUN166]

We learn in DEVI that Holmes was once engaged in the study of the ancient Cornish language. This somehow led to an interest in the ancient fishermen who inhabited the Cornish coast. Reading one of the books on this subject one April evening, the Great Sleuth remarked:

"Watson, here's a rather interesting fact. Did you know that the ancient Cornish fishermen bartered with fish rather than with money?"

"Fascinating," replied his friend with the wandering wound, "I guess you could say they were the first people to use credit cods."

This was written by "The Rascally Lascar."
It was first published in Plugs & Dottles, Issue #182, November,

1993.
It was later published on the Shamlockians' List on April 17th, 2005.

Breathe, Push...Breathe, Push [SHPUN168]

It was a warm evening in April when Dr. Watson was summoned to the bedside of the Earl of Wickingham's wife who was heavy with child and soon to be delivered thereof.

As Watson entered Lady Wickingham's bedroom, he heard a series of low, protracted groans followed by "don't," "can't," "won't," "couldn't."

"Ah," observed the good doctor, "she's going through her contractions!"

This was written by "The Rascally Lascar."
It was first published in Plugs & Dottles, Issue #178, July, 1993.
It was later published on the Shamlockians' List on April 18th, 2005.

Amour du Derrière [SHPUN169]

One fine April evening, Holmes and Watson were rehashing the aspects of the caper known as "The Golden Pince-Nez."

"Yes, Watson," remarked London's famous gumshoe, "Anna Coram must not only be held responsible for the death of Willoughby Smith, but also for the most selfish of acts -- her suicide. I say selfish, because in killing herself she left all who loved her behind."

This was written by "The Rascally Lascar."
It was first published in Plugs & Dottles, Issue #177, June, 1993.
It was later published on the Shamlockians' List on April 19th, 2005.

Just Another Fish Story [SHPUN172]

"Well, Watson, have you found anything of interest in today's paper?"

"Dreadfully dull stuff it seems. The biggest item appears to be the conference between Britain and France over fishing rights in the Channel, and that has temporarily been postponed by both parties, no reason given."

"The reason, my good fellow, should be obvious. The two parties simply want to mullet over."

This was written by "The Rascally Lascar."
It was first published in Plugs & Dottles, Issue #202, July, 1995.
It was later published on the Shamlockians' List on April 22nd, 2005.

Update on Texas History [SHPUN173]

"I Say Holmes, that was a brilliant bit of deduction, finding that Texas oil man's wife."

"Indeed, Watson, Texas makes me think of the old slogan 'Remember the Alamo,' particularly this case."

"I say, Holmes, why is that?"

"It seems that during that battle, the officer in charge put his wife, of all people, on the battle line. She was shot by the enemy, shattered her patella, and had to be removed on a stretcher."

"After the fighting was over, she divorced her husband, and sued for Alamo knee."

This was written by "The Absent Hound."

It was first published on the Shamlockians' List on April 26th, 2005.

Moriarty Foiled [SHPUN177]

As you may have suspected, Professor Moriarty was indeed behind the events of "The Red-Headed League." The arrest of his gang members, particularly the clever John Clay, was a severe blow to the Professor's world-wide criminal operations.

"With John Clay out of action," lamented Moriarty to his second in command, "we shall have to postpone indefinitely the armoured car heist we had planned for Boston, Massachusetts."

"But why, Professor?" asked Colonel Moran. "Couldn't we send someone else to do it?"

"It's no use," answered his chief, "I cannot take Brinks without Clay."

This was written by Rosemary Michaud.
It was first published in Plugs & Dottles, Issue #222, March, 1997.
It was later published on the Shamlockians' List on May 1st, 2005.

Foiled Again [SHPUN184]

One dismal November evening, Holmes and Watson were in pursuit of the crazed members of a murderous religious sect. The courageous duo followed the zealots to a seedy corner of London, where, through the yellow reek of the fog, they could just discern a house, the doors and windows of which were emblazoned with the strange signs and symbols of the fanatical order. Holmes paused and gripped Watson by the arm.

"My dear fellow," said he, "I fear that out trail has reached a dead end."

"How can that be, Holmes?" Watson protested. "We are within yards of the villains and there evil temple."

"Precisely, Watson! We have come upon a cult-de-sac!"

This was written by Rosemary Michaud.
It was first published in Plugs & Dottles, Issue #204, September 1995
It was later published on the Shamlockians' List on May 28th, 2005.

The Adventure of the Desperate Colonel [SHPUN185]

"So you caught me, Holmes", snarled Colonel Sir Warrender Despard, VC, KCB as he cringed in the grasp of two stout Constables. The shocked faces of the members of the Royal London Stamp Society looked at their erstwhile patron like so many startled rabbits.

Even I could see that it was useless for the colonel to deny that he had been caught in the act of removing exhibits from the Golden Jubilee Stamp display at the Crystal Palace. A set of burglary tools and a litter of transparent envelopes filled with the choicest and rarest specimens of fifty years worth of adhesive stamps from many countries were either protruding from the pockets of his evening dress or lay scattered about his feet.

"I regret seeing a noble servant of the British Empire and hero of half a dozen glorious military campaigns brought so low," said Holmes. "Why did you stray from the path of duty and honour?"

"I needed the money and that is all I will say," hissed the Colonel.

"But I could have told you stealing stamps was futile," said Holmes.

"Why so, Holmes" I asked.

"Because philately will get you nowhere."

This was written by Richard Milne.
It has never been published before.

The Adventure of the Soft Cell [SHPUN186]

"Holmes," I said dropping the *Times* in my excitement. "Edward Turnell, the man you gave evidence against at his trial, has escaped from Dartmoor!"

"Indeed," said Holmes, displaying little concern at my dramatic news.

"Don't you remember that he swore he would get even with you and so did that young slattern who claimed to be his wife... What was her name?"

"Susan Hope," said Holmes. He stifled a yawn and thrust his hands into his dressing gown.

"It says here that some of his old gang may have assisted in the escape..."

"Nonsense, Watson, only one person helped him break out,"

"Who?"

"His fancy woman obviously did it"

"Of course," I groaned, clapping a hand to my forehead. "Hope springs E. Turnell."

This was written by Richard Milne.
It has never been published before.

The Adventure of the Card Playing Cats [SHPUN187]

Of the many cases that Holmes dealt with over the years I knew him, probably none was so quickly solved yet so bizarrely presented as the Adventure of the Card Playing felines. I had risen late as was my want after a hard night at my Club and found Holmes in solemn conclave with a white haired middle-aged man wearing a white overcoat.

"Ah Watson!" said Holmes, "This is Professor Watts Watt formerly of the London University…"

"How do you do?" said the Professor vaguely eyeing me askance, "Mr. Holmes was, er…, was about to explain how he knew I was an absent minded professor… "

"It is simplicity itself, sir. When I see a man with three days growth, a grimy white coat, odd socks, odd shoes and no hat or overcoat it is highly suggestive of concern with matters other than normal decorum, dress and the weather. But pray tell me your problem, Professor. I am rather busy with the case of the upturned spike – I certainly don't wish to fall down on it."

"Er, quite so, …since I was forced to retire from my chair at University owing to a confusion of lighting a match to detect a gas leak, and some footling nonsense with a female student, I have devoted myself to teaching animals to behave more like humans. Monkeys are easy but my greatest triumph has been training a number of large wild cats to play poker. Each night they settle down to a few hours serious play. I give them all the same number of poker chips but for some reason only one cat wins. I can't understand it – marked packs, changed seating, spiked milk – it makes no difference – always the same winner."

"The lion," I suggested.

"Er, no…." murmured the professor.

"The leopard," I continued.

"Too easily spotted," said the Professor.

"Pray pay attention, Watson," said Holmes interrupting, "it is surely obvious to the meanest intelligence that the cat that wins continually has to be a cheetah!"

This was written by Richard Milne.
It was first published on the Shamlockians' List on May 30th, 2005.

Three Little Indians [SHPUN190]

"I say, Holmes," remarked Watson, glancing up from his copy of the *Evening Standard*, "I see here that three sons of an American Indian chief have all graduated with honours during the past four years from Yale University, and have been admitted to an exclusive yacht club in Boston. I bet their father is extremely proud of them."

"For sure, Watson, every Indian chief would like to see his red sons in the sail set."

This was written by "The Rascally Lascar."
It was first published in Plugs & Dottles, Issue #041, February 1982.
It was later published on the Shamlockians' List on June 1st, 2005.

Your Slip Is Showing [SHPUN193]

It was in the spring of '95 that the late Sir Thaddeus Warburton III had dinner at his club, a few brandies after, and was never more seen alive!

The following day, to the shock of all fashionable London, his body was found in one of the lowest alleys of Whitechapel -- more specifically, in a room inhabited by one of the district's many demimondes, an Elizabeth Atkins by name. Miss Atkins could not be located, and remains a mystery to this day. Just as mysterious (and certainly bizarre!) was the condition in which Sir Thaddeus' body was found. He lay in Miss Atkins' bed, his head propped up by two dirty pillows, with a half-drunk cup of tea resting on his chest!

The cause of death was obvious. A petticoat, obviously Miss Adkins', had been used to garrote the poor man, and still remained tightly wrapped around his throat.

Called in to investigate, Holmes remarked to his Fidus Achates: "These are, indeed, mighty deep waters, Watson. This case may never be solved, but the condition of the body DOES prove one old adage."

"What's that?" asked Watson.

"'Tis most obvious, you dunce! You are no doubt familiar with the old saw that goes:

'There's many a slip 'twixt the cup and the lip.' I believe it's attributed to the Greek sage Palladas."

This was written by Howard E. Burr*.
It was first published in Plugs & Dottles, Issue #055, April 1983.
It was later published in the Gaslight Gazette; V11, #06, 05/2005.

It was later published on the Shamlockians' List on June 3rd, 2006.

*Even more rascally than his son!

Come Blow Your Horn [SHPUN194]

"Here's an interesting article in the paper, Holmes."

"How's that?"

"It seems there are four carpenters in Kent who can really play those huge Ump-Pah horns, and have decided to form a quartet."

"Interesting! Do they have a name?"

"Yes, they're known as 'The Tuba Four'."

This was written by "The Rascally Lascar."
It was first published in Plugs & Dottles, issue #52, January 1983.
It was later published on The Shamlockians' List on June 4th, 2005.

Stick With The Prose, Doctor! [SHPUN198]

"Watson, you appear to be in poor spirits. I suppose it's this accursed heat."

My friend Sherlock Holmes had correctly diagnosed my state of mind one blazing hot day in late June.

"The heat, Holmes, yes -- plus this check which I have just received from *the Strand*. For something different, I wrote up your latest case, that of Lord Bromley's prosthesis, in the form of verse and submitted it to the editor. 'Twas accepted, and I have received the check for same in the amount of a measly two pounds! Can you believe it?"

"Seems quite fair to me," replied Holmes.

"Fair, my deerstalker! They have always paid me at least ten pounds for an adventure!"

"Well, Watson," came the reply from my smart-ass friend, " having worked with me these many years, you should know by now that rhyme does not pay."

This was written by Robert Brodie.
It was first published in Plugs & Dottles, Issue #142, 07/1990.
It was published on the Shamlockians' List on June 28th, 2005.

Ouch! [SHPUN199]

Dr. Watson arrives at 221B Baker Street and is stunned to find his friend Sherlock Holmes out front in an overall, applying a pale yellow gloss to the front door.

"Holmes what is it?" cried the stupefied Watson.

"A lemon entry, my dear Watson!", replied Holmes.

This was written by "The Absent Hound."
It was first published on the Shamlockians' List on July 28th, 2005.

Things Go Better With Coke [SHPUN203]

It was one of those wild, tempestuous Baker Street evenings, with pea soup fog dripping down the windows, the wind screaming like a ruptured banshee, and Mrs. Hudson sobbing like a child in the chimney, having been stuffed there by Holmes after she had served us scrapple for supper for the third straight night.

"I say there, great deductive detective," remarked I, "I see here in the *Evening Standard* that there has been a murder committed at the local Coca-Cola production facility. Do you think you will be called in by Lestrade and the Yard to help solve the case?"

"Well, if I am, old fidus Achates, I have already solved the case!"

"Jumpin' deerstalkers and coal scuttles, you mean you know who the murderer is?"

"Absolutely, you old saw bones ... the bottler did it!"

This was written by "The Rascally Lascar."
It was first published on the Shamlockians' List on August 11th, 2005.
It was later published in The Log of The Survivors of the Gloria Scott, Vol. 11, Issue #8/9, August/September, 2005.

The Itinerant Detective [SHPUN206]

After his return from the dead as reported in "The Empty House", Holmes was very active. I have only written up a few of the cases from that busy time and mentioned several more. I had moved back to the Baker Street rooms and had given up my practice to spend more time helping him with this heavy caseload. Unfortunately, that 'help' more often consisted of receiving unscheduled callers and fending off inquiries from the official police force than in assisting with investigations.

One case involved a criminal ring that operated out of Northern Germany, in the mountains south of Halberstadt. They were engaged in receiving stolen goods and converting those items into more easily sold forms. Items made of precious metals were melted down and recast, gems were reset and artworks were redone in slightly different forms to be sold to unsophisticated American and middle eastern buyers.

At one point, Holmes was tracing the site of this work by masquerading as a professor on a hiking and mountaineering vacation wandering the wilds of rural Germany. Needless to say, the communications arrangements were complex and time-consuming so that I could only send wires to some accomplice in Westphalia who relayed the message to Holmes whenever he could check in and who also returned such occasional, belated replies as Holmes could make and maintain his persona.

Inspector Lestrade was handling the investigation for Her Majesty's Government and became increasingly frantic for news as the weeks passed with Holmes out of touch. One Friday afternoon he arrived in Baker Street demanding to know where Holmes was and when he would provide information Lestrade could pass along to his superiors.

Naturally, all I could tell him was that "Holmes is where the Harz is."

This was written by "An Ill-dressed Vagabond."
It was first published on the Shamlockians' List, on August 18th, 2005.
It was later published in The Gaslight Gazette, Vol. 11, Issue #6, October, 2005.

Hearth Warming [SHPUN207]

When Holmes retired to the Sussex Downs, I saw little of him from years end to years end. After the events in "His Last Bow" and the advent of the Great War, I volunteered for service and was accepted for limited duty in a field hospital in France. I need not go into details of the wounds and deaths, but the introduction of poison gas on the battlefield only brought new horrors to my already over-supplied trade.

I heard little from Holmes during those dreadful years, but we did manage to meet twice in London to share meals and he told me that his brother, Mycroft, had set him several tasks that were keeping him quite busy. By 1918, when the Americans came in on our side, it was apparent that the Hun would be defeated, but the War dragged on and the injured kept coming to our hospital. My own health began to fail and Influenza completed the task begun by too much work and too little rest, so the Army requested I go home and cease infecting the injured and the rest of the Medical Service.

I had retired from active practice before the Great War and had acquired a small detached home in Tunbridge Wells, which sported all the so-called "modern amenities", with heating gas, electricity and hot and cold water laid on. However, my illness did not allow me to manage on my own, so I asked Holmes if I could recover with him on the Downs.

His reply was immediate and he arranged for a car to meet my train and drive me to his cottage. The combination of sea air and good British grub, with a lot of rest began the repairs to my constitution and chats with Holmes beside the snug fireplace began to restore my belief in the essential goodness of the universe. I commented on the colourful flames and distinct odours of the sea coal fire and Holmes agreed.

"Yes, Watson. There's no fuel like an old fuel!"

This was written by "An Ill-dressed Vagabond."
It was first published on The Shamlockians' List on August 39th, 2005.
It was later published in The Gaslight Gazette, Vol. 12, Issue #5, May, 2006.

Nautical Story [SHPUN209]

As is well known, Watson was a great fan of sea tales. What is less known is that, besides his Beaune, he also enjoyed his rum.

One evening Holmes returned to 221B Baker Street, to find Watson in the loo, reciting "The Ancient Mariner" between bouts of projectile vomiting.

"Aha, Watson, rhymes fly when you're heaving rum."

This was written by "The Absent Hound."
It was first published on the Shamlockians' List on September 7th, 2005.

Tibetan Musings [SHPUN210]

It was the middle of January after Holmes return from the dead and a steady snow was falling on London, covering up the soot and making it into a place of gentle beauty. We looked out from our cozy sitting room and felt no need to be anywhere else but in front of our sea coal fire with drinks and tobacco and good friendship.

Holmes looked out and mused on his recent travels:

"It was just such a night that I wandered into a small village in Tibet as the snow was beginning to fall in earnest and shelter was becoming a concern. Unlike most of Asia, Tibet is, in many ways, a matriarchal society. Most property is owned by women and passed to daughters, rather than sons. This particular village was the property of one woman, whose nieces and daughters held most of the farms and the single, communal mill."

"The woman, herself, was rather odd and lived in an old watch tower infested with bats. She professed to admire the flying creatures and dressed all in black robes and scarves that made her seem like a bat herself. Her oddities did not extend to hospitality, so I was made quite welcome and invited to stay in the largest house in the village, which belonged to her niece, who was also the storekeeper. I suspect that news of the outside world, such as Lhassa, was in very short supply there."

"As the snow fell, I was pressed for every scrap of information I held and many cups of tea were drunk and pipes smoked during the long night. Heavy shutters covered all windows and the snow muffled all sounds until we could think ourselves to be the only persons alive in all the world. A gradual lightening of the smoke filled gloom heralded the approach of morning and I made as if to go outside, but was stopped by the niece."

"'No!' she said. 'The snow is still falling. Wait.'"

"Later, as it must have been early afternoon, I tried again to look outside and was told to 'Wait.' Yet again."

"Finally, as dusk was creeping onto the heights, a loud series of clanging noises shattered the calm. The niece said that the snow was now over, so I asked how she knew."

"She said 'The snow's not over till the bat lady rings'."

This was written by "An Ill-dressed Vagabond."
It was first published on the Shamlockians' List on September 9th, 2006.
It was later published in The Gaslight Gazette, Vol. 12, #03/04, March/April, 2006.

Rah! Rah! Rah! [SHPUN212]

Mrs. Hudson's niece, Prunella, took cheerleading lessons so she could inspire the members of her favorite soccer team. Her efforts were most successful, with the team going onto win the championship.

Pleased with her cheerleading success with the soccer team, she then asked her coach if she might cheer for the local rugby team.

"Sorry," replied the coach, "that is a course of a different holler."

This was written by "The Rascally Lascar."
It was first published on the Shamlockians' List on September 22nd, 2005.

The Weather in Mexico-- [SHPUN213]

"Good Lord, Watson, whatever have you been fooling with there?"

"Holmes, it's the greatest thing since sliced scrapple! It's a short wave radio. Would you believe that right now I am getting the weather report from Tijuana, Mexico?"

"Well, stomp my deerstalker, what does it say?"

"Elementary, my dear Sleuth — 'Chili Today, Hot Tamale'."

This was written by "The Rascally Lascar."
It was first published on the Shamlockians' List on September 23rd, 2005.

Here's Looking At You! [SHPUN214]

'Tis a little known fact, but after his literary relationship with Dr. Doyle had been established, the Good Dr. Watson decided to return to medical school and study for a specialty in ophthalmology.

He then convinced his literary agent that they should establish a joint medical practice for the treatment of diseases and surgery of the eye.

The joint venture worked but for a few months before there was a falling out of the two. It seems that when it came to running the practice they simply could not see eye to eye.

This was written by "The Rascally Lascar".
It was first published on the Shamlockians' List on September 24th, 2005.

The Best of British Grub [SHPUN215]

Holmes once noted that Mrs. Hudson "had as good a notion of breakfast as a Scotswoman" and that was a high compliment from him. In point of fact, the food at our Baker Street lodgings was always well-prepared and usually served in timely fashion, so long as Holmes was willing to eat at scheduled times. Even when kept waiting, our landlady was ingenious in keeping our meals in fine state.

Certainly we had a lot of traditional English fare, Pease pudding, roast beef and the like, but sometimes the menu featured French and Scottish dishes. Holmes especially appreciated the former, with his French background and the summers his family spent on the Continent. For my own part, a diet of veal and sauces seems petty fare, but I must admit that Mrs. Hudson produced tasty dishes and did not abuse our palates with frequent foreign kickshaws.

Probably her best efforts went into her baking where she produced many of my favorites; Bath buns, Banbury cakes, scones with clotted cream and the inevitable Christmas puddings. She even baked French and German cakes and rolls. I recall commenting to Holmes about some lovely shaped German cakes with a soft filling that were a real heavenly treat. I wondered how she managed to carve the cakes into such lovely shapes without disturbing the filling.

He explained:

"Mrs. Hudson has the latest thing in bakeware, bundts of steel from Vienna, that she uses to bake those treats." he told me.

This was written by "An Ill-dressed Vagabond."
It was first published on the Shamlockians' List on October 8th, 2005.

The Plague Spot [SHPUN216]

Early in 1895, Holmes arranged the arrest of Wilson, the notorious canary trainer. This case was something of an oddity, from its subject matter to the way it was introduced to Holmes' attention. Wilson trained canaries, but few people knew of the specialized uses to which he put his little pets. The birds could sing, of course, but some were taught a darker trade. Select birds were encouraged to revert to their normal nesting behavior and to bring back insects to feed their non-existent broods. Normally, this would pose no problem for anyone, but Wilson operated in a specialized milieu.

Wilson's birds had been taught to focus their insect taking talents on demand and he used these birds to terrorize the flea-circus community. A trio of trained, terrorist termagants could devastate a single enterprise in moments, and all such enterprises that wished to continue in operation were forced to pay "protection money." Wilson managed a tidy little income from tithing the numerous street shows and small time "raree palaces."

This uncomfortable situation had endured for some time before Wilson overstepped the bounds of common sense and tried to expand his clientele. A certain Mr. Corcoran operated on the fringes of this entertainment community by providing a service to the various operators. Mr. Corcoran was the proud owner and trainer of a pair of larger, docile insects whose services he was used to rent out to flea circus proprietors who wished to stage a particularly spectacular event. His protégés were trained to act as "bulls" in a flea circus "Corrida" that allowed all of the circus members to participate in a massed show to finish off a successful run. The docility of his "Bulls" prevented any harm to the circus staff while their size made them seem quite menacing to the spectators.

In any case, Wilson got around to demanding his "mordida"

from Corcoran, who promptly told him how and where to stuff his birds. A Serinian Hit Team was accordingly dispatched and Mr. Corcoran was left without a source of income. In his anguish, he turned to Holmes, as none of the cowed flea circus proprietors had been willing to do. They had staff yet to lose, whereas Corcoran was bereft of working capital assets.

Holmes quickly dealt with the matter by staging a raid on Wilson's school which captured the whole operation, red-beaked, as it were. Thus, he removed a plague-spot from the East End of London and restored the vigor of an important segment of the British Entertainment Industry. He was even able to secure compensation for Corcoran from the seized assets of Wilson's business, allowing that worthy to acquire and train a new brace of "bulls."

When I mentioned to Holmes my intention to write up this tidy little investigation, he suggested that I name it after Mr. Corcoran, the injured party, as "The Case of the Lessor of Two Weevils."

This was written by "An Ill-dressed Vagabond."
It was first published on the Shamlockians' List on October 11th, 2005.

The Botanical Holmes [SHPUN219]

After our brush with "The Devil's Foot," Holmes gave himself over to increased study of exotic plants and their medicinal qualities. He made frequent trips to the Royal Botanical gardens and was often in correspondence with plant hunters from all over the world. His objective, of course, was to become acquainted with as many of the poisons in use by humans as was possible. It had galled him that he did not immediately recognize the source of the Tregannis poisonings.

Our rooms were cluttered with strange plants from time to

time and Holmes would concoct noxious brews from the oddest ingredients. I often found my appetite disappearing after he completed yet another distillation or reduction and Mrs. Hudson's complaints were loud and frequent. The six months or so that Holmes devoted to this phase of his chemical education were among the most uncomfortable of our association, but by the time autumn arrived, we were having fewer such incidents.

It was late in September when Holmes brought home some ferns reputed to be from the Amazon jungle that native "doctors" used as a purgative. At a time when English physicians were prescribing "high colonics" and such for every digestive problem they encountered, I felt that Holmes new plaything was somewhat passé, and I said so.

He replied: "Watson, with fronds like these, who needs enemas?"

This was written by "An Ill-dressed Vagabond."
It was first published on the Shamlockian's List on January, 18th, 2006.
It was later published in the Pleasant Places of Florida Communication #260; V09, #02, March/April, 2006]
It was also published in The Gaslight Gazette, V12 Issues 01/02, January/February, 2006

Poor Miss Kitty [SHPUN222]

"I say, Watson, now that the Gruner affair is history, have you had any success, as you had hoped to do, of instilling a bit of genteelness in our friend Kitty Winter?"

"Alas, my good gumshoe, my efforts have all been to no avail."

"Well, old sawbones, it just goes to prove the old adage -- you may lead a horticulture, but you can't make her think!"

This was written by "The Rascally Lascar."
It was first published on the Shamlockian's List on March 8th, 2006.

The Masquerade Ball [SHPUN223]

In the year 1895, Holmes was engaged in a number of investigations and I was able to accompany him on many of these. One of the strangest involved death threats to several literary figures.

The charges brought against the playwright, Oscar Wilde, by the Marquis of Queensbury ignited a storm of controversy which resulted in a general condemnation of that part of the Literary Set assumed to be homosexual. There were denunciations from numerous pulpits and outraged Letters to the *Times* by "old English Values", "Home and family" and such as well as rallies by various societies that sprang up denouncing "pederasts" and "sodomites."

Holmes became involved at the request of his brother, Mycroft, when threats, which seemed to have some substance behind them, were made against a some-time poet-Laureate. The person in question informed the Prince of Wales and indignantly requested protection, all the while protesting his innocence of the accusations. Mycroft was instructed to look into the matter and was able to determine that the threats had been made by one particularly virulent group of sporting men who were all members of a single "Gentlemen's Club."

Sherlock was asked to follow up and to find if any specific plans were in train to take action. After a fortnight, Holmes determined that an upcoming Masquerade Ball was to be the chosen arena for "action to cleanse these perversions from English Society." I suspect that Holmes joined the club in question under a disguise, but he never told me his method for gaining the information.

On the evening of the Ball, I found myself costumed as Vulcan, in company with Holmes as Hermes, attending a lavish affair at the home of wealthy but not socially prominent peer. The guests' choices of costume seemed to draw heavily on classical themes, with goatherds and goose girls interspersed with Olympians and earth deities such as Fawns and Satyrs. The food and drink were quite good, but I found the company and the entertainment tedious.

Meanwhile, Holmes kept moving about and telling me to watch first one person and then another, so I was not overly bored.

At Midnight, several skits and tableaux were to be presented with prominent artists and poets as participants. As the first of these was underway, Holmes suddenly attacked a group of servants who were moving some furniture into the presentation area. The furniture turned out to conceal several whips, flails and swords which the "servants" apparently planned to use on the participants in the activities. These same "servants" later proved to be members of the suspect Club and, in fact, proclaimed their mission to rid polite society of the "degenerates" by public beatings and humiliation.

Holmes seemed quite proud of his achievement in preventing this outrage until the next day's newspapers arrived.

The Headlines proclaimed "Gods Save the Queens!"

Thereafter, he refused to discuss the matter.

This was written by "An Ill-dressed Vagabond."
It was first published on The Shamlockians List on May 23rd, 2006.
It was later published in The Gaslight Gazette, V12, Issue #06,

June, 2006.

The Case of the Matilda Briggs [SHPUN226]

The case of the "Matilda Briggs," which I mentioned elsewhere, was investigated by Holmes before our association began. It was cited in a letter from a firm of insurance appraisers, at the beginning of another case (SUSS), as having been successfully concluded by Holmes. At the time, Holmes dismissed the reference with the comment that "Matilda Briggs was not the name of a young woman, Watson. It was a ship which is associated with the giant rat of Sumatra, a story for which the world is not yet prepared."

Naturally, I attempted to find out more about this intriguing set of events, but Holmes remained reticent. Finally, I asked him what possible connection a firm of industrial insurance appraisers could possibly have with such a bizarre subject.

After considering the request, he said:

"The Captain of the Matilda Briggs died while the vessel was in transit from the Far East with a cargo that was insured by a client of Morrison, Morrison and Dodd. The vessel was later caught in a storm and much of the cargo was lost and the rest damaged. Since the insurance contract had been accepted on their recommendation, the firm asked me to investigate the situation and to determine the cause of the losses."

"I found that the death of the Captain and the incapacitation of his first officer led to the damage and losses incurred. The sequence of events was purely fortuitous and was not the result of sabotage or incompetence. The cargo was properly stowed and the ship well found, but the remaining officers and crew were simply unable to cope with the series of natural disasters they encountered after the Captain's death and the injury to the first officer."

"Surely, Holmes, the cause of the Captain's death was not

natural." I said. "You spoke of "the giant rat of Sumatra" when you first mentioned the case. What was the meaning of that? Why is the world not yet prepared for this story? What killed the Captain?"

Holmes said, "He disagreed with something that ate him."

This was written by "An Ill-dressed Vagabond."
It was first published on The Shamlockians' List on July 5th, 2006.

Interlude at Baker Street, #02 [SHPUN235]

It was one of those typical Fall evenings in Baker Street, the equinoctial gales having set in with exceptional violence. Holmes and I sat on either side of our usual cheery fire while the wind screamed, the rain beat against the windows, and little children blubbered and bleated in the chimney. My friend was deeply engrossed in a copy of the *Evening Standard*, while I sat nursing a brandy and reminiscing of my experiences of women which extended over many nations and three separate continents. Holmes's voice suddenly interrupted my rather lubricious thoughts.

"You know, Watson, I believe I may have said this once before, but my life is definitely stranger than anything which the mind of man could invent."

"Yes, Homes," I replied, "I recall you making a similar statement just prior to our introduction to Miss Mary Sutherland and the missing Hosmer Angel."

"Well, it's true, Watson – so *very* true. I have just read an account here in the *Standard* which tells of the recent passing of a Mr. Tobias Popp. He made no great mark in life, was a tobacconist by trade, and died quietly in his sleep at the age of eighty-two. His demise would not have merited the space that it commands in this evening's paper were it not for the strange request he made in his will."

"Strange request? How's that, Holmes?"

"It seems that Mr. Popp desired his coffin to be closed and that it be encircled with an azure sash of pure silk. Now what do you make of that, good fellow?"

"Well, Holmes, I really can't say what I make of it. The man was obviously an eccentric. I only wish that there had been some sinister or criminal feature connected with the event and you had been consulted."

"Good Lord, Watson, what do you mean by that?" Holmes replied, staring at me dumbfoundedly.

"Well, I was just thinking that when I came to present the story to the public I could have entitled it *The Strange Case of Popp's Blue Ribbon Bier.*"

This was written by "The Rascally Lascar."
It was first published in Wheelwrightings; Vol. 3 Issue #01, May, 1980.

The Adventure of Sir Reginald Falmouth and the Giant Rooster of Woking (or, Fowl play in Surrey) [SHPUN236]

It was on a bleak November night in the year 1889 that my friend, Mr. Sherlock Holmes, was introduced to the sinister circumstances surrounding the death of Sir Reginal Falmouth. The weather had turned cold and unpleasant that day, and the evening brought with it the wind and rain which so often lashed our windows in Baker Street. I was seated before our cheery fire, smoking a second pipe and musing over the experiences that I had suffered during the Afghan War, while Holmes was slumped in his decrepit arm-chair, lazily bowing out some of

Mendelssohn's Lieder on his Stradivarius.

"I say, Watson," Holmes suddenly remarked, laying aside his violin, "if my ears don't deceive me, I believe Mrs. Hudson has just admitted a visitor. Let us hope that it is someone to see *us* instead of our good landlady. I am sorely in need of some little problem to challenge my mind, which has begun to stagnate of late."

We had not long to wait before Mrs. Hudson ushered in a tall, middle-aged gentleman with hawk-like features and a magnificent crop of jet black hair.

"Allow me to introduce myself," said he, advancing on Holmes, his hand extended. "My name is John Falmouth. My home is in Woking, Surrey."

"Woking? – Yes," replied Holmes, "Dr. Watson and I had occasion recently to assist an old school chum of his in a rather delicate matter. He, too, was from Woking. But pray, remove that horribly wet coat and tell us what brings you to Baker Street."

Our visitor shed his soggy apparel, moved closer to the fire and began his strange story.

"I'm here tonight, Mr. Holmes, because of the recent death of my father, Sir Reginald Falmouth. His name may not come to your mind, but for many years he was one of Parliament's leading Conservative members, following in the tradition of my grandfather, who led the Conservative cause during his own time. Father was forced to retire from public life some five years past due to a rather serious heart condition. From that time, until his death two weeks ago, his life was a most unhappy one. Because of worry over his health and boredom from lack of both mental and physical activity, he became very morose and extremely argumentative with all who came in contact with him.

This was especially true of our neighbor, Mr. Venuccio."

Holmes crossed over to the fireplace, dug his index finger into the toe of the old Persian slipper, and proceeded to fill his cherrywood with fresh shag. Turning to Falmouth, he begged him to continue his narrative.

"We have known Mr. Venuccio for some years, Mr. Holmes, and have always been on the best of terms with him. He was born in Italy and came to this country when he was a boy. He is something of a gourmet cook, and many's the fine Italian meal my father and I had at his table. But all that came to an end with father's change in attitude; and mostly because of the chickens."

"The chickens?" Holmes's expression was one of bewilderment as he paused in the act of lighting his pipe with a live coal extracted from the fireplace.

"Yes – chickens. Mr. Venuccio is a retired farmer, and is noted throughout Surrey for the fine chickens he raises. This he does mainly as a hobby, but I'm sure he realizes a small profit from the sale of some of the birds as well as their eggs. Through various selective breeding techniques he has managed to produce some of the biggest chickens I have ever seen. The roosters are extremely large and their meanness matches their size. Why, not to long ago, a youngster in the neighborhood was teasing the birds, and one of the larger roosters flew at him and managed to inflict some serious lacerations on the poor lad's body with this spurs."

A cloud of acrid, foul-smelling smoke arose from Holmes's pipe as he tamped and puffed the odious shag into satisfactory ignition. "This is all very interesting, Mr. Falmouth," he said, "but I know you didn't come out on a night such as this for a paltry discussion of poetry. What has all this to do with your father?"

"Well, as I have stated, my father had become irritated by all who dealt with him. With Venuccio, however, the irritation took on the semblance of all-out war, mainly due to two disparate reasons. My father's conservative background could not brook Venuccio's Liberal philosophy. This, coupled with the noise from the chickens which, my father insisted, awakened him before dawn each morning, was enough to push him to the breaking point."

At this juncture, a sudden violent gust of wind brought a long mournful moan from the chimney. The fury of the November storm was increasing, and I was most happy when Holmes suggested a round of whiskies before Falmouth proceeded with his story. After a number of rounds – the exact number escapes me – he continued.

"My father lost all sense of reality. He became convinced that Venuccio was bent on harassing him to his grave. His actions became irrational and irresponsible. He had reached the conclusion that his only source of satisfaction against Venuccio would be the slow and systematic destruction of the chickens. Well, father began stealing out in the dead of night, wringing a chicken's neck or two, and leaving the carcasses for Venuccio to discover the next day and fret over. I'm sure the old farmer knew what was going on. It was certainly clear that no wild animal was devastating the flock, since none of the chickens were ever eaten or left bloodied.

"I tried reasoning with my father, but to no avail. I realized that if he continued in this venture he would soon be caught by our neighbor and charges brought. My mind was made up – I would have to have my father committed."

"A most unhappy decision to be sure," Holmes interjected, "but better a wringing of hands than a wringing of necks." When the raucous laughter that greeted this *bon mot* by Holmes had subsided, we had more rounds while Falmouth continued his story.

"Commitment, however, became unnecessary due to events of just two weeks ago tonight. We had both retired for the evening, when I awoke about two o'clock. I thought I had better check on father before going back to sleep. Well, sure enough, his bed was empty. I realized this was the last straw. I hurriedly dressed and took out towards Venuccio's, hoping to stop the old man before he dispatched any more chickens. The moon was full that night, so I had no trouble following the narrow path which leads from our house to our neighbor's. It was at a point in the path some fifty feet from the coops that I spotted my father. He was lying on his back just to the side of the path. His face was bathed by pale silver moonlight and was frozen in death with a look of indescribable horror.

"There were no marks of violence upon his person, so I assumed that his heart had finally failed him – an assumption which was later borne out by the authorities. The horrible expression on his face was explained by the doctor as resulting from the severe pain which probably presaged the attack. The reason I'm here tonight, however, is the footprints which were so clearly visible around the body."

"Footprints?'

"Yes, Mr. Holmes, footprints."

"A man's or a woman's?"

John Falmouth looked strangely at us for an instant, and his voice sank almost to a whisper as he answered:

"Mr. Holmes, they were the footprints of a gigantic rooster!"

■■■

I must admit that a shudder passed through my body at the

sound of those last words, and it was with great effort that I refrained from calling for another round. Holmes, however, appeared to be unmoved until, in searching for his pipe, he discovered its charred remains in the fireplace where I had noted he carefully placed it after our last series of rounds. Turning testily to our guest, he said:

"Well, Mr. Falmouth, what exactly is it you would like me to do? You, yourself, state that your father's death was from natural causes."

"I realize that, Mr. Holmes, but is it not possible that Venuccio trained that rooster to attack my father? If so, then he would be indirectly responsible for his death. Might we not have a case here which we could present to the authorities?"

"My dear man, I'm afraid not." Holmes was most emphatic.

"But certainly, Holmes," I joined in, "there might be a possibility..."

"No, Watson – none whatsoever. And if you would recall to mind some English history and some Italian cuisine, you would know why."

"Good heavens, Holmes!" I exclaimed. "What in the devil does that have to do with the case in hand?"

"Everything, my dear fellow – everything! You have been informed by our guest that Sir Reginald was a staunch Conservative. You may also recall that the Conservative Party in England was originally known as the Tories."

"You know my methods, Watson. Use them, and it all becomes obvious – there can be no possible cause for action."

"And how's that?" I asked, somewhat miffed by Holmes's

air of superiority, and rather devilishly happy that the fire had destroyed his damned pipe.

"Because, Watson, you simply cannot condemn a man, especially an Italian, for wanting to have some chicken catch a Tory."

This was written by "The Rascally Lascar."
It was first published in Wheelwrightings, Vol. 01, Issue #02, September, 1978.
It was later published in Plugs & Dottles, Issues 90 & 91, March/April, 1986.

VARIATIONS ON A THEME

Some themes are simply too much fun to leave to someone else's ministrations. Sherlockians are noted for not being able to leave well enough alone. There's always a little bit more to be wrung out of an idea. The temptation to redo another's (or even one's own) effort is often overwhelming. These next items are the originals and efforts at "punching up" those earlier tries, maybe even someone's rework of another's still earlier gem.

Esmerelda's Revenge [SHPUN309]

Sherlock Holmes and Doctor Watson were doing their usual investigative business one day, when they uncovered an amazing painting.

At first glance, it looked like a picture of a normal oak tree, in the middle of a wilderness, but if you looked closer, you could see that it was a very surreal painting. The tree's trunk was actually made of fire and its branches were made of ice, clouds and earth.

"What is it" asked Watson in awe.

"It's an element tree, my dear Watson," Holmes replied.

This was written by Sandy Kozinn "Esmerelda."
It was first published in The Gaslight Gazette, Vol. 13, #10, 10/2007.

Weekend Groaner [SHPUN108]

Sherlock Holmes and his trusted Dr. Watson were on duty. They were
trying to get into a house they needed to search.

"Oh, no, Sherlock," exclaimed Watson when he tried the

doorknob. "We'll never get in. It's locked!"

Holmes removed a bright yellow citrus fruit from his pocket and squeezed
the juice into the keyhole. The door clicked open with ease.

"I say, how did you mange that?" asked Watson.

Holmes turned to his pal.

"A-lemon-entry, my dear Watson."

"Calgary Sun", News section, page 6 [02/19/2005]

This was written by Karen Murdock (May Blunder)

Cogito, Ergo Sum [SHPUN055]

"I say, Watson, here is certainly a change of direction!"

"How's that, Holmes?"

"Well, I read here in the paper of a Madame in Paris who has forsaken her house of carnal pleasures and its accompanying demimonde, and has instead become an avid student of the French philosophers. Seems she has always been very keen of mind, and but for a series of personal tragedies, would have pursued a loftier and more intellectual occupation than the one she now deserts.

"In fact, she possesses rather exceptional talents in the realm of mathematics, and has taken a special interest in the seventeenth century French philosopher/mathematician who developed the analytic geometry. You know to whom I refer?"

"Of course," I replied, "the old 'Cogito, ergo sum' guy. And it would appear that the madam in question is guilty of an age-old adage."

"And what might that be, my good fellow?"

"'Tis quite obvious, Holmes, that she is putting Descartes before the whorcs."

This was written by "The Rascally Lascar."
It was first published in Wheelwrightings, Volume 08, issue #01, May 1985.
It was published on the Hounds of the Internet List on July 26, 2003 and on January 14th, 2005.

Untitled [SHPUN200]

"I say, Holmes, here is an interesting story in today's news.

It is about a remarkable horse owned by one of our own hansom cabbies. It is very smart, and anything that is shown it, it masters easily, except one day, its teachers tried to teach it about rectangular coordinates and it couldn't understand them. All the horse's trainers, and even experts from the London Academy of Sciences tried to figure out what was the matter and couldn't. Do you have any idea what could be the problem?"

"Elementary, my dear Watson. Of course he can't do it. Why, they're putting Descartes before the horse!"

This was written by "The Absent Hound."
It was first published on the Shamlockians' List on July 30th, 2005.

Just Trying To Get Ahead [SHPUN197]

"Here's quite a story, Holmes."

"And what might that be, my good fellow?"

"A French Count was recently found guilty of spying for Germany and was sentenced to death by the guillotine. The authorities offered to spare his life if he would only name his German contacts, but the count adamantly refused -- at least until it was too late."

"Too late?"

"Yes, the Count's head was placed on the block yesterday, and just as the deadly piece of steel began its swift descent, the condemned lost his courage and cried out, 'wait a min...', but not soon enough, and the blade performed its sanguinary ritual with its usual speed and efficiency. I believe, Holmes, that the moral to the story is that treason does not pay."

"True, Watson, but there is a second moral to the story which you have missed."

"Which is?"

"Elementary, Watson – don't hatchet your Counts before they chicken."

This was written by "The Rascally Lascar."
It was first published in Plugs & Dottles, issue #42, March 1982.
It was published on the Shamlockians' List on June 14th, 2005.

Weg Von Mit Seinem Kopf [SHPUN217]

"Well, Holmes, I see here in the *Frankfurter Zeitung* that our old friend, Count Von Kramm, has been executed via the guillotine for espionage.   Seems he was caught spying for France, refused to divulge his French contact, and his head was put on the block.   His nerve did crack, however, at the last second.   He tried to yell out that he was ready to confess, but the blade beat him to it."

"Alas, Watson, it but proves an old adage."

"Pray tell, famous gumshoe, what might that be?"

"Elementary, my good MD – don't hatchet your Counts before they chicken."

This was written by "The Rascally Lascar."
It was first published on the Shamlockians' List on October 19th, 2005.

Wiggins of Moscow [SHPUN159]

Some years after his retirement, Sherlock Holmes and his fidus Achates decided to tour the Soviet Union. While being shown the many sites in the great city of Moscow, they spotted a poor, pathetic urchin who was trudging along, bent under his heavy load of newspapers.

"That poor lad is sure having a hard time of it with all those papers," remarked Watson.

"Yes, Watson, he is" replied Holmes, "but you'll note that he holds his head high with pride because he has a clutch of *Tass*."

This was written by "The Rascally Lascar."
It was first published in Plugs & Dottles, Issue #174, March, 1993.
It was later published on the Shamlockians' List on April 13th, 2005.

An Oldie? [SHPUN204]

"Great being here in Moscow on a visit, not so, Holmes?"

"Right on, Ye Olde Gum Shoe Buddy, but look at that poor newspaper boy burdened down with that enormous load of Communist newspapers."

"Burdened he may be, oh Great Sleuth, but nonetheless, he shows a clutch of *Tass*!"

This was written by "The Rascally Lascar."
It was first published on The Shamlockians' List on August 15th, 2005.

One At A Time, Please! [SHPUN131]

"You've heard me speak of my colleague, Anstruther, have you not, Holmes?"

"Many times, Watson."

"Well, all these years I thought him devoted to his lovely wife Kathryn. Today I learned that he has been leading a double life and has a second wife by the name of Edith in Bermondsey. His perfidy has been uncovered, and he is to stand trial for bigamy."

"Interesting, Watson, most interesting. And it sure goes to prove the truth of that old adage."

"Adage? What adage, Holmes?"

"Elementary, my good fellow -- you can't have your Kate and Edith too."

This was written by "The Rascally Lascar."
It was first published in Plugs & Dottles, Issue #138, March, 1990.
It was later published on the Shamlockians' List on March 8th, 2005.

A Lesson in Boating [SHPUN061]

"Watson, you can never underestimate man's ability to do the stupid and ridiculous."

"How's that, Holmes?"

"I read here of one of our astute members of Parliament who recently made a trip to Alaska. Having made friends with some

Eskimos, he asked if he might do some boating in one of their unique vessels. Permission was granted, but not being acclimated to the extreme cold of the region, our countryman took aboard a container of hot coals for warmth. All went well until the makeshift heater overturned in rough waters, burning a hole in the bottom of the boat. Fortunately, our friend was rescued with no injury except to his dignity."

"A most interesting and, I must admit, funny story, Holmes, and it certainly does support that old familiar saw."

"And what might that be, pray tell?"

"Holmes, you can't have your kayak and heat it too."

This was written by "The Rascally Lascar."
This was first published in Plugs & Dottles, Issue #81, June, 1985.
It was later published on the Hounds of the Internet List on January 26th, 2005.

Watson Makes an Ash of Himself [SHPUN048]

Holmes and Watson were naturally invited to the grand opening ceremonies of Tower Bridge on June 30, 1894. It was a splendid occasion when the Prince of Wales turned a silver cup to open the huge bascules by way of the mighty steam engines and hydraulic mechanisms.

But as the bascules were lowered, a steam launch, 'The Chrissy Rodeen,' in the Pool of London crowded too close and struck the lowering panels as they closed, shearing off its smokestack, and spraying those on the approaches and walkways with a shower of sparks and cinders, much to the dismay of the assembled onlookers in their finery.

Caught in the spray, Watson, who had lost track of Holmes in the crowd, made his own way home. Back in Baker Street, he ruefully surveyed the damage to his topper and Chesterfield. Upon spying Holmes, then returning without a mark on his impeccable attire, he exclaimed:

"I say, Holmes, where the devil were *you* when the ship hit the span?"

This was written by David McCallister.
This was first published in Plugs & Dottles, Issue #191, August, 1994.
It was later published on the Hounds of the Internet List on January 17th, 2005.

More of Watson's Practice [SHPUN242]

In the year of '95, the Shah of Imiridu's son, who was officially known as the Shan, paid a visit to his cousin in the London Borough of Kensington. While at dinner one evening, he suffered a violent, epileptic seizure. Being the closest discrete medico to the scene, Dr. Watson was called to lend assistance.

When he entered the cousin's flat and saw the prostrate body of the Shah's son, he exclaimed:

"Good lord! What has happened here?"

To which, the cousin replied:

"Where were you when the fit hit the Shan?"

This was written by "The Rascally Lascar".
This was first published in Plugs & Dottles, Issue #37, October, 1981.

Don't Be Chicken, Watson! [SHPUN130]

It was in the spring of '88 that Holmes and Watson were invited to the country estate of Lord and Lady Beaverbrook, for whom Holmes had recently been of service in a delicate private matter. Before their final meal before returning to London, the Beaverbrooks decided to serve their cook's specialty, Chicken Marengo.

Unbeknownst to the Beaverbrooks, however, was the fact that Watson had once become violently ill after eating this dish, and since that time could not stand the sight, taste, smell, or thought of said fare.

"Holmes, I am not going to be able to eat that chicken," he whispered to Holmes, as the call to dinner was announced.

"Come now, Watson," replied Holmes, "it can't be all that bad."

"Really, Holmes, ever since that one bad experience with the dish -- well, I'm afraid if I try to eat any I'll lose my crumpets."

"Nonsense, Watson," was Holmes's rather stern reply. "You simply can't offend the Beaverbrooks by refusing the specialty of the house. You're just going to have to be brave and bite the pullet."

This was written by "The Rascally Lascar".
It was first published in Plugs & Dottles, Issue #137, February, 1990.
It was later published on the Shamlockians' List on March 7th, 2005

Too Much of a Good Thing [SHPUN299]

As they had for innumerable evenings past, our beloved

Baker Street duo were awaiting the arrival of yet another of Mrs. Hudson's suppers one stormy, tempestuous evening in April.

"Well, Holmes, what's it going to be tonight? Queried Watson.

"I believe Mrs. Hudson spoke of roast chicken earlier in the day."

"Chicken again, Holmes?" Watson's voice expressed considerable irritation. "Drat it! Last night it was chicken stew: the night before that, chicken fricassee; before that, chicken cacciatore. This is getting a bit old."

"I know, Watson," Holmes rejoined, "but unless we opt for Simpson's, there's nothing we can do about it. We're just going to have to bite the pullet."

This was written by the "The Rascally Lascar."
It was first published in Plugs & Dottles, #199, April, 1995.

<u>Water, Water Nowhere</u> [SHPUN120]

"Watson, this article on Sir William Gasperson's solo trek across the Gobi Desert in the latest *National Geographic* is incredible. What a wild and desolate place the Gobi must be. At one point in his journey Gasperson writes that he didn't pass any water for five days!"

"Really, Holmes? Well, as a doctor of medicine all I can say is that Sir William was in dire need of a good diuretic."

This was written by "The Rascally Lascar". It was first published in Plugs & Dottles, Issue #123, December, 1988. It was later published on the Hounds of the Internet List on February 27th, 2005

<u>Water, Water Nowhere II</u> [SHPUN297]

'Twas shortly after the end of The Great War that Holmes and Watson, both long retired, returned to London to hear a lecture at Albert Hall by the famous archaeological scholar, Lawrence of Arabia. The highlight of Lawrence's talk was his disturbing account of being lost for some days in the desert area South of Cairo, Egypt.

As they discussed the lecture over dinner at Simpson's that evening, Watson remarked: "What a harrowing experience, Holmes! And, to add to their problems, how devastating that Lawrence and his party should all come down with kidney failure."

"Kidney failure?" queried Holmes. "I don't recall Lawrence mentioning anything to this effect."

"Why, he certainly did," returned Watson. "Don't you remember Lawrence remarking that while lost in the desert he and his party didn't pass any water for seven days?"

This was written by the "The Rascally Lascar."
It was first published in Plugs & Dottles, #176, May, 1993.

Soups On! [SHPUN133]

It was in the early spring of '88 that my friend Sherlock Holmes was called upon to investigate the strange affair of Lord Roodensham's glass eye. The case was a brief one, a mere two days, but of such a taxing nature that Holmes, as he was wont to do at such times, refused any nourishment (even scrapple!) for a full forty-eight hours. It was no surprise, then, that my friend suggested something a little nutritious at Simpson's following the successful conclusion of the case.

We had just been served our cock-a-leekie soup, when Holmes, reaching for the salt shaker, clumsily knocked over his cup, spilling the contents into the center of his lap. Somewhat embarrassed, he summoned the waiter for assistance.

"Is there something wrong, sir?" queried our friendly garcon.

"Yes," replied Holmes, "there's a soup in my fly."

This was written by "The Rascally Lascar."
It was first published in Plugs & Dottles, Issue #153, June, 1991.
It was later published on the Shamlockians' List on March 10th, 2005.

Soup's on II [SHPUN287]

Despite Holmes's recent, embarrassing experience with his cock-a-leekie soup while dining at Simpson's, the exertions he underwent in conjunction with the recovery of Lady Stanhope's truss were of such an extreme nature as to suggest another visit to this famous Strand restaurant at the successful conclusion of the case.

My friend was just about to partake of his Soup du Jour, a hearty Scotch Broth, when to his utter disgust he espied a huge black fly floating therein. Needless to say, he immediately summoned our waiter.

"What, sir, may I ask, is this fly doing in my soup?" queried Holmes, with more than a touch of annoyance in his voice.

Our waiter stared inquiringly at the bowl held before him, and after careful scrutiny replied:

"I'm not absolutely certain, Mr. Holmes, but it looks to me like he's doing the backstroke."

This was written by "The Rascally Lascar."
It was first published in Plugs & Dottles, Issue #154, July, 1991.

Soup's on III [SHPUN288]

Undaunted by his last two encounters with insect-laden soup at Simpson's, Holmes returned once again for something a little nutritious following the exertions of another trying case. Eschewing the cock-a-leekie soup and Scotch broth of bad memory, he ordered a highly touted bouillabaisse. But, alas! No sooner had the dish been placed before him, than he spotted a dipterous creature floating therein.

"Waiter," he yelled," there's a fly in my soup!"

"That's not surprising, sir," replied the waiter, "our chef was at one time a tailor's apprentice."

This was written by W. W. Higgens.
It was first published in Plugs & Dottles, Issue #155, August, 1991.

Let the Chips Fall Where They May [SHPUN225]

In their retirement, Holmes and Watson attended one of the elegant dinners catered by the British Culinary Institute. The theme of the meal was a nautical one, with courses ranging from shrimp cocktail to fish and chips. The piece de resistance was, however, the ice sculptures.

Each diner was served a replica of a boat or ship made from frozen sherbet.

Just as Holmes was preparing to enjoying his edible sailboat, a busboy slipped on a slick spot on the floor, causing one of the plates he was carrying to disgorge fish and chips all over the table at which the Baker Street Duo were sitting. One of the pieces of potato landed on the deck of Holmes's nautical creation.

Looking somewhat miffed at this development, Holmes called out in his most strident voice:

"Waiter, there's a fry in my sloop!"

This was written by "The Rascally Lascar" from a suggestion by William Ballew.
It was first published in "Plugs & Dottles – Issue #156, Sept, 1991.
It also appeared on the Shamlockians' List on June 18th, 2006.
It also appeared in The Gaslight Gazette, V12, Issue #07, July, 2006.

Forbidden Chemistry [SHPUN283]

"Holmes," I remarked one snowy December evening, "I see here in the *Times* that a chemist in Ipswich has been given an award by the Royal Society for his work on the salts of acetic acid – the acetates, that is. I recall your work on the acetones during the affair of the Copper Beeches. Have you ever done any experimenting with the acetates?"

"No, Watson, I haven't," was my friend's reply, "and I don't intend to do so."

"And why not, may I ask?"

"Elementary, Watson. He who acetates is lost."

This was written by "The Rascally Lascar."
It was first published in Plugs & Dottles, Issue #147, December, 1990.

Westward How? [SHPUN100]

The party of westward migrants including John Ferrier and little Lucy got lost somewhere on the Great Alkali Plain. "There was somethin' wrong; compasses, or map, or somethin'" John explains to Lucy.

History records that the problem stemmed from the compasses used by the Ferrier party, which were all manufactured by the Tate Watch Manufacturing Company of Philadelphia.

Now, the Tate Watch Manufacturing Company made fine watches, but their venture into the compass-making business was a disaster. The compasses pointed any old which-way and westward-bound immigrants were liable to end up anywhere from Canada to Mexico, if not lost utterly somewhere on the alkali flats.

This led to a well-known expression at the time:

"He who has a Tate's is lost."

This was written by Karen Murdock "May Blunder."
It was first published on the Hounds of the Internet List on
February 17th, 2005

The Case of Something Fishy [SHPUN282]

One day Stamford and I had finished our rounds at Bart's, and were setting out for dinner.

"Come, Watson," said he, "Let's get some pasties at Ye Olde Scalpel and Syringe."

"No," said I, "Sherlock Holmes will be waiting for me at Baker Street. He promised to fry up some fish and chips for us while Mrs. Hudson is away."

"Is he a good cook?" queried my friend.

"Oh yes, and I wouldn't miss this masterpiece for the world. Why don't you come along? Surely you know Holmes's reputation with our native seafood, don't you?"

"No, what is it?"

"Elementary, there's no plaice like Holmes's."

This was written by David R. McCallister, who says "Upon my sole, this must flounder, as it was written by a hake."
It was first published in Plugs & Dottles, Issue #145, October, 1990.

Good Neighbor Policy [SHPUN205]

Early in our tenancy at Baker Street, I noticed that Holmes often entertained guests of somewhat dubious character. After one such visit that included service of a complete fish dinner for ourselves and the guests, I queried Holmes:

"Who were that odd couple we had to dinner, Holmes?"

He replied; "the man was an American, an itinerant dentist, and, I suspect, a gambler. The woman with the big nose and

Hungarian accent was only introduced as "Kate" so she may be his wife."

"Yes, yes, Holmes. I gathered that from the conversation, but why were they here. Is this some case you are working on?"

"Oh no! They just drop by every time they come to London. They seem to enjoy my hospitality."

"What makes you think that, Holmes?"

"Well, the man remarked as they left that 'There's no Plaice like Holmes' for the Halidays'."

This was written by "An Ill-dressed Vagabond."
It was first published on The Shamlockians' List on August 15th, 2005.

Eggs Benedict [SHPUN224]

Wishing a respite from Mrs. Hudson's breakfast fare, our famed Baker Street Duo decided to dine at Simpson's one morning.

Much to their surprise, their eggs benedict were served in shiny hubcaps instead of the usual china.

When queried about this, the waiter replied,

"There's no plate like chrome for the hollandaise!"

This was written by "The Rascally Lascar" from a suggestion by Dr. James Taggart.
It was first published on the Shamlockians' List on May 26th, 2006.
It was later published on the Hounds of the Internet on May 27, 2006.

It was in the spring of '95 when my friend Sherlock Holmes was called upon to investigate the strange happenings associated with the Egyptian Exhibit at the British Museum. One of the highlights of the vast display included the mummified bodies of three of Egypt's ancient rulers -- Mernep-tah, Rodenhotep IV, and Hatshepsut. It was during the third month of the showing that Rodenhotep IV began to shed his coverings. Slowly, but most surely, the linen bandages which encased the body of this Egyptian ruler were found to be unraveling!

The most accepted explanation for the strange phenomenon was that some person, either a prankster or a necrophile, was somehow gaining entrance to the museum after closing hours, and was slowly doing a peel job on old Rodenhotep IV.

"What do you make of it, Holmes?" I asked. "Is it the work of someone of this world or," I jokingly added, "the manifestation of some four thousand-year-old curse?"

"Neither, Watson," replied my friend. "My examination has been most thorough, and I can assure you no one has been tampering with the body. No, Watson, the explanation for what has been happening is so simple as to be obvious."

"Obvious to you, Holmes, but not to others. Pray tell me, why are those bandages unraveling?"

"Elementary, my good fellow ... most elementary. Old Rodenhotep simply got a bum wrap."

This was written by "The Rascally Lascar."
This was first published in Plugs & Dottles, Issue #65, February, 1984.
It was later published on the Hounds of the Internet List on December 19th, 2004

Lexical Lucubration [SHPUN174]

"Godfrey, my brainy barrister, I am assembling an Anglo-American Glossary and need your assistance. I know that the feminine under-garment that goes by the name of panties in America is known here as knickers. Tell me, is it possible that there exists here in jolly old
any other term for that item?"

"Interesting that you should ask, my adorable adventuress. As a matter of fact, I do believe that down at Old Bailey I have heard some of our clients speak of a bum wrap."

This was written by Frank Darlington.
It was first published in Plugs & Dottles, Issue #203, August, 1995.
It was later published on the Shamlockians' List on April 28th, 2005.

Ship Ahoy! [SHPUN248]

All of you who have been so kind to follow my chronicles of Mr. Sherlock Holmes will no doubt recall the bizarre case of *The Five Orange Pips* and the mysterious loss of the barque *Lone Star* along with the nefarious Captain James Calhoun. The ship, you will recall, was lost in '87, but it wasn't until some three years later that Holmes and I learned the true fate of Captain Calhoun. I cannot divulge his name, but there was one sole survivor of the *Lone Star* when she went down in a fierce Atlantic gale in September of '87. He was rescued by an American sealing vessel and eventually returned to England. An avid reader of The Strand, he read my account of the case, and immediately hastened to Baker Street to enlighten Holmes with the details of James Calhoun's death.

My readers will be much surprised to learn that the Captain met his end some two days before the storm which destroyed the *Lone Star*. It all happened in the following way… Desiring a little sport, it seems Calhoun put out in a longboat one afternoon with the hopes of harpooning a whale. He soon sighted one, but when he hurled the harpoon he failed to note that his left foot was encircled by the coils of the rope, and he was precipitated overboard. The Captain was momentarily stunned by the accident, but could easily have swum back to the longboat had the *Lone Star* not been so close. Before he could regain his senses, the huge vessel bore down upon him and he was never seen again.

"Ha!" exclaimed Holmes, on hearing these details, "I guess you could say in the case of Captain James Calhoun that his barque was worse than his bight."

This was written by "The Rascally Lascar" from a suggestion by Dr. Neil Taylor.
This was first published in Plugs & Dottles, Issue #47, August, 1982.

The Dog Who Did Bark [SHPUN135]

'Twas a rather mild and pleasant evening in early March, but despite the good weather and that fact that Holmes had just brought to a successful conclusion the baffling mystery of the disappearance of lady Stannet's bidet*, my friend was in the foulest of moods.

"Watson," he remarked, with obviously restrained rage, "if that accursed dog of Mrs. Hudson's keeps me awake one more night with his damnable yapping, I'm going to seek other quarters."

"I've also heard it, Holmes, but the poor creature is suffering from distemper and worms."

"Maybe so," Holmes snapped back, "but his bark is definitely worse than his blight!"

*Unfortunately, Watson fails to tell us whether the bidet in question was a small horse or an intimate bathing device.

This was written by "The Rascally Lascar".
It was first published in Plugs & Dottles, Issue #148, January, 1991.
It was later published on the Shamlockians' List on March 13th, 2005.

If I tend to refer to 1895 as the *annus mirabilis* of Mr. Sherlock Holmes's career, it is with very good reason. A succession of the most astounding and highly-publicized cases during this period had caused my friend's name to become a household name in England and, at the same time, had shown to what heights of effulgence his amazing powers of deductive reasoning could rise. I have only to mention the already chronicled case of Lady Chattingham's prosthesis and I'm sure my readers will agree with my appraisal of this remarkable year.

We were barely into '96 when a most ferocious snowstorm hit London. My notes tell me it was the third of January. Holmes and I had remained indoors all day, mainly because of the storm, but also because no great cases of import were at present demanding my friend's attention. We had just finished one of Mrs. Hudson's famous dinners – one which would have received the praises of the most discriminating gourmand – and had settled ourselves before a cheery, crackling fire with our brandies and our pipes. The windows were covered with a thick layer of ice which, in spite of its cold appearance, tended to act as a comforting shield against the Winter's storm which raged without. Holmes had picked up the *Evening Standard* and was perusing its contents when he suddenly remarked:

"I say, Watson, this is rather a sad article here on page five concerning the Chitworth family. Have you read it?"

"No, Holmes, can't say that I have. What's it about?"

"Well, it seems that a hardworking collier by the name of Jabez Chitworth recently lost his wife after a long and lingering illness. He was very attached to her and her death, according to friends, left his mental state somewhat in question. To compound the problem, he had two sons, both in their twenties, who, to his great disappointment, refused to enter the mines when they came of age. Instead, they decided to engage in pursuits of the mind as a means of livelihood, finally settling on, of all things, the writing of poetry! Their poetic endeavors met with very little acclaim and brought in even less in the way of money to help support the Chitworth household. The father would have sent them packing some time ago, but demurred because of his wife's deep affection for the boys.

"His wife's death, however, relieved him of this restraint, and last week, in a very angry mood, he ordered the boys to find gainful employment or leave his house forever."

"Can't say that I blame him one bit," I replied.

"Well, the sons refused to do either and the situation went from bad to worse. The poor colliers' mind finally snapped."

"Suicide?"

"No, Watson – murder!"

"Oh, how dreadful!"

"Yes, my dear fellow, most dreadful. It seems his sons were very fond of oatmeal biscuits. Two days ago, just before supper, Mr. Chitworth laced one of the biscuits with a powerful vegetable alkaloid and served half to each son. Death was almost instantaneous. The poor fellow then notified the authorities and gave a full confession of guilt.

"As I once before remarked, Watson, what is the meaning of it? What object is served by this circle of misery and violence and fear?

"I'm afraid I don't know, Holmes," I replied. "I feel, however, that the case in point is unique in one respect."

"And how's that, Watson?"

"Well," I continued, "to the best of my knowledge, this is the first documented incident of someone killing two bards with one scone."

Holmes groaned and reached for the brandy bottle.

This was written by "The Rascally Lascar".
This was first published in Wheelwrightings, Vol. 03, Issue #03, January, 1981

Sticks and Scones may... [SHPUN152]

"I've said it before, Watson, life is definitely stranger than anything which the mind of man can invent."

"Uh ... how's that, Holmes?" queried the old medico, laying down the latest catalog from Victoria's Secret.

"I read here in the paper that a baker named Barker in Bermondsey got so fed up with his two sons who refused to work and who sat around all day jotting down silly, immature bits of poesy, that he baked a large oat cake, laced it with strychnine, fed it to the two wastrels, and killed them."

"Really! Now there, my good fellow, is a perfect example of killing two bards with one scone. By the way, how about these latest bloomers from Vicky's Secret? Bet Mrs. Hudson would be shocked!"

This was written by "The Rascally Lascar."
It was first published on the Shamlockians' List on April 7th, 2005.

<u>Murder The Ump!</u> [SHPUN115]

"Really, Mr. Holmes, I don't know what's come over the boy," remarked Mrs. Hudson one evening after serving the Great Detective a generous portion of Bubble & Squeak*.

"Well, let's try to approach the problem in the usual deductive fashion," replied Holmes. "You say that your nephew has of late absolutely refused to sit on his father's lap?"

"That's right, Mr. Holmes. Little Chrissy's dad, you know, is Thomas Rooten, the famous rugby umpire. A nicer man you couldn't hope for, at least up to about a month ago. Don't know, sir, but something's gotten into that man. He's become as mean and nasty as a hornet. He's provoked arguments with the rugger players, and off the field has acted in a bullying fashion with many he has come in contact with."

"Ha," exclaimed Holmes, "that's it! It's quite obvious now why Chrissy refuses to sit on his father's lap."

"Pray tell, why?"

"Elementary, my dear Mrs. Hudson! Every good Englishman knows that the son never sits on the brutish umpire."

*This genuine British Grub recipe is available without charge from Gourmet Bob's, 419 Bangers St., Peoria, IL 61614. Recipe will be sent in a plain brown envelope.

This was written by "The Rascally Lascar" from a suggestion by Suellen Kirkwood.
It was first published in Plugs & Dottles, Issue #121, October, 1988.
It was later published on the Hounds of the Internet List on February 26th, 2005.

I had risen late and found Holmes in solemn conclave with Sir Sphairystike Raquet, President of the Wimbledon Lawn Tennis Club.

"Ah Watson," said Holmes. "Sir Sphairystyke is consulting me about the problems of holding the tennis championships at Wimbledon."

"Indeed," said the club president [well I wasn't going to print that name again.] "Since the competition was thrown open to players from other countries several years ago we have not been able to complete a championship due to bad light and rain."

"I see," I said. "What about roofed courts and artificial illumination?"

"Holmes suggested that," said Sir Sphairystike. "Sadly our finances don't permit us to take those steps."

"Tell me." said Holmes, "Do you use court officials from other countries?"

"I fear we have to under the rules – less too many foreign players complain of home capital decisions."

"You must insist on the use of United Kingdom officials," said Holmes, "otherwise you will never complete a championship until you have money to cover the courts."

"Why?" asked the puzzled president.

"Because the sun never sets on the British Umpire."

This was written by Richard Milne.
This has not been published before.

Calling A Spade A Spade [SHPUN112]

Holmes and Watson, out for a London stroll one evening, were approached by two heavily painted women, both exhibiting considerable décolletage. Ignoring the wiles of the two obvious strumpets, the great detective and his Boswell continued on their way.

"I'm afraid, Watson," remarked Holmes, "that London has more than its share of such women, the so-called soiled doves."

"Soiled doves? 'Tis certainly a euphemism for ladies of such low character"

"To be sure, Watson, and only one of many such euphemisms. You have certainly heard of such women referred to as demimondaines, grandes horizontales, young persons, fallen women, and so on."

"Yes, Holmes, those I have heard. And having listened to you playing 'Danny Boy' on your violin all afternoon, I believe I have another metaphor for such ladies -- at least as they apply to our city."

"And what might that be?"

"Elementary, Holmes. How about 'London Derrière'?"

This was written by "The Rascally Lascar."
This was first published in Plugs & Dottles, Issue #118, July, 1988.
It was later published on the Hounds of the Internet List on February 23rd, 2005

Bottoms Up! [SHPUN034]

Taking a break from the confines of their sitting-room,

Watson cajoled Holmes into a visit to the local pub. The good doctor hitched his gluteus maximus up upon the small, hard bar stool, bemoaning to his friend: "Why is it only in London pubs that you get these beastly uncomfortable seats? They wouldn't stand for them up north!"

"Our bottoms are different from those to the north, Watson. Surely, you have heard of the London Derriere?"

This was written by "The Rascally Lascar."
This was first published in Plugs & Dottles, Issue #188, May, 1994.
It was later published on the Hounds of the Internet List on January 5th, 2005.

The Sultan's Souvenir II [SHPUN155]

This was probably the problem of the pregnant concubines which Abdul the Damned referred to Holmes.

Given the Sultan's express permission to enter the Seraglio to pursue his investigations, Holmes soon returned, to report that the recently appointed Eunuch was not cut out for the job.

This was written by "Anonymous".
It was first published on the Shamlockians' List on April 11th, 2005

Christmas Presents [SHPUN065]

During BLAN (The Adventure of the Blanched Soldier), Holmes told Watson he had a commission from the Sultan of Turkey which was apparently of great importance. We have never been told what this was, however, I do know that, whilst in Istanbul, the Sultan asked Holmes to investigate a rather delicate matter -- how was it that so many of the women of his harem were becoming pregnant.

With special permission, Holmes entered the zenana, or women's quarters, to try to solve the mystery.

A few hours later, he reported to the Sultan – "Your excellency, the problem is your new eunuch, Abdullah. I'm afraid he is not cut out for the job."

It was as a result of this visit that, on his return, Holmes regaled Watson with the following ditty :-

"It was Christmas day in the harem,
With the Eunuchs at the door,
With hundreds of lovely women

Lying naked on the floor.
In walked the grand old Sultan,
Whose voice rang through the halls,
Saying 'What do you want for Christmas, lads ?'
And the Eunuchs answered 'Balls'!"

This was written by "Anonymous."
It was has never been published before.

Singers? Yes. Fathers? Never! [SHPUN170]

"What a damnably accursed practice!" shouted Holmes.

"What's that?" asked a rather startled Watson.

"Were you aware that the majority of 18th century male opera singers were castrati, the eviration often done without the consent of the child? For sure, it produced a voice of extraordinary power and unique tone quality, but at the expense of the singer's man-hood. Heavens!"

"Well, Holmes, opinions no doubt vary concerning the ethics of the practice, but I'm sure all would certainly agree that said castrati were cut out for their work."

This was written by "The Rascally Lascar."
It was first published in Plugs & Dottles, Issue #179, August, 1993.
It was later published on the Shamlockians' List on April 20th, 2005.

<u>How Dry I Am</u> [SHPUN268]

On a blustery May afternoon, I happened by my old lodgings in Baker Street and decided to take refuge from the rains in the company of my old friend, Sherlock Holmes. As I stepped into those familiar rooms, I was taken by surprise as I nearly tripped over the strangest doormat I had ever seen.

"Ah, Watson!" said Holmes, rising from his chair in a cloud of acrid, blue smoke. "So good to see you again."

"Holmes, what is this contraption?" I asked, looking at the thing at my feet. It consisted of a board, about three feet by four feet, across which were arranged metal twines in criss-cross fashion. To these was attached an array of magnets and rods.

"Watson, you know my methods. What does it appear to be?"

"Well, the twines appear to be conductors of a sort, and I can only guess from my practical but limited background in Physics that the magnets somehow produce some sort of electrostatic charge."

"Excellent!" he exclaimed in a fashion akin to fatherly pride.

"But I'm afraid I'm quite bewildered as to what it actually does," I continued.

"These wires will, when charged, evaporate any moisture clinging to the bottoms of shoes. You know how Mrs. Hudson hates people tracking in water."

"Ah, I get it now, Holmes," I replied, "these are the twines that dry men's soles."

This was created by Bret D. Wortman, of The Lying Corn-

Chandlers (Ames, IA).
It was first published, in Plugs & Dottles, Issue # 092, May, 1986.

With Apologies To Thomas Paine [SHPUN128]

It was in the summer of 1900 that our Baker Street Duo decided to attend the Second Olympiad in Paris. At the start of the 400-meter run, Holmes, observing the many officials with their stopwatches, pointed to the assembled crew of timers and said to Watson:

"Those, my good fellow, are the souls which time men's tries."

This was written by "The Rascally Lascar."
It was first published in Plugs & Dottles, Issue #133, October, 1989.
It was later published on the Shamlockians' List on March 5th, 2005.

All the Prints That Fit the News [SHPUN008]

'Twas late in the afternoon on a cold, wet day in December when Watson returned to Baker Street after visiting a sick patient who was suffering from food poisoning, the result of eating raw scrapple for breakfast.

"Ah, Watson, my good fellow, you are finally back," remarked Holmes. "Is it still raining, might I ask?"

"Of course it is," replied Watson testily. "Why do you think I'm standing on this newspaper? These are the *Times* that dry men's soles."

This was written by "The Rascally Lascar."
This was first published in Plugs & Dottles, Issue #149,

February, 1991.

It was later published on the Hounds of the Internet List on December 8th, 2004.

Good Girl...Bad Knee [SHPUN140]

It was in the early spring of '88 that Dr. Watson was summoned to the country estate of Sir Christopher Roodenswaite to treat the famous barrister's daughter who had injured her knee in a riding accident. The attractive, well-mannered, and cultured young lady was unable to walk on the injured limb, and was in some pain.

Watson's examination revealed a highly swollen and inflamed area surrounding the patella, conclusive evidence of torn ligaments and muscles. The good doctor, having completed his examination, sadly asked the demure damsel:--

"What's a joint like this doing in a nice girl like you?"

This was written by "The Rascally Lascar."
It was first published in Plugs & Dottles, Issue #163, April, 1992.
It was later published on the Shamlockians' List on March 20th, 2005

Watson Is At It Again [SHPUN144]

In VEIL (The Veiled Lodger), Watson feigned ignorance of the original investigation into the death of Ronder, the wild animal trainer, but in fact, he and Holmes actually did travel to Abbas Parva on the day following the tragedy. While Holmes investigated the rampage of Sahara King, Watson became distracted by Angelo, the knife-thrower, or rather, by Angelo's fearless assistant and target, his lovely daughter Cecilia. The good doctor was last seen walking with Cecilia toward her tent, where he was overheard using a pickup line that has been popular with young blades ever since:

"What's a knife girl like you doing in a joint like this?"

This was written by "The Rascally Lascar" from a suggestion by Rosemary Michaud.

It was first published in Plugs & Dottles, Issue #207, December, 1995.

It was later published on the Shamlockians' List on March 28th, 2005.

Smoke, Smoke, Smoke That Cigarette [SHPUN196]

'Tis a little known fact, but Sherlock Holmes forsook his cocaine habit in the late '90s, and took up the smoking of marijuana. As he and Watson strolled the Strand one June evening, they spotted an East End slattern in the seamiest of attire, advertising her "wares," with a reefer hanging from her painted lips.

Walking up to her, Holmes ripped the smoke there from, looked soulfully at it, and murmured: "What's a nice joint like you doing in a girl like this?"

This was written by "The Rascally Lascar."

It was first published on the Shamlockians' List on June 6th, 2005.

The Whitechapel Floozy [SHPUN202]

This trollop, this soiled dove from the gutters of Whitechapel, was ushered into our Baker Street lodgings one night of tenebrific and stygian gloom, a cannabis reefer dangling from her scarlet painted lips.

Sherlock Holmes, who was familiar with three hundred and forty-two varieties of marijuana smoke, could tell at an instant this demimondaine was smoking the very best. Walking up to this hussy of a whore, he yanked the smoking fag from her mouth, gazed at it soulfully, and said:--

"What's a nice joint like you doing in a girl like this?"

This was written by "The Rascally Lascar."
It was first published on the Shamlockians' List on August 8th, 2005

NOT REALLY PUNS AT ALL

Some of these formulations are not, strictly speaking, Puns at all. They may involve wordplay, but they are not simple transpositions or mis-pronunciations. Nevertheless, they are Sherlockian (????) and they involve word mis-interpretation, so we cannot ignore them but must bring them along as a form of PUNishment.

Bees and Strawberries [SHPUN178]

Unbeknownst to most Sherlockians is the fact that in addition to raising bees when he retired to the South Downs, Sherlock Holmes also took up the cultivation of strawberries. His retirement cottage happened to border on the grounds of an insane asylum. One morning, as he tended to his berries, an inmate from the institution was watching him through the fence.

"What are you doing?" queried the patient.

"Putting manure on my strawberries," replied the famous sleuth.

"Manure?" came the puzzled reply. "I put sugar on mine, and they've got ME locked up!"

This was written by "The Rascally Lascar."
It was first published on the Shamlockians' List on May 2nd, 2005.

New Scotland Yard Cooperation [SHPUN314]

One day early in our association, I asked Holmes about the ferret-faced fellow who had been coming by with increasing frequency in the last few weeks. I asked if he had a difficult problem or if he was an agent for some client and Holmes looked at me as if I had asked him why the rain was wet.

He recovered his composure and explained that the gentleman in question was a recently promoted Inspector for the Metropolitan Police who was consulting him on a possible smuggling case. He said that he thought that Mr. Lestrade's occupation was so self-evident that he had never bothered to mention it, simply assuming that I understood the situation. I then asked him why a Scotland Yard official would consult him about smuggling and asked if he had been to sea.

It was at this point that Holmes explained his professional work as a consulting detective and went on to relate some examples of earlier 'cases' that he had handled. I found the entire subject most fascinating and kept asking for more details and examples until Mrs. Hudson brought up the tea tray. After we had tasted the scones and clotted cream and sampled the robust Darjeeling she had brewed, I asked about the current investigation.

Holmes explained that it seemed an enormous amount of un-taxed Cognac had been showing up recently in the London metropolitan area. Normally, the brandy smuggling trade was conducted by fishing trawlers and coastal traders and traveled to various seaports on the Channel and in the Broads, and was kept in rough control by the Customs Service cutters. This recent traffic seemed to be passing through the Port of London or through some nearby area and it was very difficult to identify what vessels might be bringing in the spirits in question.

Holmes went on to say that he had spent a great deal of time in bars and among drinks retailers listening for gossip that might be related to this illicit trade. He had finally been able to identify some links to a group of 'Yachting' nudists with a compound somewhat East of the Metropolis and had found a few holes in the walls of their fences. Apparently, Lestrade and his men were looking into them.

This was written by "An Ill-dressed Vagabond."
This was first published on the Shamlockian's List on May 30th, 2009.
It was later published in "The Formulary," [#20, 12/2010].

Planning For Saturday [SHPUN032]

The good Dr. Watson, having heard of the formation of the Salvation Army in the East End of London in 1865 by the Rev. William Booth, desired to learn more about the inner workings of the charitable organization. He, therefore, made an appointment with the Reverend himself.

Booth went into great detail concerning the feeding and housing of the poor and homeless, the caring for of orphans, attempts to resurrect those from the evils of the demon rum, etc. Finally, Watson asked: "Tell me, Reverend, do you also make efforts to save London's bad girls, our so-called 'soiled doves'?"

"We certainly do," came the reply.

"Excellent," replied Watson, "save two for me and my friend Sherlock Holmes for this Saturday night."

This was written by "The Rascally Lascar."
It was first published on the Hounds of the Internet List on January 3rd, 2005.

The Perfect Anthelmintic [SHPUN290]

'Twas in the Summer of '97 that Sherlock Holmes decided that his good friend Watson was worshipping too frequently at the font of Bacchus. Holmes himself had given up the consumption of alcohol and, concerned over his friend's health, decided to give him an object lesson. Having obtained an earthworm from the grounds of the nearby Hyde Park, he proceeded one evening to set two glasses on the table before Watson, one glass filled with water, the other with whiskey.

"Now please observe, my good fellow," said Holmes. The great fathomer first dropped the worm in the glass of water and then withdrew it, whereupon it continued to wriggle with considerable vitality. The procedure was then repeated using the glass filled with whiskey, the result being a very dead member of the Phylum Annelida.

"Now, Watson," remarked Holmes, "does this tell you anything?"

"It indeed does, Holmes," replied the old Afghan campaigner. "'Tis quite evident from what you have demonstrated here that if I drink enough whiskey, I'll never have worms."

This was written by "The Rascally Lascar."
It was first published in Plugs & Dottles, Issue #159, December, 1991.

Pure Hogwash [SHPUN285]

'Twas in the early Spring of the year 1891 that Sherlock Holmes and I spent an enjoyable week in the small Surrey town of Godalming at the invitation of an old college chum of mine named Percy Natwick. While there, a local farmer friend of Percy's reported to both Percy and the Godalming constabulary the theft of his prize Berkshire boar. Having had such amazing success recently with the recovery of another missing animal, the famous race horse Silver Blaze, Holmes offered to investigate the boar's disappearance.

To everyone's surprise, the animal was found wandering the countryside a few days after its disappearance, having obviously got loose from whomever had stolen it. No one held out much hope in discovering who the culprit was, but after a few minutes alone with the porker, Holmes announced the name of the thief – a neighbor of Percy's who eventually confessed under questioning by the authorities.

"This is amazing, Holmes," I remarked, "however did you

determine the identity of the guilty party?"

"Elementary," was my friend's reply – "The pig squealed."

This was written by Dave Galerstein.
It was first published in Plugs & Dottles, Issue #151, April, 1991.

It's All in the Syntax [SHPUN037]

Mrs. Hudson, though a long-suffering and kind landlady, never had the advantage of a formal education. This was most evident when it came to her writing abilities. So one day when she wished to dispose of one of her many mixing bowls (used, of course, in the preparation of British Grub), she asked the good Dr. Watson to compose an ad for same for the local papers. This, Watson happily agreed to do.

Before composing the add, Watson felt a chill coming on, and sought to remedy the situation with some fine brandy from the Rhodonne region of France. As chills go, this was a rather stubborn one, requiring a considerable quantity of the fermented grape distillate before warmth was restored to the aging Doctor's body. But, compose the ad he did, sending it off to the papers.

Alas, there was not one reply to said ad. Could it have been the wording? ---

For Sale
Mixing bowl designed to
Please a cook with a round
Bottom for efficient beating.

Inquire: 221 Baker St.

This was written by "The Rascally Lascar."
It was first published in Plugs & Dottles, Issue #217, October,

1996.
It was later published on the Hounds of the Internet List on January 15th, 2005.

Was Mrs. Hudson's Face Ever Red! [SHPUN038]

You would think Mrs. Hudson would be hesitant in asking Dr. Watson to compose another ad for her after yesterday's mixing bowl fiasco, but nonetheless, she did.

The good landlady had acquired another terrier to replace the one which Holmes put to sleep in *A Study in Scarlet*. She became very attached to the new pooch, named "Rodie," so was extremely upset when the dog happened to wander away from Baker Street one day.

"Would you please write a 'Lost' notice for me and send it to the local papers?" she asked Watson.

Holmes's companion was more than happy to do so, but once again may have spent too much time at the font of Bacchus before doing so.

Herewith is the ad presented:--

LOST: Small gray and white terrier. Reward. Neutered. Like one of the family. If found, contact Mrs. Hudson, 221 Baker Street.

This was written by "The Rascally Lascar."
It was first published in Plugs & Dottles, Issue #218, November, 1996.
It was later published on the Hounds of the Internet List on January 16th, 2005

Canonical Tongue-twister [SHPUN047]

Mrs. Hudson was called to the door of 221b by an itinerant tinker, who asked if she had any pots or pans that needed repairing.

She went down to the kitchen, and returned with a couple of pans which she handed to him.

Staying to watch the tinker at work on his bench at the rear of his little donkey cart, Mrs. Hudson asked:

"Are you copper-bottoming 'em, my man?"

To which he replied "No, I'm aluminiuming 'em, Mum".

This was written by "Anonymous."
It was first published on the Hounds of the Internet List on January 17th, 2005.

Sisters of Mercy [SHPUN076]

Watson was going about his rounds in his little A Model Ford (LAST) when he saw a notice by the wayside - "Sisters of Mercy Bordello - 5 miles."

Intrigued, he drove on, and passed another - "Sisters of Mercy Bordello - 1 mile" until eventually "Sisters of Mercy Bordello - next right."

He turned into a parking lot outside a building which was obviously a nunnery, went up to the front door and rang the bell.

The door was opened by a girl in nun's habit, who held out a collection box, saying – "It's going to cost you five pounds."

He put in the fiver, and she told him "Go down this corridor, take the first right, and go through the door at the end of the passage."

All eagerness, Watson followed her instructions, went through the door, and found himself back outside in the parking lot.

Facing him was a notice, reading "Go in Peace. You have just been screwed by the Sisters of Mercy."

This was written by "Anonymous."
This was never published before.

Chinese Dental Clock [SHPUN080]

Holmes returned from a visit to the dentist, and told Watson "While I was in the waiting room, a Chinaman came in and sat down. What time was it ?"

"I've no idea" said Watson

"Tooth hurtee" replied Holmes.

"A second Chinaman came in - what time was it then ?"

"I've still no idea"

"Tooth hurtee too."

This was written by "Anonymous."
It has never been published before.

Watson's Practice #2 [SHPUN083]

Watson was examining a male patient, known to him as having a drinking problem, who presented at the surgery complaining of a general malaise, and of simply "feeling

Rotten".

Having given him a thorough examination, Watson said "I can find nothing at all wrong with you. It must be the drink."

"OK, doctor," replied the patient, "I'll come back when you're sober."

This was written by "Anonymous."
It has never been published before.

Holmes and Watson, at the Opera [SHPUN084]

Holmes and Watson attended a performance of the Mozart opera *Don Giovanni* at Covent Garden.

The performance went swimmingly until the final act, up to the point when the Don was supposed to descend into Hell to pay his debt to the Devil.

That is when the stage trapdoor failed to operate, leaving the unfortunate actor stamping his feet in an effort to make it work.

Then came a cry from the audience - "Praise the Lord, Hell's full."

This was written by "Anonymous.".
It was first published on the Hounds of the Internet List on February 7th, 2005

Plain Tales from the Raj [SHPUN090]

During his convalescence in the Military Hospital at Peshawar, Watson spent many an evening in the Officers' Mess, enjoying a quiet smoke and a chota peg among his fellow invalids.

One evening, those present were discussing the drawbacks to life on the sub-continent.

One young subaltern declared that, in his view, the worst aspect was the climate, where one could be baked to death in the summer, and washed away when the rains came.

A grizzled old major responded, that, in his opinion, the biggest drawback was religion, because the Hindu and the Muslim would never live together in peace, preferring to cut each other's throats at every opportunity.

Yet another suggested the biggest drawback was the agitators, who roamed the country, inciting rebellion by preaching independence to the ignorant masses.

Colonel Sebastian Moran, the well known heavy-game hunter, his left arm in a sling, knocked out his pipe on the ashtray, and addressed his fellow convalescents:

"As I am sure you are all aware, I have traveled the length and breadth of this country, from the plains of the south to the jungles of the north, in pursuit of just about every species of indigenous game animal.

Gentlemen, it is my considered opinion that the greatest drawback in India is the elephant's foreskin."

This was written by "Anonymous."
It has never been published before.

Watson's French Lesson [SHPUN092]

Holmes and Watson were discussing the difference between "savoir faire" and "sang froid", when Watson said "I can give you an example from my own, personal experience."

"One afternoon last week, my neighbor came home unexpectedly, and caught me 'in fragrante delicto' with his wife."

"Instead of shouting at us, he stood at the foot of the bed and said, 'Don't mind me. Just carry on what you were doing'."

"That was 'savoir fair'."

"Now, if I HAD been able to carry on what I was doing, that would have been 'sang froid'."

This was written by "Anonymous."
It has never been published before.

A Cornish Sermon [SHPUN097]

The Rev. Mr. Roundhay, vicar of Tredannick Wollas (DEVI), complained to Holmes that someone had stolen his bicycle.

Holmes suggested that the Rev. should include the Ten Commandments in his sermon on Sunday, and scan the faces of the congregation when he got to "Thou shalt not steal," when the guilty party would perhaps reveal himself.

The Vicar did as Holmes suggested, and after the service, the detective asked whether he had been able to identify the thief?

Mr. Roundhay replied, "As a matter of fact, when I got to 'Thou shalt not commit adultery', I remembered where I'd left it."

This was written by "Anonymous."
It has never been published before.

Watson's Diagnosis [SHPUN102]

Dr. Watson was examining a young woman who presented with a number of green rings on the inside of her thighs.

Puzzled by these symptoms, he consulted a textbook or two, then rang a colleague to see if he could help in diagnosing the problem, but to no avail.

Then he had a brainwave.

"Are you having an affair with a gipsy ?" he asked.

"As a matter of fact, I am." she replied.

"Then tell him his ear-rings are not made of gold."

This was written by "Anonymous."
It has never been published before.

Watson's practice #3 [SHPUN109]

Watson was treating a patient who was suffering a severe attack of hemorrhoids.

"I'm prescribing suppositories - place one in your back passage every night. Come back and see me in a week."

The patient duly returned, and Dr. Watson asked how he was getting on.

"Well" said the patient, "I put one in the back passage, one in the front hall, and one at the foot of the stairs, but for all the good they've done, I might just as well have stuck them up my arse."

This was written by "Anonymous."

It has never been published before.

I Sea What You Mean, Holmes [SHPUN110]

"You know, Holmes, they say that the submarine will be incredibly advantageous to have if we are ever engaged in another war."

The famous gumshoe stretched out his long legs, reached for his pipe, and responded with a noted lack of enthusiasm. "That may be, Watson, but I do not think much of the idea."

"Come now, Holmes, the practicality of it must appeal to your logical mind. Be honest now, how do you view the concept of the submarine?"

"I don't, my good fellow—it's beneath me!"

This was written by "The Rascally Lascar" from suggestion by Marla Elmore.
It was first published in Plugs & Dottles, Issue #117, June, 1988.

Flagrante Delicto [SHPUN176]

'Twas another bitterly cold night in January. Holmes and Watson were comfortably ensconced before a cheery fire which was slowly incinerating all of the Lascar's irritating posts to a certain discussion group across the Pond -- an act of courtesy on Holmes's part to the list owner of that group.

As usual, the wind screamed like a banshee without, but the sobbing little brat in the chimney was quiet, having been removed by the sweep the following day. Watson was questioning Holmes about his latest case. Emitting a horrendous, eruptacious belch (Mrs. Hudson's bangers & mash), the good doctor asked:

"You say the woman shot her husband with his pistol at close range?"

"That is correct, Watson."

"Any powder marks on the body?"

"Of course, you dummy, that's why she shot him!"

This was written by "The Rascally Lascar."
It was first published in Plugs & Dottles, Issue #221, February, 1997.
It was later published on the Shamlockians' List on April 30th, 2005.

The Uniqueness Of Victor Hatherley [SHPUN175]

'Twas a bitterly cold evening in January. Holmes and Watson were comfortably ensconced before a cheery fire following a delicious supper of Bangers & Mash (one of those accursed British Grub dishes banned from certain Holmesian discussion groups in the Colonies). As usual, the wind screamed without, and that ever-present, nasty little brat was blubbering in the chimney.

Holmes was reminiscing over some of his more *outré* cases, and had come to the one anent the hydraulic engineer, Victor Hatherley.

"You know, Watson," he remarked, "that case possesses a unique feature not found in any of the cases you have seen fit to chronicle."

"Ha, you mean Hatherley's near demise in the hydraulic press?"

"No, my good amanuensis, I refer to the fact that Hatherley was the only individual in my many cases ever to give someone the finger."

This was written by "The Rascally Lascar."
It was first published in Plugs & Dottles, Issue #220, January, 1997.
It was later published on the Shamlockians' List on April 29th, 2005.

Watson's Fourth Honeymoon [SHPUN162]

By the time Watson married for the fourth time, he was somewhat past middle age, and his new bride considerably younger.

In the weeks prior to the wedding, Watson called at the Naval and Military Stores, in an effort to purchase some pyjamas with his old regiment's crest on the breast pocket, but without success. He settled for a pair with the Union Jack on the pocket, instead.

After the honeymoon, the bride's mother had a long chat with her daughter, asking her whether, being an older man, her new husband had come up to expectations, in bed?

To which the new bride replied, "Oh, Mummy, everything was fine in that department. In fact, although he hasn't said anything, I think he used to screw for England."

This was written by "Anonymous."
It was first published on the Shamlockians' List on April 14th, 2005.

Why No Mr. Hudson? [SHPUN114]

For those who wonder what happened to Mrs. Hudson's husband, he left home after the following episode, which took place one Boxing Day, shortly before Holmes and Watson appeared on the doorstep at 221b.

Mr. Hudson returned home from an office party, to find his wife in the hall, drawers around her ankles, being 'attended to' by a strange man.

"What the hell's going on ?" he shouted, as the man made good his escape.

"I was just giving the milkman his Christmas Box." she replied.

"What the hell do you mean?" he yelled.

"Don't you remember, dear", she said, "We discussed this only a couple of days ago. You said to give the coalman a bottle of Guinness, and the postman a couple of cigars."

I asked you "What about the milkman?" and you said "F--k the milkman!"

This was written by "Anonymous."
It has not been published before.

Watson and Mary's Honeymoon [SHPUN161]

For their honeymoon, Watson took Mary to hotel in a pretty, little village in the New Forest.

On the morning after their first night, Watson stood on the balcony of their room, admiring the surroundings, when he saw on the next balcony a young curate, who was honeymooning there, too.

"Delightful little spot, isn't it ?" he remarked.

"Yes, indeed", replied the curate, "And so cunningly concealed."

This was written by "Anonymous."
It was first published on the Shamlockians' List on April 14th, 2005.

Those Telltale Wrinkles [SHPUN121]

"Good heavens, Watson, why the downcast look? I trust Mary is not ill."

"No, not ill, but she's so angry with me she asked me to leave the house this evening. I'm afraid I've done it, Holmes."

"Not another woman?"

"No, no, not that. But probably worse. We were getting ready to go to the theater this evening, and I remarked to Mary that her stockings were wrinkled."

"I don't know why that should upset her. I would think a woman would want to be told by her husband if some part of her dress were not quite right. What was so bad about telling her that her stockings were wrinkled?"

"She wasn't wearing any, Holmes!"

This was written by "The Rascally Lascar."
It was first published in Plugs & Dottles, Issue #124, January, 1989.
It was later published on the Hounds the Internet List on February 28th, 2005.

Interlude at Baker Street #6 [SHPUN240]

It had been a blustery day in Late November, and I had not seen Holmes since morning when, bundled against the weather, he had left our Baker Street lodgings without informing me of his destination. 'Twas near four o'clock when I heard his familiar step upon the stair. Bursting into the room, he tossed his top coat and hat on the rack, poured himself a stiff glass of whiskey, and exclaimed with great satisfaction: "Watson, I've solved it!"

"Solved what, Holmes?" I queried.

"The bogus laundry affair, good man, the bogus laundry affair."

"Fake laundry, Holmes, whatever ...?"

"A clever and diabolical scheme, Watson, and definitely the workings of Moriarty. Picture this – a newly established laundry here in London, catering strictly to British nobility, and with the most devious intentions in mind. Coming from the nobility, most of the pieces of dirty clothing contain the owners' monograms. Trusting that one laundry item out of many per customers will not be missed, the evil operators have been stealing such, cutting out the portion containing the monogram, and selling same to a rare group of collectors who, for some reason, are willing to pay quite a price for the noble insignias.

"And, Watson, the monogram which appears to have gone for the highest price is that of Sir Cedric Waithegaite, a former weaver and *very* close friend of Oscar Wilde. *His* monogram is definitely unique."

"Unique" How's that, pray tell?"

"Well," Holmes replied, with a half-restrained chuckle, "it reads 'Fruit of the Loom'."

This was written by "The Rascally Lascar."
This was first published in Wheelwrightings, Vol. 11, Issue #01, September, 1988

A Sad Case [SHPUN244]

Sherlock Holmes was leisurely perusing a copy of the *Daily Telegraph* one blustery November evening when he suddenly remarked:

"I say, Watson, here's a rather sad case."

"How's that, Holmes?"

"Well, they give no names for obvious reasons, but it seems a baby was born yesterday at Bart's, and the poor little blighter doesn't have any ears."

"Hum … how unfortunate," replied Watson. "What about it's eyesight?"

"Eyesight? Well, the article states that the child is normal in every other respect."

"Ah, that's good," remarked Watson, "because he'd surely never be able to wear glasses."

This was written by "The Rascally Lascar."
This was first published in Plugs & Dottles, Issue #35, August, 1981.

Watson the Deafer [SHPUN116]

At the local market, Watson found a stallholder selling hearing aids for 5 shillings each.
Being a little hard of hearing himself, he handed over his 5 bob, and was given a small brown
envelope.

When he got it home, he opened it, to find nothing but a

short piece of white string inside.

Next day he took it back to the market, and demanded an explanation from the spruiker.

"It's simple", he was told. "Just place one end of the string in your ear, and the other in your top pocket, and when they speak to you, people will SHOUT UP!"

This was written by "Anonymous."
It was first published on the Hounds of the Internet List on February 25th, 2005.

A Tent Joke [SHPUN117]

Sherlock Holmes and Dr. Watson wanted to examine Professor Presbury's dog to see if there was any reason for this formerly friendly animal to snarl and snap at his master. They couldn't see him on the grounds, but Holmes suddenly stopped, then moved quickly over to a small tent that for some reason had been set up under a tree. He emerged, triumphant, with the dog docilely following him at heel.

"My goodness," cried Watson, "you amaze me. How in the world did you know he was there."

"You constantly amaze me, Watson," came the cool reply. "I thought surely even you would know enough to seek out a dog in a pup-tent."

Adair - who obviously would only have sent this on a dare.

This was written by Don Dillistone.
It was first published on the Hounds of the Internet List on February 25th, 2005.

That Old Wound [SHPUN118]

A crisp February evening found our Baker Street Duo dining at Simpson's famous hash-house in the Strand. Watson had ordered his favorite dish, *jambes des grenouilles*, and was voraciously gnawing away at one of the golden fried delights.

"And how is your frog's leg?" queried the famous private dick.

"Just like I wrote in The Sign of Four," replied his Fidus Achates — "it aches wearily at every change of the weather."

This was written by "The Rascally Lascar."
It was first published in Plugs & Dottles, Issue #122, November, 1988.
It was later published on the Hounds of the Internet List on February 26th, 2005.

THE STONES, et al.

Variations of "Leave no stone unturned" seem to fascinate Sherlockians, who have a real penchant for beating a theme to death. Over the years, puns on this line seem to turn up at every drop of a punch line. As the Internet Lists have become more popular, variations pop up at odd intervals with depressing frequency. As ever, the last word is provided by the lovely Esmerelda.

<u>Determination</u> [SHPUN002]

Holmes's investigation into the disappearance of herring fisherman Thaddeus Kipperman eventually brought the great sleuth and his fidus Achates to the tiny village of Worthing on the southern coast of England. While searching for clues along the shoreline, Holmes suddenly picked up a handful of rocks and began hurling the missiles at a flock of sea swallows which were gracefully flitting above the water's edge.

"Good heavens, Holmes," cried Watson, "why are you harassing those poor birds?"

"Because," replied Holmes, "I promised Kipperman's wife that in searching for clues as to his whereabouts, I would leave no tern un-stoned."

This was written by "The Rascally Lascar."
It was first published in Plugs & Dottles, Issue #31, April, 1981.
It was later published in Plugs & Dottles, Issue #110, November, 1987.
It was later published on the Hounds of the Internet List on August 6th, 2004.
It was later published on the Hounds of the Internet List on February 8th, 2005.

Those Funny Red Rumps [SHPUN188]

Holmes and Watson were spending a few idle hours at the Bond Street Picture galleries, viewing the works of the famous baboon painter Sir Joshua Simian.

"Remarkable, Watson, remarkable!" exclaimed Holmes. "Simian' use of colors is simply breathtaking."

"Absolutely," replied Watson, "this painter has left no stern un-toned."

This was written by "The Rascally Lascar."
It was first published in Plugs & Dottles, Issue #32, May 1981.
It was later published on the Shamlockians' List on May 30th, 2005.

Beer Drinking Songs [SHPUN189]

In the winter of '89, Sherlock Holmes temporarily forsook his Strad and took up the playing of musical beer mugs. Each evening, before playing, he would carefully adjust the liquid level in each mug so as to produce exactly the right pitch. Following one of his more brilliant performances one evening, Watson remarked:

"Marvelous, Holmes, simply marvelous! The accuracy of the notes produced by each mug is nothing short of incredible. How do you do it?"

"Elementary, Watson," came the reply, "it's simply due to the fact that I make sure to leave no stein un-tuned."

This was written by "The Rascally Lascar."
It was first published in Plugs & Dottles, Issue #34, July 1981.
It was later published on the Shamlockians' List on May 31st, 2005.

<u>This One's for the Birds</u> [SHPUN191]

Once again Holmes had worn himself out with overwork and underfeeding, not to mention lack of sleep. Watson convinced him to get away from London and took him down to Brighton, hoping that the sea air and walks along the rocky beach would work wonders with Holmes's health.

The two were out for a pre-breakfast stroll one morning when Watson noticed that the sea birds were not wheeling in the sky as was their wont, but were huddled closely together on the beach, appearing to fill the entire area. He remarked upon this to Holmes, noting that he saw no sign of a predator bird and wondering what had caused the phenomenon.

"You see but you do not observe, Watson. Not only are there many birds, but each bird is perched on a separate rock, and no rock is uncovered. These birds are merely determined to leave no stone unterned."

This was written by Sandy Kozinn "Esmerelda."
It was first published on the Shamlockians' List on June 1st, 2005.

<u>The Farewell Tour</u> [SHPUN218]

After the war, Holmes returned to the Sussex Downs and his semi-retirement gradually changed to a full withdrawal from the world. My Medical efforts during the war had exhausted me and I found it increasingly difficult to even attempt to keep up with the progress of Medicine, more or less to continue in practice. My wife and I settled down to a comfortable retirement, supplemented by occasional lectures and appearances.

With the death of my literary agent in 1931, our lives became even more circumscribed and my wife's death in 1933 drew a curtain over that happy part of my life. Holmes, sensing my loss of interest in life, invited me to move in with him and, for lack of any strong inclination to do anything else, I acquiesced. Under the influence of his questing mind, life again provided challenges and appeal and we both felt a renewed desire to grasp at events around us.

Unfortunately, we both had problems with ordinary travel but felt "Penned up" in the quiet society of the Downs. After some effort, we located trustworthy and efficient help, a butler cum chauffeur and a nurse/housekeeper, to simplify our problems with day-to-day living. Charles was a grandson of Wiggins, an early member of the Baker Street auxiliary of the official police force and Miss Chambers was a grand-niece of our faithful Mrs. Hudson.

With such help available, we were able to undertake a less sedentary lifestyle and found ourselves able to travel to London regularly and to make visits to the Continent with some frequency. In 1937, Holmes asked if I would like to travel to America and see some of the sights he had visited in his earlier travel(s?) there. I neglected to remind him of my own American expeditions and said that I would be delighted to accompany him.

In due course, after much planning and fuss, we embarked at Southampton and sailed for New York. Fortunately, the crossing was swift and the weather accommodating, so that Dr. Bell and Mr. Sigerson were not seriously inconvenienced. We arrived in "Gotham on the Hudson" as Holmes insisted on calling New York and spent several days in a fine Hotel resting from our voyage.

One evening, the concierge informed Holmes that the Town Hall was holding a recital by a newly popular American violinist, one Isaac Stern. Holmes ordered tickets and we were bundled into a Hotel limousine and whisked away with only two porters and one bell captain having to help Charles and Miss Chambers manage the expedition.

I found the concert quite pleasant and felt well enough afterward to sip a sherry with Holmes in our suite and ask his opinion of Mr. Stern.

Holmes admitted the man had talent, but did not like Stern's "Bowing," which he characterized as "Busy." In fact, Holmes commented that "he attacked the music with fervor, seemingly determined to leave no tone "un-Sterned."

This was written by "An Ill-dressed Vagabond."
It was first published on the Shamlockians' List on November 4th, 2005.
It was later published in The Gaslight Gazette, Vol. 11, Issue #11, November, 2005.

The Trained Cormorant [SHPUN220]

I have mentioned elsewhere the story concerning the Politician, the lighthouse and the trained cormorant and I do not propose to recount that affair as many features about it are still confidential. However, one aspect that may be of interest to the public can be revealed at this time, since the man involved has recently died.

The trained cormorant in question was quite a remarkable bird. It formed an otherwise untraceable linkage between the politician and the lighthouse (no matter which politician and which lighthouse). The manner in which Holmes discovered this linkage is quite mundane, a tip from an informant with a grudge and Holmes was on the scent.

The real interest in the matter was the methods used by the trainer. The activities performed by the cormorant should not be discussed, even at this late date. Suffice it to say that the bird was an efficient and effective participant, although quite innocently, in the conspiracy that rocked cabinet circles. Training the bird to perform the required actions was done by a true genius.

Holmes was looking for the source of the bird which had been cited as the connecting link, but with little success. He knew it must be tamed and trained in order to participate so effectively, but he had no idea who was involved as trainer and handler. We were haunting seaside resorts in the area of the lighthouse for clues as to the home of the cormorant with no particular direction, merely trolling, as it were, for clues.

One day Holmes became fascinated by a crowd of seabirds surrounding a lone beach loafer. Some were sitting quietly on the ground and others were flying gracefully about the man's chair and screeching at him. The man seemed to be tossing items into the air for the birds to catch and then waiting for them to bring the items to him. Upon receiving the items, the man would uncover a cup and allow the bird a drink from it.

Holmes became convinced this was the trainer of the cormorant and arranged to have him watched at all times. Within a few days, Holmes had all the information he needed to confront those involved and to demand their cooperation. Since then, the matter has not been reopened, pending proper behavior by those concerned.

I asked Holmes what about the seaside scene had drawn his attention.

He explained that the man on the beach was training those seabirds to return articles thrown away and he was using beer to reward the birds that performed well. Almost all learned quite quickly what was required and persisted in returning thrown items until they could no longer fly, for having drunk so much beer. He said it was quite clear that the man was a thorough and competent trainer. When I asked why, he replied:

"The man left no tern unstoned."

This was written by "An Ill-Dressed Vagabond."
It was first published on the Shamlockians' List on January 25th, 2006.
It was later published in The Gaslight Gazette, V12, Issue #08, August, 2006.

Voodoo in Cornwall [SHPUN227]

Holmes' brush with Voodoo was occasioned by some rather odd events in Cornwall. In the late Summer of 1904, Holmes asked me to accompany him to Truro, where the Chief Constable had asked him to look into a series of disappearances. My wife was glad to see me get away from the minor monotony of my practice at a time when most of my patients were on Holiday and my presence around the house was, I suspect, becoming a burden. So Holmes and I settled in on the train to the West country.

At Truro, the Chief Constable met us at the train and had us driven straight to the local Police offices. He told us that more than a dozen people, from several households were missing. That so many were missing only became apparent recently, as in each case, the entire family had disappeared all at one time, leaving no one to inform the Police until workers arrived at the farms on Monday. It was now two weeks since the disappearances and no progress had been made by the local officers. Holmes requested the particulars of each event and we retired to an excellent Inn for dinner and a solid night's sleep.

In the morning, we were assigned a Police Trap and driver and we began a journey to each of the isolated farms where the disappearances occurred. The first farm was really a small estate, owned by one Hezekiah Stone, a retired West Indies trader. Mr. Stone lived there with an elderly, spinster sister and had only daytime staff who worked the farm and a housekeeper who lived on a nearby farm. The Housekeeper had reported both Mr. Stone and his sister missing when she came to work on a Monday and found no one in residence. There were no signs of violence and only the fact that there were no lights burning and no doors locked at the farm seemed significant.

The same was true at each of the next two farms. Farm hands reporting for work reported no family members at home at the Cadwallader farm, where Mr. Cyrus Cadwallader, his wife, Leah Stone Cadwallader and their two, grown daughters had seemingly vanished into thin air. The St. Just farm followed the pattern. Mr. Armand St. Just, his wife Sarah Stone St. Just and their teenaged daughters were missing and the many cattle at the farm were all still in pasture when the hands arrived in the morning. The final farm which belonged to the younger Hezakiah Stone offered more clews. Apparently Hezakaiah junior, his wife and his two, grown sons had put up a fight as there were indications of a large scuffle and some marks which might be blood in the dust of the extensive yards.

After returning to the Inn and spending the afternoon abusing the hospitality of the Inn's parlour with several pipes of noxious shag, Holmes used the telephone at the Inn to call the Chief Constable and ask if anyone notable had moved into the area in recent times. The only newcomer was a Haitian expatriate who had taken up a large estate to the North of town and Holmes pounced on this news with glee. He suggested an immediate descent on this estate with a large force of police, which was arranged.

At the Estate, a large staff of Haitians was found and arrested along with the missing persons, all of whom seemed stupefied and who had been working the fields under direction of the owner's overseer for the last two weeks. My examinations indicated that all had been extensively drugged, apparently as part of a ritual in which they had been "turned into zombies" for ease of control. The owner apparently had known the senior Hezekiah in the Islands and had developed some grudge against him. No doubt, he was the victim of sharp business practices, as old Hezekiah was noted for his cheese-paring ways.

On our way back to London, I commented to Holmes that the Haitian had been most thorough in his vengeance.

Holmes replied, "Yes, he left no Stone 'unturned'!"

This was written by "an Ill-dressed Vagabond."
It was first published on the Shamlockians' List on August 8th, 2006.

<u>In a Carriage in Scotland</u> [SHPUN228]

Holmes' latest case had taken us further and further into the wilds of Scotland, and we were being shaken unmercifully as our carriage swept over the unmetalled roadbed.

"I say, Holmes," I complained, "did some lunatic just dig up this road for fun."

"Not quite, Watson," he replied. "You remember passing the stone quarry a few miles back, don't you? They've spread gravel from there over the road. If they did not, the constant rain would turn it into a soggy morass."

"Then there will be not one second of relief until we are back in civilization, I suppose," I grumbled.

"Not altogether, Watson, not altogether. There'll be a short respite now and again."

"Did they run out of gravel, then?"

"Not at all!" he laughed. "You've felt what I've felt, Watson, but you've not observed. On the straightaway, the bumping is constant, but as we turn, the bumping is less rather than more as we might expect."

"So it is, but why?"

"In parts of the road they leave the gravel off the sharp s-curves to reduce skidding, so some turns are left unstoned."

This was written by Sandy Kozinn "Esmerelda."
It was first published on the Shamlockians' List on August 8th, 2006.

The following version was written at the same time as being more suitable to the tastes of the general public.

Rural Roads Still Exist
by Our Lifestyles Correspondent
Hicksville, Iowa, August 8, 2006

Outside the urban scene, suburbia and exurbia seem to have taken over the whole world, with only a few dedicated square miles here and there left in a rural state. The same concrete paving and black tar surfaces sprawl endlessly across the continent, punctuated here and there with the same MacDonald's and Burger Kings and Krispy Kremes and K-Marts that could be Anywhere, USA.

Still, here and there in this great country there are still a few spots that seem to have dispensed with calendars years ago, in our parents' or grandparents' or perhaps great-grandparents' time. Here there are great swaths of green between houses, each with a barn and a hen house and fields of corn or wheat or soy beans. Here, among the paved quarterings of the sections laid out when the land was first settled by farmers wind little lanes of dirt, rutted and dusty in summer, muddy and almost impassible in spring and fall, snow covered and rarely accessible in winter, short cuts from neighbor to neighbor.

Now and again, where the land has been subdivided and a farmer's sons' and grandsons' houses share a quarter section with the older generation, a small bit of progress may be found. Someone, likely enough the landowners themselves, have covered the worst of the roads with gravel to soak up the rain in wet weather and keep the dust down in bad. Not all the roads have received this loving attention, only those where the houses are within easy sight of each other.

Someone with a real understanding of what it's like to drive on narrow roads with no police patrols to monitor the speed has spread the gravel on these roads, for it seems to have been left off where a tilt in the terrain would result in all the gravel washing off onto the fields at the side. The decision to gravel or not to gravel seems to have been a judicious one, for where the road goes around a stand of trees or a small pond suitable for watering livestock and forms sharp s-curves, to reduce skidding when the teenage boys with brand-new drivers' licenses are prone to go far too fast, some turns are left unstoned.

Also from MX Publishing

Close To Holmes

A Look at the Connections Between
Historical London, Sherlock Holmes and
Sir Arthur Conan Doyle.

Eliminate The Impossible

An Examination of the World of
Sherlock Holmes on Page and Screen.

The Norwood Author

Arthur Conan Doyle and the Norwood Years
(1891 - 1894) – Winner of the 2011 Howlett
Literary Award (Sherlock Holmes book of
the year)

www.mxpublishing.com

293

In Search of Dr Watson

Wonderful biography of Dr.Watson
from expert Molly Carr – 2nd edition
fully updated.

Arthur Conan Doyle, Sherlock Holmes
and Devon

A Complete Tour Guide and Companion.

The Lost Stories of Sherlock Holmes

Eight more stories from the pen of John H
Watson – compiled by Tony Reynolds.

www.mxpublishing.com

295

297

Also From MX Publishing

The Outstanding Mysteries of Sherlock Holmes

With thirteen Homes stories and illustrations Kelly re-creates the gas-lit, fog-enshrouded world of Victorian

Rendezvous at The Populaire

Sherlock Holmes has retired, injured from an encounter with Moriarty. He's tempted out of retirement for an epic battle with the Phantom of the opera.

Baker Street Beat

An eclectic collection of articles, essays, radio plays and 'general scribblings' about Sherlock Holmes from Dr. Dan Andriacco.

www.mxpublishing.com

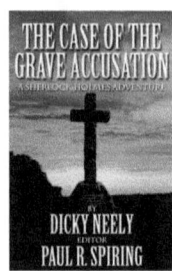

The Case of The Grave Accusation

The creator of Sherlock Holmes has been accused of murder. Only Holmes and Watson can stop the destruction of the Holmes legacy.

Barefoot on Baker Street

Epic novel of the life of a Victorian workhouse orphan featuring Sherlock Holmes and Moriarty.

Case of Witchcraft

A tale of witchcraft in the Northern Isles, in which some long-concealed secrets are revealed including about the Great Detective himself.

www.mxpublishing.com

Also From MX Publishing

The Affair In Transylvania

Holmes and Watson tackle Dracula in
deepest Transylvania in this stunning
adaptation by film director Gerry O'Hara

The London of Sherlock Holmes

400 locations including GPS co-ordinates
that enable Google Street view of the
locations around London in all the Homes
stories

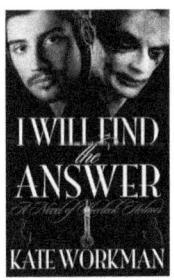

I Will Find The Answer

Sequel to Rendezvous At The Populaire,
Holmes and Watson tackle Dr. Jekyll.

www.mxpublishing.com

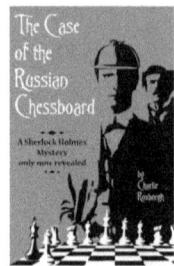

www.ingramcontent.com/pod-product-compliance
Lightning Source LLC
Chambersburg PA
CBHW052001020726
47501CB00004B/956